THE SAME JOURNEY ALL ALONG

BEVERLY BOW

ISBN: 979-8-9911436-0-8

Published by Two Hawks Haven

ACKNOWLEDGEMENTS

With deep gratitude to the team that has guided me through this process, my publishing consultant Robert Henry, editor Chandi Lyn Broadbent, proofreader Anne Broadbent, and cover designer Nada Orlic. Special thanks to fellow author Sethyn Bryant for her encouragement, and for helping me to understand the ins and outs of the child protective services world.

To my husband, Don Fries,
my son, David Bow,
and my sister, Susan Harrington,
with gratitude for their loving support

May 4, 2014

"He's dead, isn't he?" Maggie said, pinning them with her piercing blue eyes. "George is dead."

Ceci and Toby turned to each other, both drawing a breath to speak at once. Then they exhaled in unison. Ceci's face crumpled. She and Toby closed in on opposite sides of the bed and the two sisters and son wept together in a huddle.

With a shuddering breath, Maggie said, "What made you think you could keep this from me?"

"Oh honey," said Ceci, "we didn't want to, but you were barely conscious yourself. You've been in and out for four days."

"Well, neither of you is any good at deception."

Ceci opened her mouth to speak, and closed it again when she saw Toby's tiny shake of the head.

May 7

The tall young woman with perfect skin and a single braid of long blond hair was intolerably chipper. She leaned over the bed. "Mrs. Berry, I'm Tess from Physical Therapy. Do you feel like taking a walk with me this morning?"

My husband, the man I've shared my last 50 years with, is dead, thought Maggie. *I don't feel like doing anything with you.* She closed her eyes, then slowly opened them and looked at the young woman. "Tess from Physical Therapy," Maggie said. "I'd have thought you would be from d'Urbervilles."

"From where?" said Tess.

"Never mind dear," Maggie sighed, "It's a literary reference—Thomas Hardy. I don't imagine they teach it in school anymore."

"I've always been in Physical Therapy," said Tess. "I've never been to Durberville—although I've been to Burgerville," she said brightly with a giggle. "That's probably not the same place though."

"Not exactly, but that's just as well. Things didn't work out too well for the other Tess."

"Anyway Mrs. Berry, are you ready for a walk?"

"Not really," said Maggie, continuing to stare at the ceiling and wishing this annoying person would disappear. "It hurts to stand."

"I know," said Tess. "This is the hard part of my job—getting you to do it anyway. Can you tell me, on a scale of one to ten, what's your pain level now?"

Unbearable, Maggie thought. *George is dead. There is no level, no number on a scale, for this kind of pain.*

"About four," Maggie said, "but that's just sitting in bed."

"Well, let's give it a try. We've got to get you walking so that you can go home."

Home? Is it still home without George?

"Up you go," chirped Tess, using one hand to push the button to bring the bed to a sitting position while wheeling a walker into place with the other. "Can you swing your legs over the edge of the bed?" She peeled back the covers and Maggie felt the rise of goosebumps as a rush of cool air hit her bare legs.

"It's cold," she shivered.

"I'll get your robe, as soon as you get your legs over the edge here," Tess said firmly.

Lacking energy for a confrontation, Maggie wrenched her legs to the edge of the bed with a groan of pain. Teeth clenched in silent protest, she put weight on each foot. Gripping the walker with both hands, she allowed herself to be tied into her robe before starting the halting trek down the hallway. The corridor was abuzz with scrubs-wearing staff darting in and out of patient rooms or pushing carts and equipment hither and yon. She felt like someone in slow motion landing in a world on fast forward.

Pain from her cracked pelvis and ribs jabbed her with each step. When they reached the end of the hall, she was breathing heavily.

Tess smiled and bent to match Maggie's 5 foot 2 inch height. "You are doing so good! You're doing awesome!" she cheered.

In her irritated state, the retired English teacher in Maggie suddenly rose to the surface. She turned the walker to face Tess. "One doesn't '*do* good' in this situation, or '*do* awesome' in any situation," she chastised. "Did you take English in school?" Tess straightened her back, eyes widening and smile fading.

Maggie's blue eyes focused fully on Tess. "Mother Teresa *does* good, or at least she *did*, but that's quite different from anything I might accomplish walking down this damnable hallway. You could say one "does *well*," or you might say a person "*is* awesome," although that certainly does not apply to me here and now."

She clamped her lips together and faced back down the hall.

"You seem to be feeling a bit more like yourself," Toby said with an amused smile, joining them in the hallway.

"Humph," she replied.

May 8

Maggie felt small and surrounded. Ceci had gone back to Eugene, needing to return to her job. Now Toby, Heather, and the two grandchildren encircled her bed like diners waiting to be seated at a table. They all looked too big in the tiny room. Eric, at 16, was athletic, still boyish with touseled brown hair, shifting uncomfortably on his oversized feet, not sure what to do with his hands. Amy, just 14, was a late-bloomer, tentative and sweet in her conversation with Granny. She had her mother's blond hair, worn long and straight, and a smattering of freckles across her nose.

Heather moved toward the mass of flower arrangements and cards on the shelf by the window. "You've certainly got some friends out there."

"Yes, it looks that way," said Maggie.

"Haven't you read them?" she asked while touching the top of an unopened envelope.

"Well, no, I just haven't really felt like it," she said. "I guess that's rude of me, I really should…"

"Let me put them over here on your bed table," said Heather. "Then when you're feeling up to it, they'll be within reach."

Maggie had done her best to avoid talking about the accident. She had asked to have no visitors other than family. It was as if encasing herself in this bubble, where nothing seemed real, could protect her from the truth of her own life. Nevertheless, the outside world was intruding.

"It looks like they're going to let you out of here in three days," said Toby. "I talked to the doctor, and she said that if you can get around okay with the walker, you should do all right."

"So, if I want to stay longer, I should refuse to walk," said Maggie.

"Mom, of course you want to get out of here. I asked about the concussion, and they said that as long as you don't fall and bang your head again, you're probably safer at home than you are here."

"What about my memory?" asked Maggie. "I still don't remember anything about the accident."

"Apparently that's normal. In fact, they said you very likely never will, although memory of the time leading up to the accident may eventually return."

Maggie tried to picture herself at her house—just her, alone in her house. She made a mental tour, and in every room, she saw George. On his favorite barstool in the kitchen. In his over-stuffed chair reading a book. At his desk in his office, studiously going through paperwork. In the bathroom brushing his teeth and talking to her with a mouth full of toothpaste. On his side of the bed waiting for her to turn out the light.

"And what am I to do with my time at home?" Maggie said.

Toby took her hand. "I can't believe you're saying that. You've always had more to do than hours in a day." But Maggie was serious. She couldn't think of anything she wanted to do, of any aspect of her life she wanted to "get on with." It was as though that former life belonged to the Maggie of George and Maggie. Now that the cord was severed, she was adrift.

"Toby and I were thinking maybe you'd like to come stay with us for a couple of weeks," Heather spoke up, "just until you're definitely back on your feet."

Maggie looked at Heather. She loved them deeply, and

treasured Eric and Amy. But if she went to their home she would need to put on a brave face, be grateful for their attentions, make the valiant effort. She didn't have it in her. "No, I appreciate the offer, but I've already disrupted your lives enough," she said. "Besides, your guest bedroom is on the second floor."

"You can have my room Granny," said Amy. "We talked about it. I'll sleep in the guest room. Anyway, what about at your house? Your bedroom is on the second floor there."

"Sweetheart that is so kind of you." She reached for her granddaughter's hand. "But I've got to face my house sooner or later. I can stay in my own guest bedroom, which *is* on the first floor. Heather, if you and Toby can do some grocery shopping for me, and drive me to appointments, I think it would be easier on all of us if I was in my own space."

"I can shop for you Granny," said Eric, suddenly coming to attention. "I've got my license now. That is if Dad lets me use the car." He tried to catch his father's eyes across the bed.

"Okay Mom," said Toby, ignoring Eric. "But if you change your mind, the offer stands. Ceci said the same thing."

"I know," said Maggie. "I practically had to push her out of here so she could get back to her job. And Eric, I will take you up on your offer of shopping. And no need to borrow your dad's car, I have a car too." Eric grinned and pumped his fist in the air.

"Well, with all that covered, I think we need to get home. These kids have some homework to do." His words elicited groans from the teenagers.

Maggie's son, daughter-in-law, and grandchildren soon left. And she was alone. Again. She was going to have to leave.

She was going to have to be alone. Steeling herself, she used the walker to tread the ten painful steps to the tiny bathroom and to even more painfully lower herself onto the toilet seat. In some strange way she welcomed the pain. Pain was the one thing that seemed real about her situation. It was something to overcome, a purpose for her life. She looked at her reflection in the bathroom mirror. "I have to do this," she told herself silently. "What other choice do I have?"

It was in this strengthening mood that she learned the information that would once again send her spinning and ultimately derail her life.

May 9

Initially Maggie had avoided asking about the accident. She remembered none of it, and she didn't want to picture it. George was dead. His body had been cremated. What else mattered?

No one pushed details on her, but like the niggling buzz of insects, the details intruded. And there was the stack of greeting cards now confronting her on the bed table. She picked them up one at a time and started to read. Some oozed sympathy, others cheered her efforts to get well. She read them all with numb detachment.

All except for the card from Ginger Benson.

Of all her friends, Ginger was the least likely to say the correct thing, and therefore the most likely to convey the truth in any situation. Married to Pete Benson, a local attorney, Ginger went through life apparently oblivious to the social graces that constrained most people in Maggie's and George's circle of friends. She said what came to her mind, and people either accepted it and loved her for it, or avoided her. She didn't care either way. Maggie was among those who loved her, and was more amused than offended by Ginger's straight-shooter comments.

The front of Ginger's card was a photograph of bright purple and yellow pansies. Inside she had written in her scrawling hand: "I'm so sorry for the loss of George and for your injuries. Given the possibility of legal issues, please don't hesitate to contact Pete. We're both here for you and willing to help. Sending our love. Ginger and Pete"

Maggie read the card several times, trying to make sense of the "possibility of legal issues" phrase. Then she reached for the bedside phone and punched in Toby's cell phone number.

"This is Toby Berry," he said in his business voice.

"What else haven't you told me?" Maggie demanded.

"Mom? What's the matter? What are you talking about?"

"You and Ceci, about the accident," said Maggie. "What's the part you haven't told me?"

"I'm not sure what you want to know," said Toby. "Dad was killed. You were hurt."

"I got a card from Ginger Benson that mentioned the possibility of legal problems. What was she talking about?"

She heard Toby let out a deep breath and then silence. Finally, he said, "I'll come over."

Maggie set the remainder of the cards aside and waited, trying to construct in her mind the possible meanings of Ginger's card. Why did Toby have to come in person? Why couldn't he just tell her on the phone? In the twenty minutes it took him to get there, a myriad of possibilities cycled through her thoughts. Had they damaged someone's property in the accident? Was someone else hurt? Was she being sued for some reason? And why was Toby keeping it a secret from her. What right did he have?

When Toby walked into the room, he was carrying a newspaper. He handed it to her without comment. She saw the headline midway down the page:

Weekend Crash Leaves Two Dead

A head-on collision on SW Winter Hill Road late Friday night left a Portland man and a Sunset High School student dead and two others injured. George Berry, 75, of Portland died when the Lexus sedan he was driving collided head-on with a Jeep driven by Cameron King, 17. King was hospitalized and released with minor injuries. King's passenger, Jason Foster, 16, was taken to a local hospital where he died of his injuries. King and Foster were returning home from a high school basketball game. Both were wearing seatbelts. Berry's wife, Maggie Berry, 76, was hospitalized in serious condition. It appears that alcohol was a factor in the accident. Toxicology reports indicate that George Berry's blood alcohol level was .17, more than twice the legal limit.

Maggie sank back into her pillow. A boy dead. Jason. The same age as Eric. Alcohol a factor. George's fault. She closed her eyes. All of the air was sucked from the room.

"Why didn't you tell me this?" she rasped as her throat constricted. Opening her eyes, she could see on his face the toll that the last week had taken.

"You were already dealing with so much Mom. I knew you needed to know, but I just couldn't find a good time or good way to tell you."

"Are they certain your dad was at fault? It was an accident, wasn't it?"

"Dad crossed the center line Mom. He drove into their lane and hit the car head on. You guys were coming back from a party. And he had been drinking. The roads were dry. There really isn't another explanation for why he was on the wrong side of the road."

"What does this mean? What's going to happen?" She was unmoored, the room spinning around her, tears welling in her eyes.

"I don't really know. I've been contacted by an attorney, and he said the family of the boy who died…"

"Jason," she said, her voice breaking.

"Jason," he said, "…by an attorney for Jason's family, the Fosters. I think they could sue Dad's estate."

She stared blankly at the wall.

"You have to not think about this. At least not right now. We'll get an attorney. I think your insurance company will get involved, so hopefully we can defend the estate against this."

"I don't care about the damned estate," she wailed. "How do you make up for the loss of a life? Of a child?"

Toby's shoulders sagged. "I know, I know. I think about that all the time," he said, taking her hand. "I look at Eric and think, what would I do if this happened to us?" He hesitated, then said, his voice quavering, "I've even thought that it's a blessing that Dad didn't live, because I don't think he could have lived with this. It would have tormented him. He was such a good man, and to be responsible for this… But it wasn't *your* fault, Mom. You were a victim too."

"A victim. I don't feel like a victim. I feel like an accessory to a crime." Not only was her partner of fifty-one years gone, but now the George of her memories, the kind, thoughtful man who she so proudly called her husband, was gone as well, replaced by a drunk driver, a killer of children.

"Oh Toby," she said, weeping in earnest now. He sat on the edge of the bed and held her, rocking as she sobbed.

May 12

Maggie awoke in the guest bedroom of her west hills home. "This is fitting," she whispered. "I am a visitor in my own life."

The house was eerily quiet after the hospital. She struggled from the bed, and began the laborious process of showering, dressing and making breakfast. Toby and Heather had bought groceries and stocked her freezer with prepared meals.

Things were just as she and George had left them to go out for the evening just two weeks ago, but it felt as if a decade had passed. His reading glasses and a library book were on the end table by his favorite chair—the one that looked out over the street. "I need to take that book back," she said. "It will be overdue."

A week had passed since they'd told her about George, but part of her hadn't fully believed it. In the hospital, nothing had been real. But now, it was real. This room, this chair where he would never sit again, this ottoman that still held dents from his feet, these glasses that lay unseeing on the table, this silence—this was her new reality.

After fifty-one years of marriage, she and George had been as comfortable with quiet companionship as they had with conversation.

By the time she had forced down a few bites of breakfast and finished putting dishes in the dishwasher she was exhausted from the efforts of the morning and settled into the recliner for a rest.

Jason Foster's name cycled through her thoughts like a mantra. She tried to picture him. Faces of countless former students appeared. Some were baby-faced, some worldly and bold, some acne-covered, nerdy and awkward. If she had still been teaching, he could have been one of her students. She felt an overwhelming need to put this right—this thing that could never be made right. She drifted into a tormented sleep.

The banging on the front door startled her awake. She was still struggling to stand with the walker when Ceci came into the room toting a rolling suitcase in one hand and a grocery bag in the other.

"Ceci? What are you doing here?"

"Toby told me you were home. Sorry to barge in, but I know where you keep your spare key. Anyway, I thought you might welcome a companion for a few days. I can stay through the weekend if you'll have me."

"There's no one I'd rather have right now. But I'm in the guest room. You'll have to sleep upstairs."

"I figured," said Ceci. "The rooms are nicer up there anyway." She gave Maggie a warm hug and hauled her suitcase up the stairs.

"How's your pain?" she called from the second floor. "Did they give you meds to take home?"

"They gave me a huge bottle of them," Maggie called back, "but I'm not taking them. I'd rather have a little discomfort than be fuzzy-headed all day."

"Just so you're not in misery. You don't have to tough it out to prove your moral character."

"I'm managing." What she didn't say was that she deserved the pain. It was the one thing that seemed right, that she should feel this hurt, this misery.

Having another human in the house relieved Maggie more than she wanted to admit. She needed the sound and presence of another person. After Toby and Heather had left last night, she felt like the stillness had swallowed everything. She was a flickering flame trying to brighten a room with too little oxygen.

Ceci came back downstairs and sat in the chair next to Maggie. She took Maggie's hand, caressing the purplish bruises still there from the IV line. "I want to know how you're doing—not just physically but emotionally," she said. "Toby told me that you know about the boy."

"I can't stop thinking about him, Ceci. I feel like there's something I should do to make it all right, but there's nothing. It's the worst I've ever felt about anything. This doesn't seem right to say this, but it's harder to take than losing George. How do people live with these things?"

"I knew it would plague you. You're the most hyper-responsible person I know. But you're not responsible for what happened. It was an accident. A tragic accident. It happened to you as much as it happened to him."

"Not really. I'm here, and he isn't. I wish it was the other way around."

"Listen," Ceci said, "don't even think that! You're my only sibling. Mom and Dad are gone, it's just us. I need you. Toby and your grandkids need you. Focus on that."

George is dead. He killed an innocent boy. That boy's family needs him. There's nothing that can make me feel worse than this. Maggie shook her head to dispel the intrusive thoughts.

It would be months before she learned how wrong she was.

May 15

Regressing from older-sister-in-charge to dependent invalid did not sit well with Maggie. Watching Ceci bustle about the kitchen and wait on her like a helpless child was too much to take. She forced herself to a standing position and steered the walker to the sink.

"I can wash my own damn dishes," she growled.

"As you wish," said Ceci with a hint of a smile as she yielded the sink.

That was how the next three days progressed. Maggie's sense of pride forced her to move despite herself.

And then there were the "counseling sessions." Ceci would plant herself across from Maggie and look her squarely in the eyes, and therapy would begin.

"How are you feeling about losing George?"

"What are you most worried about?"

"Have you thought about reconnecting with your friends so that you have a support network?"

"Do you have plans to spend time with Toby and your grandkids?"

"What about restarting your volunteering at the YMCA? They probably have a rehab program too, so you could do physical therapy there."

It was as though Ceci was running a boot camp recovery program that Maggie hadn't signed up for.

"Look Ceci," she said. "I know you're trying to help me, but I'm not ready for all that. I just need to come to terms with what's happened, and to do it in my own time."

"Okay Sis, I hear you. I just don't want you moping around here and processing all this stuff by yourself. It's a lot to deal with."

"It's mine to deal with," said Maggie.

"You're right. But promise me that if you need to talk to someone, you'll call me—or if not me, someone. There are support groups for things like this."

"It's you I'll call," said Maggie. "I promise. I'm not the support group type."

Within the hour, she was watching Ceci's red Miata disappear down the street.

She wished she could just unload her weighty emotions into her sister's willing arms, but she couldn't extricate herself from these feelings. They were all she had right now. If she let go of them, she didn't know what would remain.

This pattern of withdrawing into herself was established long ago in childhood. When she sought comfort from her mother for physical or emotional hurts her father would upbraid her for what he saw as weakness. And her mother had passively acquiesced, leaving Maggie to find her own solace.

It was a survival mechanism that had gotten her through the lesser traumas of youth, but she worried that it would not serve her well with what lay ahead.

July 4

If there was a silver lining to everything that had happened since the day of the accident, it was that Maggie had found a new closeness with Toby. The pair had worked together to plan a memorial gathering for George, which they held during the last week in June. They had spent hours going through photo albums, remembering family times together, laughing at the pictures of father and son antics from camping trips and soccer games. Toby helped Maggie remember the other George. The one who wanted to make the world a better place. The one who would never hurt another person. The George she had fallen in love with over half a century ago.

Enjoying a July 4th picnic with Toby, Heather, and the kids, the knot she was carrying inside her began to loosen. The idea that maybe she could move on with life in some fashion started to take root. Her physical pain was nearly gone now. She knew she would never fully move past the accident. And then there was the ongoing lawsuit filed by the Foster family. Jason's family. Until that was settled, the pain of that night, of George's final act, would be a daily presence.

"Granny, guess what," Amy said, breaking her momentary musings. "I made the potato salad myself this year, and it totally rocks!"

Maggie smiled at her granddaughter. "That's wonderful! I can't wait to eat it all," she joked.

She promised herself that from now on, she would focus on the happy times and try to find a way forward.

September 15

The small dog swayed joyfully from side to side as he surveyed the ever-changing scene. He perched on Minnow's lap, front paws on the dash of the pickup, head cocked to one side, right ear up and left ear down as if listening to something Billy was saying. His ears were always in these opposing positions, and together with his eyes, one brown and one green, he was over-all a lopsided critter. As Billy said, he lacked symmetry. Whatever he lacked in appearance, he made up in exuberance. His name, Bonkers, fit perfectly.

Slouching in the sun-warmed seat, a sleepy-eyed Minnow ruffled his uneven coat, humming a quiet tune. In the sun the odor of dog shampoo from last night's bath mingled with his usual doggy scent. He licked her chin, and she smelled the kibble on his breath. Suddenly she jerked upright, swiveling her head to look behind her out the side window. "Uncle Billy, stop!" she cried. "Turn around!"

Billy slowed the truck. "What's the matter?"

"I saw one. Just back there on the right. Please. I've never seen it before," she pleaded. "Please go back!"

With a sigh, Billy pulled onto a side road, turned the truck camper and its small utility trailer around, and retraced their path an eighth of a mile. This was a new stop. He didn't like new stops. He didn't like new anything. His quickening pulse was at war with his commitment to Minnow, a sense of duty which nearly always decided these internal battles.

As he rounded a curve, he saw a spot of color—flowers, a cross, a blue stuffed rabbit, a photo. A small roadside shrine to someone departed.

He swung across the road and stopped beside it. As soon as

the truck was stopped, he pulled a small tablet and pen from his pocket and checked his watch so that he could record the exact time and their location on his list for the day. Next to the location, he wrote *New roadside memorial.* Billy kept lists. He had a page in his notebook for every day of the month, and a notebook for every month.

Minnow bounded from the truck, Bonkers springing ahead of her. A fan of dark hair caught the wind and covered her face. She was tall for her twelve years. She also carried a notebook and pen. She clasped the notebook between her knees, gathered her hair into a ponytail and secured it with a band from her wrist. Then she squatted before the items, studying each as though to commit them to memory; caressing the rabbit, tracing the outline of the face in the photo, straightening a tilted vase of flowers, tickling the dead blossoms from their stems without disturbing the still vibrant ones. She walked away from the shrine and deposited the dried petals beneath a scrubby oak tree, then returned. Standing again before the collection of items she opened the notebook and wrote. Bonkers busily sniffed the perimeter, barked tentatively at the rabbit, and then lifted his leg at the base of the cross.

"Bonkers no!" Minnow chastised. She grabbed his collar and pulled him away. He looked at her with tilted head, his cocked right ear demanding an explanation.

"This is a sacred spot. This is about someone," she said. "Go pee on a tree." He did.

She saw a bit of color by a tree about twenty paces away and went to explore. It was a wilted bouquet that had been tossed aside and abandoned.

"Look Bonkers," she said. "Some of these are still beautiful." She pulled off the rubber band and separated the stems, tossing away the wilted blossoms and keeping the ones that still looked fresh. When she was finished, she held a smaller, but no less lovely, bouquet. She started to twist the rubber band around the new bouquet, but it broke, snapping her fingers.

"Ouch!" she said. Then she grabbed the base of her ponytail with one hand and released her hair, securing the hair band around the flowers before returning them to a prominent place underneath the cross.

After another minute of studying the shrine, she walked back to the truck and called to Bonkers who launched himself up the running board and scrambled onto the floor of the truck. Billy started the engine, turned the camper around and they resumed their journey.

"Uncle Billy," Minnow said, "I saw a sign for a gas station ahead. Will you stop?"

"We still have approximately 247.5 miles before we need gas," he said.

"Not for gas," she said, "just to talk to them. They probably have a restroom too. You can check it out." This stretch of road was new for Billy and Minnow and it was an out-of-character move on his part to expand their route. He had to temporarily abandon a section of Highway 18 due to construction. Changing the routine always left him off balance and out of sorts.

"I've already made one unplanned stop. If we go to the gas station that would be two unplanned stops in the same day."

Minnow persisted. "Her name was Carrie. She was 12. The same age as me."

He had calculated their arrival times for each of their planned stops and adding one more would change everything.

He would have to recalculate. But then he would have to recalculate anyway because of the stop at the memorial. In fact, he had already been recalculating in his head, but all of that would be wasted effort if he stopped again.

He wouldn't buy gas. Not with 247.5 miles worth of gas left in the tank. If he bought gas, that would mean he would buy gas nine times this month, and he always bought gas only eight times in a month. If they stopped, he wouldn't want to stay too long. The owner might not appreciate them asking questions.

After a mile, a Texaco station appeared on their right, two pumps and a small convenience store. Billy parked near the restroom doors and went into the men's. Minnow rolled down the windows halfway and shut Bonkers in the pickup, taking her notebook and pen. The store was empty except for the gas station attendant who was bent over the bottom shelves of the soft drink case, stocking sodas. His faded jeans struggled to find purchase on narrow hips and flat behind, forced down by the oversized belly bulging from the bottom of a green plaid shirt.

"How ya doin?" he asked, turning his head toward her when the bell on the door jingled.

"Hi," said Minnow, walking over to stand next to him.

"Can I get you somethin'?" he looked up.

"I saw the roadside memorial a ways back on the road," said Minnow, "for Carrie. I was hoping you could tell me what happened."

He straightened, inspecting Minnow more directly, running his hand through thinning brown hair.

"Friend of yours?" he asked.

"Kind of, but I didn't exactly know her too well. We've

been traveling lately so I just saw the memorial this morning."

"It's a heartbreaker," he said, shaking his head. "Happened a week ago on Saturday. Her older brother was driving, probably showing off. Rainy night. Just skidded off the road at that curve and wrapped around a tree. '07 Dodge Charger. He had it in here for gas just the day before. That night he comes running in here, all bloody, screaming to get help for his sister. The ambulance was quick, but there was no way. Poor kid. Poor kids I should say. The brother's not going to get over this one. I wouldn't."

"What's her brother's name?" asked Minnow.

"Well, let's see. There's three of them Baker boys. This one's the youngest, except for the girl. She was the only girl."

"Carrie," said Minnow.

"Yeah, Carrie. Sweet thing. Used to come in here for Kit Kat bars. She loved Kit Kats and Dr. Pepper. She and her friends, always giggling about boys or some such. But the brothers, let's see, there's Tom, the oldest, then John, and then the youngest, that's Danny."

Minnow opened her notebook to a page she'd headed with the words "Carrie, Age 12, Highway 20. She added *September 6* to the heading and *Baker* after Carrie's name. On the next line she wrote *Brothers: Tom, John, Danny (driver)*. Underneath that she wrote *Loved Kit Kats and Dr. Pepper. Giggled with girlfriends.*

"Thanks for telling me," said Minnow. "Can I ask what your name is?"

"I'm Henry," he said, "but most folks call me Hank. Hank Farmer. Only I'm not."

"You're not what?" asked Minnow.

"A farmer," he said with a chortle.

The string of bells on the door jingled as Billy walked in. He was just shy of six feet tall, slender with straight dark hair that fell over his forehead and onto his black-framed glasses. His movements were nervous and jerky, giving the impression of someone easily startled.

"Uncle Billy, this is Mr. Hank Farmer," said Minnow. "He's been telling me about Carrie."

"Hello Mr. Farmer," said Billy in his characteristic clipped, precise speech. He raked his fingers through his hair to push it out of his eyes, pulled out his tablet and pen and added *Hank Farmer* to his list for September 15.

"Hank," said Hank. "Mr. Farmer was my grandfather."

"That would be logical," said Billy, "assuming you're referring to your paternal grandfather, and that he had a son who was your father."

Hank looked at Billy with furrowed brow, paused, then laughed. "Well, that's just how it was. My grandfather had a son—four sons really, and one of 'em had me. So there you have it, my family tree in a nutshell."

"Your ballcock in the men's is faulty," said Billy.

"My what?" said Hank, looking at Billy with new caution.

"The American Standard in the men's. It has a faulty ballcock."

"Uncle Billy fixes toilets," Minnow interjected. "He's really good at it."

"Oh. Well, uh, thanks," said Hank, "but I can't afford no repair bills right now. It's this store that keeps my gas station above water. There's no real money in sellin' gas. But it's just barely above water. I just jiggle the handle on that thing and it's usually alright."

"He doesn't charge anything," said Minnow. "He does it for free."

Hank's eyebrows shot up. "You do it for free? Now why would you do that?"

"I already have enough money," said Billy.

"Ohhkay, well that's a new one," said Hank. "Jeff Bezos has got enough money too, but I don't see him doin' nothin' for free. But anyway, why do you want to muck around with toilets, doin' a nasty job like that if you don't need the money."

"Classification of something as a nasty job is a human bias Mr. Farmer."

"Hank."

"I do it out of respect and appreciation for Sir John Harrington, and Alexander Cummings, and Joseph Bramah."

"And they would be…?"

"Inventors," said Billy. "The basic idea for the flush toilet came from Harrington in 1596, over 400 years ago. Only he didn't think of the "s" shaped pipe that keeps the sewer gases from escaping into your restroom. That came almost 200 years later with Alexander Cummings in 1775. Then Bramah added the hinged flap and float valve three years later. Do you not think it remarkable that we're still using the same basic design today—236 years later? Think about it Mr. Farmer. How many inventions can you name that have stood the test of time like that? It's a crime when we allow a brilliant invention like this to malfunction. Toilets are designed to work correctly, even though some manufacturers have made so-called improvements that get in the way of their simple perfection. I find it distressing to see them untended and operating poorly. So I fix them."

"Well if that don't beat all," said Hank.

Billy was sixteen the first time he fixed a toilet, right after his dad died. The toilet in their house quit working, and since there was only one bathroom, this was a family crisis. He read about how the toilet worked, bought the parts and fixed it. Never before had he done something useful for other people, something that seemed important. And then it had started to bother him when he would go into a public restroom and the toilet was not being maintained in good working condition. He started carrying tools with him, compelled by the need to make it right. When he would find a faulty toilet, he'd fix it on the spot. His mother had given him a gift of white coveralls, and often people just thought he was a plumber that someone had called to come fix the toilet. Other times they didn't even know he was doing it. But one guy threatened to call the police, and at the library they did call the police. After that he always got permission to make the repairs.

"So we were talking about your ballcock in the men's," said Billy. "It's about a 10-minute job."

"Be my guest," said Hank. "And feel free to check out the ladies too, as long as there's no one in there. I don't know how clean they are..."

"I always clean and sanitize them before working on them," Billy said and walked quickly out the door toward the truck. Hank, shaking his head, said again, "If that don't beat all." Then to Minnow, "Your uncle's a strange one. He just goes around fixing toilets in gas stations for free?"

"It's his thing," she said. "It makes him feel better, and it makes the world better at the same time. I think he knows more about toilets than anybody in the world. He also makes metal sculptures that he sells."

"And you go with him? How old are you? Aren't you in school?"

"I'm 12, and I'm homeschooled," said Minnow.

"Homeschooled. In a camper?"

"Sometimes. We have a house too, near Boring. Can you believe there's a town named Boring?"

"I believe it. I've been through there. Good name. Not much to see, but then not much here either. So it's just you and your uncle at your house?"

"It used to be my grandma's house, and I went to school then. But she died two years ago, and now it's just me and Uncle Billy, and he can't stand to stay put for more than two weeks at a time, so I go with him."

"What about your mom and dad?"

"I don't know my dad. He took off before I was born. My mom's around but she's got problems, so I've been with my grandma since I was three, except for a few months back with my mom, but that didn't work out. And now I'm with Uncle Billy. We get along good. I also have my dog. His name is Bonkers. Do you want to meet him?"

"Well, why not," said Hank. Minnow dashed from the store and returned a minute later with a squirming Bonkers in her arms.

"He loves people," she said, and as if to prove it thrust him toward Hank who accepted him with surprise. Bonkers sniffed Hank's neck and then gave him a quick lick of approval.

"Well, little fella, you may not win any dog shows, but you're a friendly one." He set Bonkers on the floor and he and Minnow watched as the dog sniffed his way around the room, stopping and looking expectantly when he came to the snack isle.

The door jingled and Billy walked back in the store wearing white coveralls with "Billy" embroidered in red script above the left breast pocket. "I've replaced the ballcock Mr. Farmer. It shouldn't give you any trouble for a minimum of five years. The ladies was fine, although there's some rust on the tank lever so you'll want to watch it and replace it before it rusts through."

"Well thank you Mr. …"

"Billy Marsh."

"Can't I pay you for any parts Mr. Marsh?"

"Payment isn't necessary. I always provide the parts."

"Well then, at least take a drink from the soda case. Go ahead. One for each of you."

Minnow didn't hesitate. She pulled a can of Dr. Pepper from the cooler and then handed Billy a 7-Up. She stopped at a shelf of candy bars, grabbed a Kit Kat bar and took it to the register. When she pulled a crumpled bill from her jeans pocket Hank said, "It's on me little lady. You all take care now."

He reached down and gave Bonkers a pat as the dog trotted to the door ahead of Minnow.

"Thanks Hank!" said Minnow as the door jingled behind them.

Back on the road she cradled the candy bar with both hands, then sniffed it through the wrapper. She gently peeled off its bright red jacket, studied the four chocolate segments, and took a small bite. The milk chocolate dissolved instantly to sweet velvet, coating her mouth and tongue. Her teeth found the crispy center.

"Mmmm," she said, exploring the textures. After she swallowed, sweet satisfaction remained.

Bonkers sat at attention on her lap, one brown eye and one green eye fixated on the candy, his tail drumming against her leg.

"You can't have this," said Minnow. "Chocolate is bad for dogs."

His tail picked up its pace. She pulled a plastic bag from her jacket pocket and plucked out a bone-shaped biscuit, holding it above his nose. He trembled in anticipation and released a small whine.

"Okay!" said Minnow and he sprung at the treat, then dropped to the floor of the truck and began to demolish it.

Now she pulled the tab on the Dr. Pepper, savoring the sweet, cherry-scented hiss. When she sipped, the carbonation burst in her mouth, the tingly burning more a prickle than a taste.

"This is the best can of pop I've ever had," she told Billy.

September 22

Minnow felt the hush of the library surround her as the pair walked through the door. It was as if the air inside was held still and captive by all those words and pages. Billy made a beeline for the nonfiction section. He walked in quick steps, toes turned out, arms at his sides. Minnow headed to shelves labeled "Pick-ups for Holds" to the left of the checkout station. Her gaze locked on the eight books labeled "Marsh, Minnow." She pulled each one from the shelf, caressed the cover, read the back of the jacket, then nestled it back on the shelf.

They had been coming to this library as long as she could remember, first with her grandmother and now with Billy. The children's library, where she had spent so many happy hours in her early years, was upstairs, complete with child-size tables and chairs. She now spent her time in the "Teen Scene" and adult sections.

"Well, hello there, Minnow," the plump, round-faced librarian smiled, looking up from her computer screen. "Are you here to pick up the books you put on hold? I think eight of them are in, but we're still waiting on a couple."

"Hi Mrs. Sanford. Yes, I want to pick them up, but first I want to use one of the Internet computers."

"Okay. You know the drill."

Minnow signed up for the 60-minute computer session and settled at a vacant computer station against the back wall. She pulled up Instagram and logged in, quickly scanning the numerous posts from her friend list. She clicked the "like" button multiple times as she scrolled, chuckled at the screen, and added quick comments.

Then she typed "Carrie Baker" in the search bar. Eighteen pictures appeared, several of adults, some of girls from other states, and one of a freckle-faced girl with curly red hair from Yamhill. "Bingo" Minnow whispered. The girl had a broad smile and was standing in a victory pose, legs spread and arms stretched in a "v" above her head. There was a soccer ball between her feet.

Minnow turned to the page in her notebook that she had headed *Carrie Baker, September 6*. She wrote the word *soccer*. Then she pulled up Carrie's followers list and 78 accounts popped up. She chose ten from girls who looked to be about her age and started following them. She returned to Carrie's profile and jotted the name of her school, her dog Moby, her favorite color yellow, favorite songs, movies and books.

The computer pinged. Sophie, one of the ten girls, had followed her back. Minnow sent a message to her right away. "OMG, I just heard about Carrie! I only knew her a little because Moby played with my dog Bonkers once, but I can't believe it. How can she be dead? Were you a close friend of hers?"

"Really close," Sophie wrote back. "I can't stop crying. I couldn't make it thru soccer practice yesterday cuz I kept looking for her and then remembering that she's gone. My Mom let me stay home from school today."

Minnow felt tears gathering in her own eyes.

"I know what you mean," she wrote. "She seemed like such an awesome girl. If you ever want to talk about her you can DM me."

"Thx ☺."

She sighed, then opened her own profile. She had 237 followers. Of those 237, she had only met three of them in person. The remainder she had acquired in the same way she had picked up Sophie. They were all followers of those on her list. Friends of those memorialized along Oregon highways.

There were no photos of her on her own story page for the simple reason that she had no phone or camera. Instead, she populated the page with photos she pulled from the Internet. Now she added one of a middle school girls' soccer game. Closing out Instagram, she opened Google and searched for Carrie Baker. Several news articles about the accident showed up. She read each, adding to her notes. Before logging out, she brought up Instagram again. Two more girls had followed her back. She sent them messages similar to the one she wrote Sophie. Out of the corner of her eye she saw Billy signaling her that it was time to go.

She logged out and picked up her eight books, scanned her library card and checked them out.

"Did you get done what you needed?" asked Mrs. Sanford.

"Yeah. I had messages from some of my friends to answer. It's so sad. One of our friends was killed in a car wreck."

"Oh dear, I'm so sorry," said the librarian. "That's a hard thing to experience at your age. At any age actually."

"It's really hard. She was a soccer player, and she had a dog just like I do."

"Well, I am so very sorry." She paused. "I've wanted to ask you how your homeschooling is going? Do you ever get together with other homeschoolers? There's a group of kids and parents that meets here at the library on Thursday mornings. Do you think you'd like to join them?"

"I don't know. Uncle Billy doesn't do group stuff usually, but I'll mention it to him. Thanks for telling me." Minnow looked down at the stack of books in her arms. "He's an awesome teacher really. Anyway, I've got to go now, but I'll see you next time we come in." She could see the librarian watching her as she and Billy exited through the automatic door.

She would not mention it to Billy. While telling people she was homeschooled seemed to satisfy their curiosity about why she was not in school, she was not homeschooled in the usual sense of the term. Uncle Billy did teach her a lot about different things, and she learned all kinds of things on her own, but there were no formal lesson plans, no textbooks or workbooks.

And sadly, there would be no Thursday morning group of kids. She would have loved a group of real friends. She thought about her last year in school, before Granny Vi died, picturing herself and Amanda running on the playground, giggling at lunch, and a profound sadness settled over her. But long-term sadness was not in her nature. She knew that Billy would never agree to a parent/child group experience. If this were not the case, if she was part of something outside her own mind and the solitary world of Uncle Billy, perhaps she would have been less vulnerable to what was coming her way.

October 4

Samantha Maverick—Sam to all who knew her—was sweeping the wood plank floor of Maverick's General Store when she first heard and then saw the battered brown van pull into the parking lot. The engine died with a cough and a rattle. A slim woman, her shoulder-length hair grown out dark at the roots and bleached at the ends, emerged, slamming the door once, then with more force when it failed to latch. She wore tight fitting, hip hugger jeans and a body-hugging red sweater with a low v-neck showing ample cleavage. Her silver-strapped wedged sandals shined white in the sun.

The passenger door opened, and a man lumbered out, starting toward the store. He was dressed in faded, baggy jeans and a brown sweatshirt, sleeves cut short to reveal the dark hair covering his thick biceps and lower arms. Unruly brown hair sprang out from beneath a well-worn baseball cap, and several days of beard growth shadowed his lower face. The woman spoke sharply to him, and he went back to the van, opening the sliding door to the back seat. A pale girl with straw-colored hair that was matted in the back jumped down. She ran toward the woman, stopping abruptly a few feet away, watching and waiting.

It was a beautiful autumn day, crisp and clear, the sunlight illuminating the red vine maples woven among the evergreen trees on the hillside behind the store. The woman surveyed the scene, walking over to the side yard where metal and wood sculptures were for sale. She focused on the metal sculptures, checking the prices, inserting her hand into the spinning parts to stop their movement. Sam saw a narrative of years or of hard living etched into her face. There was something familiar about her that Sam struggled to identify.

The trio came onto the porch, the woman scrutinizing the furnishings and storefront. The store was empty of other customers as the woman came through the door, followed by the girl and man.

"Hello," said Sam. "I saw you looking at the metal sculptures. Did you find something you liked out there? They're all hand-crafted by an Oregon artist."

The woman looked around the store, taking in the neat shelves of food, hardware, kitchen utensils, and the wood stove in the corner. The little girl stood back, silent, watching the woman who Sam guessed was her mother, seeing the similarity in facial features. The man had wandered over to the hardware aisle.

The woman looked at Sam and smiled. "Nice place," she said. "All yours?"

"Yep, all mine," said Sam. "For better or for worse. You look so familiar to me. Have we met?"

The woman barked a laugh. "No, we haven't met, but I understand you know other members of my family."

Now she had it, the familiarity. "Billy and Minnow," she said. "You must be Billy's sister. Katrina is it?"

"That's right. I didn't know my big brother ever uttered my name out loud. Actually, let's just say I'm Minnow's mother and not worry about what I am to Billy," she said, eyes hardening.

"So, what brings you to Connor?" Sam asked, wary now. She saw Katrina compose her face, visibly softening her features.

"I know my brother comes here. Thanks to him, I'm not even allowed to see my own daughter. Do you know what that's like? To have your own child ripped away from you?" Sam watched as tears welled in Katrina's eyes.

"I just want Minnow to know that things aren't the same as they were. Now I have Dirk," she pointed toward the hardware aisle, "and my Sadie," she said, reaching behind her, pulling the silent girl to her side. "We're a regular family. Minnow belongs with me, and I want her to know that our family won't be complete without her." Her eyes hardened again. "It's not right for Billy to keep her from me. When you see him, you tell him that."

"How did you know that he comes here?" asked Sam.

"I keep track of my brother. It's the only way to know what's happening with my daughter. Isn't that what any loving mother would do?"

Sam nodded silently. "C'mon Dirk," said Katrina. She pulled Sadie by the arm toward the door. "You tell him," she repeated as the three exited the store and got into their van.

Watching the van speed off down the highway, Sam shivered, feeling as though a chill breeze had blown through the store.

October 6

The truck jostled and squeaked through the rutted parking lot, a scruffy brown and white head protruding from the passenger window, black nose drinking in the fir-scented air. Billy waved at the bearded man clad in jeans and a green parka as he pulled up next to the gas pump. Bonkers whined and scrabbled madly with all four paws, trying to squeeze through the partially open window.

"Hold on buddy," said Minnow, prying him from the window. "Don't worry, we're going in." She tucked him under one arm, opened the door and slid to the puddled ground. "It's wet," she told the squirming dog. "You can't get down 'til we get to the door."

Under the porch roof of Maverick's General Store, she released the dog. He waited like a coiled spring by the door. She waved to Sam through the window, then twisted the handle. Bonkers' nails slipped on the worn wood floor. Once he got traction, he sprinted to Sam and launched himself like a missile toward her chest. She was prepared for his arrival and captured the ecstatic body in her arms.

"Well hello you lopsided little mongrel!" Bonkers placed a front paw on each of her shoulders and began to lick her cheek, whimpering with happiness, his tail whipping from side to side.

"I've missed you too," she said into his upright ear, then

filled the corners of the room with infectious laughter when he nibbled her ear in return.

It was Sam who had cared for Bonkers when he was a bedraggled, abandoned pup, barely alive, and nursed him back to health. It was Sam who had recognized in Minnow the deep longing for companionship. And it was Sam, as only Sam could, who was able to convince Billy to add the dog to his home on wheels. The small dog was wholly devoted to Minnow. But his bond with Sam was of the maternal variety, deep and everlasting.

Bonkers was not her first rescued animal. Sam had a room attached to the shed out back, fully dedicated to care of the wounded and abandoned. She called it the Critter Spa. The entrance to the small graveyard behind the house was marked with a sign that said "Furry and Feathered Friends Cemetery" where those who didn't make it were lovingly laid to rest. It was a hodgepodge of small wooden crosses and cairns of stone amidst meadow flowers.

Sam set the dog on the floor and pulled Minnow into a lengthy hug. Stepping back, she stared at the girl, shaking her head. "I can't believe that you're as tall as me now! When did that happen?" Minnow shrugged, grinning.

"And where's that crazy uncle of yours?" she asked, peering over Minnow's shoulder toward the door.

"He's getting the tank filled and talking to Donovan."

"Well, he's predictably on time as usual. I don't need a calendar or clock on the days you two show up."

"I know," said Minnow. "You should try to get him to do something new or different."

"I'd like that opportunity," said Sam with a wink. "Honey,

would you go out and tell him to be sure to come in and talk to me? I've got some sales money for him. I'll hang onto Mr. Goofy here." She scooped up the dog while Minnow headed to the door.

Billy and Minnow had been coming to Samantha Maverick's store since Billy first started his rounds two years ago. Sam and Donovan were the nearest people to family in either of their lives.

Billy had met Sam during his one-year attempt at community college. He had looked up with a start when a girl from his morning history class, with wild blond hair and laughing green eyes, sat across from him at the lunch table. She smiled at him, causing him to fix his eyes on the sandwich on his plate, which he had cut into four equal squares, and the fries he lined up on the tray in pairs.

He had wanted to do groups of four fries, but there were ten total, so it had to be five pairs. He figured he would start with eating a pair of fries, then eat a quarter of the sandwich, and then a pair of fries, alternating this way and coming out even with the last pair of fries.

"I thought that point you made in study group, about the underlying causes of the Civil War, was brilliant," the girl said.

Billy looked up, startled. Was she talking to him? Then he looked back at the french fry in his hand. He didn't say anything.

"Where did you learn about that?" she went on. "It wasn't in our textbook."

"It was a library book by Paul Calore," he stammered, darting his eyes at her and then looking back at his plate. "I like to read."

"About history?" she asked.

"About all kinds of things," he said, still looking down.

"I'm Samantha—Sam actually. You're Billy, right?"

That's how it began, this first experience with friendship. She would seek him out at lunch and coax conversation from him. She stood up for him in study group when other students discounted his comments. Over the course of months, Billy became less wary and started to seek her out if she got to the cafeteria before he did. He rehearsed things in his mind that he wanted to tell her that day. He shared his unique brand of humor, and she actually got the jokes. Most people didn't get his jokes.

At the end of the spring semester she told him she was getting married to a guy from her high school. She was moving to Connor to run a store and gas station with her new husband, Mike Maverick. By that time, college had become intertwined with Sam and if she was no longer there, he didn't see the purpose of being there either.

He preferred the solitary comfort of his workshop to the strain of rooms full of people.

For Sam, marriage to Mike Maverick seemed too good to be true. As it turned out, it was. Together they remade the country store and gas station in Connor into a welcome stop for travelers and a neighborhood gathering spot. Best of all, Sam was able to devote an outbuilding behind the store to an animal rescue for small creatures in need of help.

Business picked up slowly but steadily, until they had doubled the revenues from the previous owner. It was Sam who suggested adding a sales yard on the west side of the store, featuring yard art by local craftsmen. Suddenly they were getting cars stopping just to look at the chainsaw carvings of bears and beavers, or to check out the redwood furniture. Revenues doubled again. It should have been a cause for celebration, but what Sam now thought of as the downward spiral of their marriage began with the sales yard. She was the one who recruited the craftsmen, who were predominantly men, and it was Sam they came to see when they brought in their products or collected their sales money. It was Sam they would chat with, laugh with, or present with small gifts they had made as a way of thanking her for marketing their creations.

Mike began coming into the store and standing behind Sam, grim-faced, whenever she was talking with a craftsman.

"What is going on with you?" she asked over dinner one night. "Are you jealous of these guys?"

"Only when I have a right to be," he said. "I see how those guys look at you. They don't think I'm watching, but I am, and I know how guys think."

"Look Mike, I don't care how they look at me. You're my husband, and I'm committed to you. If you don't trust me enough to know that I'm not interested in anyone else, then that's a big problem."

"It's not you I don't trust," he said. "I just don't like other guys hanging around and cozying up to my wife. It's not right. And I don't see you doing anything to discourage them."

Some version of this evening conversation echoed through their relationship month after month. Sam tried making light of his comments, teasing him into a better mood, wooing him into an embrace, reassuring him of her devotion to him alone.

That seemed to ease tensions, at least until the next visit from one of her "admirers" as Mike called them. What finally interrupted the cycle was Sam's announcement one morning."

"I've got some news for you," she said as they were eating breakfast.

Mike looked at her, eyebrows raised.

"You're going to be a father."

His quizzical look was replaced with a huge grin, and he jumped up from the table and wrapped Sam in a hug. He became solicitous and contrite, talking about his son and everything he wanted to teach him.

"What if it's a girl?" Sam asked.

"If it is, then it is," said Mike. "But I just have a feeling that it's going to be a boy."

He was wrong. When Sam had an ultrasound at four months, the technician said, "Unless it's a little boy who is good at hiding something, it's pretty certain you're going to have a daughter."

From the moment it was confirmed, she felt the bond form with the child growing inside her. It infused every moment of every day with new meaning. But the more the neighbors attention focused on Sam and the baby, the more morose Mike became until one January night, after a miserably cold and wet day at the gas pumps, the conversation turned ugly.

"You've got a sweet deal here, don't you?" he said. "Spend your days in here with a toasty wood stove, chatting with your boyfriends and having gaga baby talk with all the neighborhood bitties, while I freeze my sorry ass off out there to earn a few bucks."

"That's not fair Mike," she said. "I work all day, and it's the coziness of the store and the extra sales from the side yard that have made us profitable. That's *my* contribution. You didn't recruit those craftsmen. I did. Do you want me to shut that down? To tell folks we're not going to sell their products anymore?"

"Damn straight I do," he said.

She looked at him, momentarily speechless. "I can't believe you said that. You would give up a third of our profits, just because you have some crazy jealous fantasy going on in your mind?"

"Yep," he said. "I've had enough of seeing this shit cluttering up the place." He grabbed a two-foot tall wood carving of an owl that had been a gift from one of the carvers and stamped toward the door, preparing to heave it outside.

"What are you doing?" she yelled, lunging toward him and grabbing his arm, trying to wrench the owl from his grasp. "Are you insane?"

"No, I'm just fucking done with being used by these bastards so they can make money off me and get it on with my wife. You don't see what they're up to, but I do."

He jerked the owl out of her hands and when she grabbed his shirt to stop him reaching the door, he swung the sculpture around, hitting her squarely in the belly. She went down, gasping for breath, clutching her belly. She curled onto her side, moaning, and starting to sob.

Mike froze, stunned, then dropped to his knees beside her. "I'm sorry Sam," he said. "I didn't mean it. I just...I just can't stand the thought of other guys thinking of you the way I think of you." All she could think of was what might have happened to the baby. She jerked away when he touched her hair.

She got up, staggered into the bedroom and dropped onto their bed. She laid still, hands over her abdomen, crying quietly, trying to make sense of what had just happened. Mike walked in and out of the room, saying her name, trying without success to get her to look at him, to respond to him. Then the bleeding and cramping started. The pain was intense, and the blood more of a gush than a trickle.

"I need to go to the hospital," she said.

After what seemed like an interminable period of time in the hospital waiting room, the receptionist beckoned Mike and let him back into the treatment area. The doctor met him and motioned behind one of the curtained cubicles to a chair.

"I'm afraid I have both bad news and good news," the doctor said. "Your wife suffered a ruptured uterus. You were very lucky. Ten more minutes and she would have bled out, but you got here just in time. We're giving her transfusions and she's going to recover. That's the good news. The bad news is that the baby didn't survive. She was already gone before you got here. The other bad news is we couldn't repair the uterus – the damage was too great. We had to do an emergency hysterectomy. This means your wife won't be able to have any more children. It was the only way to save her. I'm so sorry."

Sam tried to picture how they would move on with their lives together. She tried to find the feelings of hope and devotion and love that had infused the first years of their marriage. Finally she said, "It's no use. It's over between us. It's not just a matter of what happened. It's that I don't want to live with the possibility of it happening again, walking on eggshells to keep from setting you off. And I don't want to feel like I'm owned by you."

Sam got the store as part of a divorce settlement and kept the last name figuring it still suited her even if her former husband did not. She had become a much-loved fixture in this community of Christmas tree farmers, tree-hugging hippies, millworkers, and retired folks, and they rallied to her side as she traversed the new terrain of a single woman business owner. The animals were her solace and her reason for living. When she would find a new home for an abused dog, or see a crow take flight after recovering from a broken wing, her heart soared.

Donovan, who was pushing 70, and his sons Randy and Gil, were Samantha's sole employees. They ran the gas pumps and gave her a break in the store when needed. Donovan was grateful that Oregon remained one of two states in the country where customers weren't allowed to pump their own gas.

Billy was showing Donovan the tool storage cabinet that he had recently built into the utility trailer when he heard the store's door bang shut and saw Minnow striding toward him.

"Sam wants you to come talk to her," she said.

"I always come talk to her," said Billy. "She doesn't need to remind me. Plus, she owes me some money."

"She's sweet on you, you know," said Donovan with a wink to Minnow.

"Sweet on me? You mean sweet like sugar?"

"Well yeah, kind of. It's an expression. Means she likes you."

"I like her too," said Billy, his brow creasing in puzzlement. "I think she knows that."

"I mean she *likes* you, as in likes with a capital L."

"Capital L, as in the beginning of a sentence, or a proper noun?" Billy frowned, looking at the ground as if it might clarify this conversation.

"He means she *likes* you like a girlfriend likes a boyfriend," said Minnow, giggling.

Billy's head jerked up. "I've never had a girlfriend."

"Well, that don't surprise me much," chuckled Donovan. "Let me tell you somethin' though. Sam is the salt of the earth. She deserves the best."

"I agree that she deserves the best. But I don't know what you're talking about Donovan. First you say she's sweet. Then you say she's salt. Can't you just say it directly?"

"He's saying Samantha is a good person and you shouldn't hurt her feelings," said Minnow.

Billy grasped his head with both hands. "Why would I do that? She's my friend and I know she's a good person."

"Look Billy," said Donovan, "Sometimes people hurt each other without meaning to, especially if they don't feel the same way about each other. I just don't want to see her hurt no more."

"I don't want that either," said Billy shaking his head and moving toward the store in his jerky, duck-toed gait. When Minnow started to follow, Donovan called out, "Minnow, can you give me a hand out here for a few minutes? I gotta fill these towel dispensers an' change out the window washer fluid."

"Oh, I get it," she laughed. "You want to give the lovebirds some time to themselves."

"Yer too smart for yer britches y'know," said Donovan. "Here, take these paper towels. An' be sure you put 'em in the right way so's they come outta the dispenser like they should."

Inside the store Billy found Sam straightening the housewares, Bonkers on her heels.

"You didn't have to tell me to come talk to you," he said. "I always come talk to you."

"I know you do," she smiled. "I just needed an excuse to get Minnow out of here for a few minutes."

"Because you like me with a capital L?"

"What?" she blushed.

"Donovan said you like me with a capital L."

Now her rippling laughter brightened the air.

"That old meddler," she said, still laughing. "I do like you with a capital L. But look, that's not what I wanted to talk about. I have some sales money for you. But I also wanted to tell you that Katrina was here two days ago."

"Katrina. My sister Katrina?" he said, scratching at a spot on his neck.

"Yes, your sister. I didn't know who she was at first, but then I saw how much she looks like you and Minnow and remembered that she's been trouble for you in the past. She's been tracking your movements."

"What did she want?"

"I'm not totally sure. But she had some low-life guy with her, along with Minnow's half-sister, and she was going on about how her life had straightened out and how she wants to put her family back together. She didn't come right out and say it, but I think she's going to try to get Minnow back."

"Shit!" Billy ran his fingers through his hair and beginning to pace rapidly back and forth. "Shit, shit! I don't believe her life is straightened out. Did she say what she's going to do?"

"No. I think she was just trying to get some information

on what you're up to, and send you a message, and maybe trying to get me to believe that she's somehow turned into a soccer mom. I didn't bite."

"You didn't bite who?" asked Billy, alarmed.

"I mean I didn't tell her anything."

"Oh. That's good. I don't trust her."

"Wise of you," she said. "Anyway, I just wanted you to know."

He continued to pace. Sam had a sense of gears upon gears turning behind his distant gaze. He took out his notebook and wrote *Katrina at Samantha's!* on its own page.

October 13

Home after a week on the road, Minnow was curled up in the brown, overstuffed recliner with a library book. The room was much as it had been when Granny Vi was alive. The recliner and sofa, each with a small side table and lamp, were the only furnishings except for the kitchen table and four chairs at the end of the room where it joined the kitchen. The floor was a sand-colored linoleum, clean but worn in places from years of use and scrubbing.

Minnow always cherished the fourteen-day breaks. She felt like a bird escaped from its cage, having a whole house after the confines of the camper. And the quiet, after the all-day drone of the engine, was pure bliss.

Billy, on the other hand, found the two weeks at home barely tolerable. He was like a tightly wound clock, needing to keep moving, and two weeks in the same house felt like forced confinement. He spent the days in his shop, cutting and bending metal into fanciful shapes that would catch the wind. He endured the days of staying in one place by inventing and building things that move.

The small, gray-green house, sitting crooked on the lot with its two bedrooms, was the only real home either Billy or Minnow could remember. It felt like enough.

Like Minnow, Bonkers was joyful to be home. He was surveying the yard, catching up on any changes that might have occurred in his absence. In the middle of a sprint, he halted, both ears up briefly, and tracked the crunching sound of tires on gravel from an approaching car. When the car turned into the gravel driveway, he sprung to the porch and stood at attention, watching the dusty red Buick come to a stop in front of the house.

A woman with sandy brown hair, turning to gray, sat in the driver's seat writing on a clipboard. After a few minutes she stepped out, wrestling a large, pink fabric bag containing a clipboard and other disorderly clumps of paper poking out of file folders. She paused and inspected the yard. As she approached the house, she saw the curious-looking dog who issued a low growl followed by furious barking. She hesitated, and just then the door flew open to reveal a slender, barefoot girl wearing jeans and a sweatshirt, her index finger marking her place in a book.

"It's okay Bonkers," said Minnow. She stepped onto the porch and picked up the dog. "Sorry," she said. "He's not too used to visitors."

"No problem," said the middle-aged woman as she joined Minnow on the porch. "I'm Helen Lafferty. I'm here on behalf of the Multnomah County Court," she said, handing Minnow a business card. "I'm looking for Minnow Marsh. Is that you?"

"That's me," said Minnow. "Did I do something wrong?"

"No, you're fine. I just need to chat with you for a few minutes. Is your grandmother here?"

"My grandmother? Uh, no. She died. My uncle is in the shop if you want to talk to him."

"I'm so sorry to hear about your grandmother. So now you live here with your uncle?"

Minnow nodded.

"And when did your grandmother pass away?"

"About two years ago."

Helen Lafferty wrote on her clipboard.

"Yes, I would like to see your uncle. Would you mind asking him to come in?"

"Okay," Minnow said, slipping on a pair of boots neatly placed by the door and retreating from the porch, holding the growling dog like a shield to her chest.

She found Billy under a welding hood, attaching the stem of a revolving flower to a metal stake. When she tapped him on the shoulder, he startled, then turned off the gas, set down the torch and pulled up the hood, eyes questioning.

"There's someone here. A lady from Multnomah County is here. She wants to talk to you."

"What does she want?"

"I don't know. She just said she wants to talk to you. Here's her card."

Billy glanced at the card. "Parental Evaluation Specialist. Dammit! Your mother's responsible for this."

"Are we in trouble?" asked Minnow, panic creeping into her voice. "What's Mom doing?"

"I don't know, but it's not likely to be something good."

"The lady's waiting on the porch. Bonkers doesn't like her."

"Okay." Billy removed his gloves and hood and hung them on their pegboard hooks, took off his welding apron and hung it beside them. He took the notebook from his pocket and made a short note, then walked to the house in his jerky, awkward gait.

"Hello," he said to Helen Lafferty in speech even more clipped than normal, glancing at her briefly before looking to the side.

"Hello Mr. Marsh—is it Mr. Marsh?"

Billy nodded.

"I'm Helen Lafferty. I'm a parental evaluation specialist working with the Multnomah County Court system." Again, she proffered a business card.

"Why are you here Mrs. Lafferty?"

"Could we possibly go in the house to talk Mr. Marsh?"

Billy opened the door, preceded her inside, then turned and looked at her. She looked around the tidy room, then said, "Do you mind if I sit down?"

Billy nodded, indicating the flowered sofa. She perched on the edge, setting the pink bag at her feet.

"The Court asked me to investigate a report of concern regarding your niece Mr. Marsh. It's my job to report back…"

"Report of concern from whom? My sister?"

"I'm afraid I can't reveal the source of the concern. As I was saying, the Court's interest is to make certain that children are safe and getting the care they are entitled to under the law. Your niece was placed under the care of her grandmother, I assume that would be your mother, when she was age three.

Apparently, your mother has passed on, and you are now caring for Minnow. However, we have no record of you being given custody. That's not something we would investigate unless there is a complaint or concern raised about the well-being of the child. In that case, the Court is obligated to investigate."

Billy paced back and forth in front of Helen Lafferty. Minnow stood by the recliner, watching the two adults, Bonkers growling quietly in her arms.

"My mother gave me guardianship," he said.

"How was that?"

"Before she died, she wrote in her will that I should take care of Minnow. She put the house in trust for Minnow and stated that I would live here as long as I'm Minnow's guardian."

"I see. Did your mother take any action to have the courts appoint you as guardian?"

"I don't know. She never said."

"I see that Minnow had a caseworker with CPS, Child Protective Services, an Ashley Nichols. Has she been in touch at all since your mother passed away?"

"No, I didn't think CPS was involved anymore since Minnow came back to live with us."

"Yes, that's probably right. And what is your source of income, Mr. Marsh?"

"As part of the trust, my mother left a monthly stipend. Plus, I make and sell metal sculptures. I also get Social Security Disability."

"On what basis?"

Billy looked up, but didn't speak.

"What is your disability?"

Billy paced more quickly. "I have Asperger's syndrome."

She wrote again on the clipboard. "This disability doesn't get in the way of you caring for your niece?"

Minnow inserted herself. "Uncle Billy takes care of me fine. We get along great."

"I'd like to hear from your uncle," said the caseworker.

"No. It just makes it hard for me to keep a regular job. I tend to misinterpret what people are telling me. And I don't like being around a lot of people."

"I see." She wrote on her clipboard. "I need to talk with Minnow alone for a few minutes, but I'd like your permission for me to do so. If you want to go back to the shop, I can ask Minnow to come get you when we're finished, and I can tell you where we go from here."

Billy stopped pacing and faced the caseworker. "This is my sister stirring up trouble, isn't it? I knew it! You should know, Mrs. Lafferty, that there are reasons my mother left Minnow with me." He pulled out his notebook and wrote *Helen Lafferty — Katrina.*

"I'm sure that is true Mr. Marsh. But we also don't rule out the possibility that people can change. I'm not making a judgment here. I just need to get a clear picture of Minnow's situation and make sure that she's not at risk. If the complaint is unfounded, we'll learn that in the course of the investigation. This is only about what is best for your niece."

"It's okay Uncle Billy. I'll talk with her," said Minnow.

Billy was pacing again, breathing rapidly. "You don't know my sister," he muttered, banging the front door as he stomped from the room. Minnow and Helen Lafferty could hear Billy pacing on the wooden porch, passing in the front window like a sentry. "Dammit!" they heard him cry out. Then he was down the steps and gone.

The caseworker took a deep breath and exhaled. "Okay Minnow," she said. "This should be painless. I just want to ask some questions about your life here with your uncle."

"Did we do something wrong?"

"My job is to make sure you have a safe place to live. Sometimes things can happen to make a place unsafe, even without someone trying to do something wrong. Why don't you sit down so we can talk for a few minutes."

Minnow, who had been rocking from one foot to the other, cradling Bonkers like a baby, now returned to the recliner, setting the small dog in her lap.

"You're not at school today. Are you ill?"

"No, I'm homeschooled by my uncle."

"Really? Do you usually conduct your homeschooling with your uncle in the shop and you in the house?"

"I'm doing my reading right now. My uncle works with me on math, science and history, but I do literature on my own."

"I see. And why did your uncle decide to homeschool you?"

"He travels for his work, and I go with him, so he can teach me while we're traveling. I'm learning algebra and botany right now, and the history of the Roman Empire. Did you know that the ancient Romans built sewer systems and had public toilets with water running underneath to carry away the waste? And they all peed in buckets and the urine was sold to fullers who used it in making wool into cloth."

"No, I can't say that I knew that. Very interesting. And just what is your uncle's work?"

"Like he says, he makes metal sculptures and sells them to different places around the state. He also fixes toilets sometimes."

"And you go with him?"

"Yep, me and Bonkers. This is Bonkers." She rubbed the dog's head.

"Are you on the road overnight when you go?"

"Yes. We go for a week at a time."

"Where do you stay when you're gone overnight?"

"We have a truck camper. Uncle Billy made it from plans he got on the Internet. It's awesome! You can see it out the window there." Minnow pointed out the front window to the pickup with camper mounted on its bed.

Helen Lafferty added to her notes.

"And what are the sleeping arrangements in the camper?"

"Well, Bonkers and I have a bed that's over the cab. Uncle Billy sleeps on the table—only it's not the table when he sleeps on it. The table part goes underneath and the seats fold into a twin-sized bed. We use sleeping bags so we don't have to mess with sheets and blankets."

"When you and your uncle are out on the road, what arrangements do you have for privacy when you're getting dressed in the morning or ready for bed at night?"

"We don't have much privacy, but I don't mind. I've lived with Uncle Billy almost my whole life."

"So does your uncle watch you while you get undressed?"

Minnow looked at the caseworker quizzically.

"Not really. He's usually sitting at the table reading.

"I see. Can he see your sleeping area from his bed?"

"Well yeah, you can see everything from everywhere in

the camper."

"What about when he gets dressed and undressed? Does he do that in front of you?"

"I guess so. I mean, like I said, there's no place to go really. But we both sleep in our underwear and t-shirts, so we just take off our shoes and pants and get into bed."

Helen Lafferty scratched with her pen on one of the papers protruding from her bag trying to get ink to flow. She tossed it into the bag and rummaged underneath the papers, coming up with another pen. She wrote several more lines on the clipboard.

"How do you and your uncle keep clean when you travel?" she asked.

"Some days we just wash with a washcloth, but we also have friends at some of our stops who let us use their showers and washing machines if we need them."

"In all the time that you've lived with your uncle, even when your grandmother was still alive, has he ever touched you in ways that made you uncomfortable?"

"What do you mean?" asked Minnow.

"Has he ever put his hands anywhere on your body that made you uncomfortable?"

"You mean like on my private parts?"

"Yes, or anywhere else that just didn't feel right to you."

"No!" Minnow frowned, looking down at Bonkers and scratching his ears. "Uncle Billy doesn't really like to touch people. He's the one who gets uncomfortable." She looked squarely at the caseworker. "Why are you asking me these questions? Did someone say he touched me? Is someone trying to get Uncle Billy in trouble?"

"I know these questions might make you uneasy. These are things I have to ask about when following up on a concern. I don't want you to feel distressed. But I do want you to know that you can be honest with me and tell me about anything that doesn't feel right in your relationship with your uncle. My job is to be someone on your side to make the situation better if you're having difficulty."

"I'm not having difficulty. Uncle Billy's always treated me good," said Minnow with finality.

"Okay." More writing. "Tell me, did you go to school in the past?"

"Yeah, when my grandmother was alive. I went to East Orient Elementary."

"Do you miss school?"

"I miss being with other kids sometimes. But I have a lot of Instagram and Snapchat friends I keep in touch with, and sometimes I get to visit them. And Mrs. Sanford at the library told me about a group of homeschoolers that gets together once a week, so I may start doing that soon."

"If you did find yourself in a difficult situation and didn't feel you could talk to your uncle about it, is there another adult you could talk to?"

Minnow looked up at the ceiling while she pondered the question. "Well, there's Sam, that's Samantha. She's a good friend that we visit. She gave me Bonkers. And there's Jenny. She's a friend's mom. I don't see her that often, but she's told me she loves me, and she always gives me a big hug when I see her. I think I could talk to them."

"Okay, that's good. You also have my card with my phone number, so you could call me if you have trouble as well."

Minnow pulled the card from her jeans pocket and studied it. "Okay," she said, shoving it back in her pocket.

"Is there anything else you want to tell me about before your uncle comes back in?"

Minnow shook her head.

"All right. Why don't you go get him then."

Billy was standing in the shop door glaring at the house when Minnow came out. When she beckoned him to come, he shook his head and motioned for her to come toward him.

"What did she ask you about?" he asked Minnow as she approached.

"Just a bunch of stuff about what we do when we're traveling. Where we sleep and stuff. And she wanted to know if I miss school."

"What did she ask about me?"

"She wanted to know where you sleep and where I sleep. And she wanted to know if we watch each other get undressed, and if you ever have touched me in a bad way."

"Shit!" said Billy. "What did you tell her?"

"The truth," said Minnow.

"Did she say anything about Katrina? I know she's behind this."

"No."

"Okay, let's go back," he said, pounding the ground on the way to the house with deliberate steps.

"Thank you for giving us that time Mr. Marsh," said the caseworker. "I know this isn't easy, but it's the way we need to proceed at this point. I have a couple more questions for you."

Billy stared past her out the window.

"Minnow tells me that in addition to your metal sculptures

you do plumbing repair work."

"Toilets," he said. "I fix toilets."

"I see. You didn't mention this when I asked you about your source of income."

"I just do it because I like to, not for money."

"Oh, well that's… unusual." More notes. "And you travel for a week at a time?"

"Yes, we go one week out of every three. I have different routes with regular stops where they count on me."

"One of the concerns was that Minnow is not in school. She says she is homeschooled."

"Yes."

"Are you aware that parents and guardians are required to register with the ESD—that's the Educational Services District—if they withdraw a child from school and commence homeschooling?"

"No."

"If Clackamas County ESD has no record of Minnow being registered as a homeschooler, she is considered truant under the compulsory school attendance law."

"I can register with them. I just didn't know."

"That's a good idea. I believe there are also testing requirements you need to be aware of."

"Okay. Minnow can pass tests."

"These are important things to do, but this is really between you and the educational system. It doesn't have particular bearing on our investigation."

"So what happens now?" implored Billy, pacing once again.

"That's not for me to decide. I'll file my report and the

court will determine next steps. We may investigate further if we need more information. Just remember that our goal is to do what is best for your niece. We all want the same thing here, right?" She fixed him with her gaze. He looked at the floor and continued to pace.

"As soon as there is a determination, someone will be in touch," she said. Helen Lafferty made some final notes on her clipboard, wedged it between the file folders in the giant pink bag, and let herself out. Bonkers escorted her to the car, resuming his guttural complaint until she was out of the driveway.

October 16

Inside the tiny two-bedroom house with peeling yellow paint, Katrina stood at the bathroom sink applying eyeliner. She was dressed in a clingy, low-cut orange sweater, short black skirt and black patterned nylons.

The bathroom smelled of the brownish mildew that crept along the wall above the shower base and around the faucet spout and knobs. The plastic shower curtain hung in uneven scallops where it had torn free of the rings. As she painted a clean dark line around her left eye, Dirk appeared in the mirror behind her. He placed his hands on her hips and began to rub rhythmically against her. She could feel his hardness against her buttocks.

She wrenched free and turned around. "Knock it off you horny bastard. Can't you see I'm trying to get dressed? You just messed up my eyeliner!" She ripped off a square of toilet paper and worked at the smudge on her right eye.

"You can get dressed anytime," he said, reaching for her

breasts. "How 'bout makin' me happy first."

She swatted his hands away. "I said knock it off! Look, I'm trying to get us a permanent place to live and some money to live on. Do you want to live in this dump forever?"

"It's not so bad," he said. "C'mon. Just a quickie."

"Fuck off. You know this only works if I can convince the court that Minnow belongs with us, which she does. That means you gotta act like a normal human being for once. Instead of trying to get your rocks off, why don't you clean up this pigsty. It can't look like this if they come for a home visit." She turned back to the mirror. Dirk reached out and tweaked the nipple on her right breast, then shrugged and left the bathroom.

Pale light filtered into the living room from the bent venetian blinds covering the two front windows, highlighting a column of dust. Sadie sat in her pajamas on the lumpy beige sofa watching TV and sucking her thumb. Her chin-length blond hair was permanently matted. A splash of freckles across her nose peeked from beneath her index finger.

"Whatcha watchin' Sadie girl?" Dirk asked.

She removed her thumb long enough to say, "Cartoons," then returned it to her mouth.

Katrina's heels clicked on the kitchen floor. "I need the key to the van," she said.

"D'you really think yer gonna get yer brother to give her up?" Dirk asked, handing her a silver key ring shaped like a fist with a raised middle finger.

"I don't give a shit what that freak does. I know some stuff about him that'll make it so he has no choice."

"Go git 'em tiger," said Dirk as Katrina opened the door.

"Just wash the dishes." She walked through the door, "and get Sadie dressed before I get back. She has afternoon kindergarten," she yelled back as she walked away.

After he heard the van drive away Dirk turned to Sadie. "C'mere Sadie girl. Your mama said we gotta get you outta these PJs." He reached for her and unbuttoned her pajama top and then bent his head to plant a wet kiss on each of her nipples. She felt the rough stubble of his chin and smelled his tobacco breath, shivering with the wetness of the kisses. She removed her thumb from her mouth to hold the two edges of the top together.

"It's cold," she said.

"I'll warm you up," said Dirk, pulling her onto his lap. He hugged her to him and rubbed her tummy, giving her a kiss on the back of the neck. When she returned her thumb to her mouth he pulled it out and said, "Look here. I'm gonna show you somethin' better to suck than that thumb. You can pretend it's candy." Cartoon music played in the background as he slid her to his left leg and reached for his zipper.

When he was through with her, he faced her to him, holding her by the shoulders and said, "Now listen. This is our special secret. You can't tell anyone. Especially your mama. If you tell anyone, people will think you're a bad girl and they'll take you away from your mama and make you live in a home for bad kids. You understand?"

She nodded, crying.

"Are you gonna tell?" he asked, raising her chin so she had to look in his eyes.

She shook her head, crying harder.

"Good girl. Now knock off the crying and go get your

clothes on. Just remember, this is our special secret." He lit a cigarette and picked up the TV remote.

Katrina sat across from Helen Lafferty dabbing at her eyes with a tissue, smearing mascara. "I'm sorry," she said. "It's just that you're the first person in this system who's given me some hope that I might get my daughter back. I'm so worried about her, being raised by my brother and all. He's not right in the head you know."

Helen Lafferty regarded her coolly. "As I told you when we first spoke Ms. Marsh, we will look into the concerns you've raised and the court will act in the best interest of your daughter. Even if we were to determine that her situation with your brother is not suitable, that's not a guarantee that she would be placed back with you. We would need to be assured that your home is the best place for her. That means no drugs or alcohol abuse, and no one in the home who is a threat to her. Your track record on these things is not good."

"I know I've messed up in the past," said Katrina, her voice breaking. "But believe me, I've learned my lesson. Drugs are a thing of the past. And I met someone who can be the father my kids need. He loves kids. Minnow's real father never had anything to do with her. He took off before she was born, so I was left on my own trying to raise her right. It was the stressfulness of being a single mom and all that got me into drugs to begin with." She dabbed at her eyes again.

"I've turned my life around and I just want a second chance to be a good mom. I got my Sadie back, but the family won't be complete until Minnow comes home. Sadie doesn't even know her big sister. And I miss her so much! It breaks my heart every day. Can you help me?" she beseeched.

"The judge will take all information into account, Ms. Marsh, and make a decision in Minnow's best interest. That's our job."

"What would happen," said Katrina, "if my brother decided he couldn't take care of her anymore? Would you let me take her then?"

"CPS and the court would consider any and all possible placements at that point."

"Doesn't it mean anything that I'm her mother?"

"The court always prefers to return a child to the original parents if we're assured that the situation is safe and suitable. However, you need to understand that at age twelve, what Minnow wants is an important component of the decision. Judges are reluctant to place a child of that age in a situation against her will. It just doesn't work out well. And you have a more difficult battle because your parental rights were previously terminated."

Katrina thought about the yellowed newspaper clipping in her handbag.

"What about if you learned that my brother is a threat to her?" asked Katrina, looking directly into Helen Lafferty's eyes.

"Once again, we would investigate and act in the child's interests."

"Okay," said Katrina. "Well, I know some things about my brother that you probably ought to know, but I haven't wanted to get him in trouble. He's my brother after all. But I may be forced to tell you about them so you can act in Minnow's interests."

The caseworker raised her eyebrows. "If there's something

we need to know, please share it."

Not now, thought Katrina. Let her worry about it. Bring it out when it will have the most impact.

"I need to think it over. It wouldn't be fair to my brother not to warn him that I'm going to tell you. I promised my mom I would protect him—him not being normal and all."

"I feel like you're playing games with me Ms. Marsh."

Katrina shook her head, dark streaks of mascara running down her cheeks as tears spilled over. "Please don't say that. I just want my daughter to be home where she belongs and to make sure she isn't gonna get hurt. But I don't want bad things to happen to my brother in the process. He is family after all. It's just so hard to know the right thing to do! I need to think about it. I'll be back in touch." She gave her eyes one last dab with the tissue and stood up to leave.

"You know that if we're to consider recommending that Minnow be placed back with you we'll need to make a home visit," said Helen Lafferty as Katrina walked to the door.

"No problem," said Katrina. "You'll see that it's where she belongs."

Sitting in the van, Katrina blew smoke from her cigarette and considered her next move. All in all, things were going as she'd hoped. But this next part would be tricky. Like a chess player, she was thinking three moves ahead, and trying to anticipate all the possibilities. In truth, she loved this kind of game. It was what she did best. She pulled her phone from her handbag and called Dirk.

"Hey you sexy bastard, what's up?"

"Not much. When you comin' home?"

"I need to do a couple more things," she said. "I want to

go see that lawyer who's the trustee for Minnow, and I may have one other stop."

"So what happened? Did it go like you wanted?"

"Yeah, it went pretty good. I think she's getting the picture."

"So we're gonna get the money?"

"All in good time. Anyways, I need you to make sure Sadie eats some lunch and is ready for the bus for kindergarten."

"How'm I supposed to know what she wants for lunch?"

"Just make her a peanut butter and jelly sandwich and some potato chips."

"Yeah, okay."

"And I meant it about cleaning up the place. They're going to do a home visit. If they don't like what they see, we're screwed."

"It's your kid making all the mess."

"Don't give me a raft of shit. Just do it."

"Right."

Katrina had been to Rick Johnson's office only once before, when her mother died. This is when she learned that there was no inheritance—at least not for her.

"Your mother left it all in a trust for your daughter," Mr. Johnson had said. "That includes the house, its contents, and her savings. Your daughter's guardian controls the trust. Your mother designated your brother as that guardian."

This news was salt in the wound she had nursed all her life. Her brother, who stole the mother's love and attention that should have been hers, now had the money, the house, and her own daughter, all things that should have been hers.

"I just want to get one thing straight. You said my daughter's guardian controls the trust. So, if they were to decide that my brother wasn't a fit guardian, and to appoint a different guardian, then that person would control the trust?"

He hesitated. "Your mother specifically appointed your brother."

"I know that," Katrina interrupted. "But if the courts decided I was the better guardian and gave her to me, what would happen with the trust?"

"In that scenario," he said, "you would control the trust."

"And so I'd get the house and money every month, right?"

"The purpose of the monthly stipend is for the care of your daughter."

"But it would come to me if I was the one caring for her, right?"

"That is correct."

"That's all I need to know. Thanks."

October 17

In her dream Maggie and George were on the beach in Hawaii. She called to him, holding out the bottle of sunscreen lotion. "You'll be burned if you don't stop!" she yelled. He didn't stop. He didn't turn around. He just moved away faster still. She was running now, furious, but the hot sand pulled at her feet and slowed her. "You need to listen to me!" she yelled, starting to cry. She dropped to the sand, feeling it burn her palms and shins.

With a shrill ring, the phone on her nightstand jarred her awake. Disoriented, she knocked the receiver to the floor. She retrieved it, her face wet with tears, her heart thudding against her chest.

"Hello?" she rasped, trying to clear her head.

"Mrs. Berry?" The intensity of the voice brought her fully awake.

"Yes, this is Mrs. Berry."

"This is Zach Sanderson. I'm sorry to call so early, but there are some additional things we need to go over in preparation for the deposition today. I expect the Fosters' attorney to play hard ball today and I want to make sure you feel ready for their line of questioning."

Zach Sanderson was the attorney for her insurance company. She pictured him now, trim and intense in his black suit, white shirt, subdued tie, his short dark hair gelled into soft spikes.

"Do you have time to talk right now?" he asked.

"Can you give me 15 minutes?" she said, willing the fog from her brain.

"Sure, I'll call you back in 15."

Maggie used a warm washcloth to bathe her face, brushed her hair, and started a pot of coffee. She tried to slow her breathing. George had been so real. She could have touched him if only she had been able to reach him. And flames of anger continued to lick at her consciousness. Why did he ignore her? Why was he moving away from her? She realized with shock that she *was* angry at him. He had, in fact, left her. And he had left her to deal with all of this. Not on purpose, of course. She knew it was not on purpose, but the feeling persisted. She pushed these thoughts aside and forced herself to concentrate on the day ahead.

Coffee in hand, Maggie wrapped her robe tightly against the morning chill and perched on a barstool at her kitchen counter surveying the silent room. It had been five months since her discharge from the hospital and she couldn't shake the feeling that she was standing outside, viewing her life through a window, her own reflection blocking her view of things.

She kept waiting to hear George's baritone booming from upstairs, "What's for breakfast Mags? I'm famished!"—expecting him to stride into the room, all business, bring his coffee and newspaper to the other barstool, and fill the room with sounds and questions and plans for the day.

Maggie had not been one of those women who structured her life around her husband, and yet, with him gone, she couldn't seem to find her center. She knew she had had a purposeful life before—at least she thought she did—but it all seemed trivial now.

She retrieved a manila envelope from beneath a stack of magazines. Pulling out a thick sheaf of papers, words jumped out at her. *Samuelson, Mertens and Collins, Attorneys. Medical expenses. Pain and suffering. Punitive damages. Driving while intoxicated.*

Driving while intoxicated.

More than once Zach had asked her about George's drinking habits. She had never thought of him as a problem drinker, or as being someone who had "drinking habits." But since the accident, whenever she tried to picture him, she saw him with a drink in his hand. She heard the ice tinkle. She smelled the amber scotch—pungent, fruity. When she and Toby had gone through the family photo albums, they had laughed at the photos of George with Toby in the swimming pool, their hair plastered flat, Toby on his Dad's back. On the next page George was at the backyard grill, spatula in his right hand, glass of scotch in his left.

She had closed the album. "I can't do this right now," she'd said. Later, after Toby had left, she went back to the album. Flipping through the pages, there it was, photo after photo, George and a glass of scotch. Not all, by any means, but enough.

In the months since the accident, she had tried to recapture her sense of George as she had experienced him throughout their marriage. They had met during in-country training for the Peace Corps in Bolivia—one of the last Peace Corps cohorts to serve that country. She had been involved in education and he in public health. She had liked him from the start but wasn't there to find a mate. She was on a mission to make the world better and viewed herself as a strong, independent woman.

George had a different idea. Every time she turned around, he was there, carrying her food tray from the mess hall, or sitting beside her in Spanish class. She tried to ignore him at first, but he didn't take no for an answer. And he was handsome and funny. At six foot one he towered over her, his dark, wavy hair glistening in the Bolivian sunlight. Bit by bit he drew her in, until one day she realized she couldn't imagine life without him.

Maggie had joined the Peace Corps to save the world. George had been a bit more practical. He'd wanted the draft deferment and the public health experience since that was his field of choice. He'd had a low draft number and was sure to be drafted into the army. His hope was that something would change during his deferment that could prevent his being sent to Vietnam. It didn't work and he was drafted, but they sent him to Germany. Maggie went with him and the two married.

She had never regretted it. He'd been a kind and loving husband and father—a positive contributor in any situation. She knew these things, and tried to hold onto them.

The ringing telephone brought her back to reality.

"It's Zach again Mrs. Berry. Is now a good time to talk?"

"Yes, go ahead," said Maggie, already weary of the conversation.

"I want to talk about our strategy for the deposition, and also about what I think the Fosters' attorney is going to do. Here's how I think it's going to come down. They're going to want to place all the blame for the accident on your husband. As we've discussed, our problem is that your husband had been drinking and it appears that he crossed into the oncoming lane and therefore appears to be at fault."

"What do you mean '*appears* to be'?" asked Maggie. "Isn't that a proven fact?"

"Maybe not," said Zach. "At least not as clearly as the plaintiff's attorney hopes to prove. You know I've been doing my own digging and I have just run across some interesting tidbits that could throw a wrench into their case."

"You mean George didn't cause the accident?" said Maggie, the thought enticing her like a wisp of cool air in a stuffy room.

"In our situation he only caused it if they can prove he did, and I'm saying they may not be able to prove it," said Zach. "You see, one thing I discovered was that there was a large pothole in your lane, about 30 feet before the point of impact. It's possible that George swerved into the other lane to avoid that pothole. I want you to think carefully. Do you remember anything about that?"

"I don't remember anything at all about that night beyond getting dressed for the party," Maggie said. She had tried to pull the memories from the recesses of her mind. What she saw was not a memory, but a fabrication based on what she now knew. What she saw was the crumpled, ruined body of a boy.

"I'm sorry, I just don't remember it."

"That's OK. In fact, that may be good—just stay with that. They're going to push you about your recollections, so just tell them you don't remember. That's the truth, right?"

"Yes. But even if George swerved to avoid something, he still was in the wrong lane so how can it not be his fault?"

"True, but here's the other thing," Zach said, excitement surging in his voice. "Apparently Jason's friend Cameron, the other driver, had a reputation for speeding and one of his favorite places to show off was Winter Hill Road. You see, speeding over the top of the hill makes your car catch some air. If George had swerved to avoid the pothole, and the kids were driving too fast over the hill, he wouldn't have had time to see them and get back into his lane, and the kids wouldn't have been able to slow down enough to avoid a crash. In other words, it could be as much their fault as his. It's a long shot, but it's possible."

"Can you prove that this was what happened?"

"I don't have to. All I have to do is cast enough doubt so they can't prove that drunken driving was the cause. Yes, he broke the law by drinking and driving, but Cameron King may have also broken the law by speeding. Anyway, I think we've got a shot, which is more than I thought we had when I first looked at this case."

"Couldn't they make a similar argument, that if George hadn't been drinking, he would have seen them coming over the hill too fast and avoided the accident?"

"That's exactly what they'll try to do, which is why I wanted to talk with you this morning. Just to remind you that they're going to ask you questions about George's drinking habits, whether he would routinely drink and drive, whether you were aware that he had had too much to drink that night. It could get nasty. We'll have some time to rehearse a bit before the deposition starts."

"Next week," Zach went on, "when I depose Cameron and two of his friends, I'm going to really pin him down about his driving habits. He's already guilt-ridden, having survived while his buddy died, so that may work in our favor, although it's not going to be pleasant."

"Is it really necessary to go after that boy? He must be suffering terribly already."

Images of classrooms full of teenage boys played like a movie in Maggie's head. She saw their exuberance, their innocent and goofy hijinks, and their vulnerability when confronted with the real world. She had often said that it was a miracle any of them reached adulthood. It wasn't their fault. They were hard-wired to take risks.

"That boy's driving habits may be responsible for the loss of your husband. Shouldn't there be consequences for that?"

"I don't know. I suppose…"

"One more thing," Zach interrupted. "Jason's parents will probably attend the deposition today."

Maggie's breath caught in her throat, her hands and feet suddenly clammy. "His parents? They'll be in the room? That's allowed?"

"As parties to the complaint they have a right to attend unless there is a valid reason to exclude them. We don't really have a reason. I just wanted you to be prepared."

"How does one prepare for that?" she said, as much to herself as to Zach.

"You'll do fine," said Zach confidently. "Is your son driving you?"

"Yes."

"Alrighty then. See you at 10, Conference Room B.

Her heels echoing on the polished linoleum, Maggie steeled herself for the plaintiff attorney's questions.

"Mr. and Mrs. Berry? They are waiting for you in there," the receptionist gestured to an open door.

The small, stuffy room was furnished with a single table and eight chairs. The walls were a uniform beige, blank except for a framed poster showing the evacuation route in case of emergency. Her head still rang with Zach's staccato coaching, hammering his point home. "Just answer the questions. Don't elaborate. Answer with yes or no if you can. You'll do fine. You got it? You okay?"

Then she saw them. Sitting at the end of the table. Jason's parents.

They looked like any of the countless couples that had sat across from her at parent-teacher conferences, anxious to know about their children's progress, concerned about their chances for college admission given their poor marks in English.

She was always firm on grading despite parental pressure.

She imagined herself saying, "It's not fair to expect less

than your child is capable of doing. If I give him a grade that he hasn't earned, just so he can get into college, what does that teach him about the real world? What happens when he gets to college, and no one is willing to cut him any slack? Better to learn this lesson now than in college or in his first job."

The best parents and students respected, even revered her, for this tough stance. Others complained to administration that she was standing in the way of their child's future. Fortunately, her principal backed her, but the same couldn't be said for the school board. In the last few years before she retired, she had been faced with calls from friends alerting her that she was being labeled a problem teacher by certain board members. As much as she loved the kids and teaching, she felt it was better to end her career with her integrity intact than to go out after caving in and violating her own principles.

But it was not anxiety over grades she saw in these parents. Their faces were road maps of grief. And anger. Raw, simmering anger. They looked directly at Maggie. She looked away as she sat, but from the corner of her eye saw Jason's mother lift something from her lap and purposefully prop it up right in front of her on the table. A photo. A beautiful boy. Lovely clear, blue eyes. Wavy light brown hair. Vibrant. His life ahead of him. His life over.

Maggie closed her eyes, tears stinging her eyelids. She heard Zach's chair scrape as he got up to talk to the opposing attorney. She felt her son's arm around her, his hand squeezing her shoulder. "It's OK Mom," he said. When she looked up again the photo was face down on the table, but it had done its business.

Zach asked for a brief recess and took Maggie and Toby

into the hall, loudly closing the door behind them.

"That was a cheap shot," Zach said. "They're just trying to rattle you. I know it's tough, but don't let them do it."

"That boy," she said, dabbing her eyes with a tissue. "I think they're just devastated. That's how I'd feel in their shoes. They want me to know what was taken from them. They want me to be as sorry as they are."

"Of course they do because they want to hurt you and get you to roll over so they can win this thing. But remember, you're a victim too. You didn't do this. You don't owe them anything. If they have their way, they'll take you for everything you've got."

"You mean take you—your company—don't you? I don't think I can do this. Can't we find a way to settle this thing and let them get on with their lives?"

"This isn't just about money," snapped Zach. "It's about your husband's reputation as well. We may have an opportunity to clear his name. We may be able to undo some of the damage that's been done."

"Mom, think about it. Dad did so much good in his life. I don't want this last act to erase everything else. I know it's hard, but do this for him, for me and Heather and the kids. Do it for yourself!"

She was surprised at Toby's vehemence.

"I didn't know you felt so strongly," she said.

"Of *course* I do. Don't you? To have it printed in the newspaper that your father was a drunk driver, who killed a kid— that's humiliating. I think it's even impacted my business." Toby, himself a certified teacher, operated an after-school tutoring program for junior high and high school kids. "Sign-ups for the fall term are down 20% from last year and I can't pin it to anything else. I'm going to have to lay off two of my tutors. Please mom, we need this win."

"Okay," said Zach, "we need to go back in there. Do you think you can handle it Mrs. Berry?"

Maggie closed her eyes, took a deep breath and nodded. The trio walked back into the room and the questioning began.

Maggie focused only on the attorney firing the questions. She felt the presence of the Fosters, smoldering embers threatening to ignite. The picture lay face down, treacherous. She tried not to see them.

After what seemed like endless, repetitive questions about George, his work habits, his drinking habits, their attendance at other parties, his driving, the attorney directed her to think about the night of the accident.

"What do you remember about that night Mrs. Berry?"

"I remember getting dressed for the Pattersons' party."

"Do you remember what you were wearing?"

She closed her eyes and pictured herself and George in the bedroom, he in his gray slacks and suspenders, she in her loose-fitting aquamarine dress. It was an unusually warm evening for May. She saw herself putting on silver earrings and bracelet, and grabbing a shawl off its hanger.

"Yes."

"Please describe what you were wearing."

"It was a light aqua-colored dress."

"Okay. What about your husband? What was he wearing?"

"Gray slacks and a sport coat."

"Did your husband have any alcohol to drink before going to the party?"

She hesitated. "I'm not sure. Sometimes he had a drink when he came home. He'd been running errands. I don't know about that night." She smelled scotch, heard the clink of ice.

"Did you have a drink before the party?"

"No."

"You remember about yourself, but not about your husband?"

"I didn't drink that night. I was on a diet and had cut out alcohol. I was upstairs in the bedroom when he came home. I don't know if he had a drink before he came up or not."

"Did he seem inebriated before the party?"

"No."

"Okay. Tell me about the party itself. What do you remember?"

"I don't remember anything after getting ready and getting in the car to go to the party."

"Was your husband driving?"

"Yes."

"Did he always drive when you went out together?"

"He usually drove," said Maggie.

"Can you think of a time when you drove?"

"I'm not…well…perhaps."

"So you can think of a time?

"Coming home from a trip to California. It was a long trip and we traded off driving."

"How often did you drive when you and your husband were out together in the evening over the past year?"

"I don't remember exactly."

"Your best guess."

"Maybe once or twice."

"Why did you drive on those occasions?"

"Well, you know, he might have been tired or something."

"Did you ever drive because he had been drinking?"

"I don't recall that," she said.

"All right," said the attorney, looking at his notes, straightening loose papers into a stack. "I want to go back to the night of the party. The Pattersons told the police that you left the party at about 11:15 p.m. Do you remember leaving to come home?"

"No."

"They said that you and your husband talked in an animated fashion for several minutes outside the house before getting into the car to drive home. Do you remember that conversation?"

"No."

"Do you remember any part of your interaction with your husband, or the ride home from the party that evening?"

"I don't remember anything," she said, tears springing to her eyes. Her breath was coming in short gasps. She sent a pleading look to Zach.

"I think we need a break here," said Zach. "This is bordering on badgering. She's told you she doesn't remember." The plaintiff's attorney responded that he was finished with his questioning for the present, reserving the right to schedule additional time if further evidence arose.

But the thing was, during this last series of questions Maggie was suddenly flooded with vivid images. All at once she *did* remember. She remembered the conversation with George outside the Pattersons'. She remembered the drive toward home along Winter Hill Road. She remembered everything except the accident itself. The flood of memories washed over her, and the truth that had been hidden stared at her as clearly as Jason Foster's face in his photo.

Maggie was silent on the ride home from the deposition, staring out the rain-spattered side window, not fully registering Toby's words of encouragement.

"You did great in there today Mom. I know it's really tough for you, but we'll get through this. Do you want me to come in?"

Silence.

"Mom? Do you want me to stay with you for a while?"

"Uh…no…no, I just need to rest. You go on home."

"You sure? I'm glad to come in for a while."

"I'm sure. I'll be fine."

"Okay, but if anything comes up, call me. Will you do that?"

"Sure. Thanks for going through that with me. Now go on home to your family."

What she wanted was time alone to process what had just happened. Once inside the house, images from the night of the accident continued to flood her brain like a repeating film loop. She closed her eyes and they became more vivid. She heard George's voice, and her own. She heard the hum of the engine as they drove, felt the car's relentless progress. The loop started again, and she saw George outside the Pattersons' as they left the party, boisterous, face flushed.

"You've had quite a bit to drink," she said.

"Yep, and I enjoyed every swallow!" he replied.

"What if I drive home?"

"I'm fine Mags. Don't worry about it."

"Seriously George, I think I should drive."

His tone changed to belligerence now. "Look Mags, I said I'm fine, and that means I'm fine. Have I ever *not* gotten us home? Ever?"

"No, but I just think…"

"You just think? You think that after fifty years of marriage, and not a single problem, you think you can't trust me to get us home? Thanks for the vote of confidence Maggie. Thanks a lot. If that's how it is then, here, take the keys. You drive." He thrust the keys in her face.

She hesitated.

"Of course I trust you. It's not that. It's…"

"It's most definitely that. Either you trust me, or you don't, and you're telling me you don't." He jingled the keys in front of her.

"Of course I trust you," she said, and walked to the passenger door.

As the loop played and replayed, it hammered home the unbearable truth. The real fault for the accident, for the death of Jason Foster, lay not with George, but with her. She could have stopped it. She could have reached out and taken the keys. They were right in front of her. But because of her fear of displeasing him, her need for his approval overriding what she knew was right, she had abdicated that responsibility.

The price of her cowardice—a boy's life.

The image of the keys dangled in her memory, taunting her. If only she could reach out and take them now, take it all back, undo what had been done. Alone in the dark house, she sat in the corner of the window seat, knees drawn up against her chest, and sobbed.

Maggie slept fitfully. In her dream she was a teenager, desperately trying to hide her report card under a stack of books when her father appeared in the room. He spotted the corner of the card poking out from beneath the books and yanked it out.

"What happened in chemistry?" he asked, his eyes piercing her.

Maggie's stomach lurched. She tried to look away but couldn't move, his eyes pinning her to the floor.

"That teacher hates girls," she replied, dry-mouthed. "And I had a lab partner who flaked out and it brought both of our scores down. I think a C+ is pretty good considering."

Her father moved in closer and held the report card in her face. "You think that do you? You think a C is pretty good? A C is an average score. Do you aspire to be average? To be an average student when you have the capability to be more than that?"

"Chemistry's really not that important to me," she mumbled.

"Listen to me Margaret, and listen closely," he said, never shifting his gaze. "None of us gets to do only what we deem important. To succeed in life, you have to do your best regardless of what the task is. And when you fail to do that, you need to take responsibility. It wasn't your teacher," he said, slapping his free hand with the report card, "and it wasn't your lab partner," another slap, "who earned that C was it?"

She stood frozen.

"You earned it," slap, "and you need to take ownership. I'm counting on this being the last time I find a C grade on your report card."

He shoved the report card into her damp, trembling hands and walked from the room.

October 18

Maggie startled awake, breathing rapidly, immediately grateful that her father's visit was only in a dream. *He's dead,* she reminded herself. She waited for his presence to fade, his smell of tobacco and aftershave lingering in her nostrils.

She stood and shuffled to the bathroom, the achy morning stiffness a reminder of her recently healed pelvis. For a moment she contemplated the still full bottle of pain medication on the shelf above the sink, the idea of numbness enticing. An involuntary shiver overtook her. She closed her eyes for a moment and then stepped into the shower, willing the hot water to wash away the residual image of her father.

The weight of yesterday's revelation followed her through her morning routine. She poured cereal into a bowl and stared at it. The sight of it turned her stomach. She poured it back into the box. The words *my fault* repeated like a mantra.

She couldn't sit still, but had nowhere to go, so she paced the kitchen. After 30 minutes she grabbed her cell phone and punched in Ceci's number.

"This is Cecelia Adams and you've reached my voice mail," said Ceci's voice. "Please leave me your name and number and I'll call you back."

"It's Maggie. I'm sorry to bother you, but I need to talk to you," she said, her voice quavering. "Please call me." She hung up and resumed pacing.

Ten minutes later Ceci called back.

"Hey Sis, what's going on?" she said anxiously. "Has something happened?"

"I've started to remember," said Maggie.

"That's great!" said Ceci. "I mean, I think it's great. I know it can be upsetting and overwhelming, but it's still good that your memory's returning. It means you're doing more healing. What do you remember?"

"Everything that night, except the accident itself."

"Wow. So it just all came back at once? What triggered it?"

"It was the deposition. The boy's parents were there. They had a picture of him Ceci. They had a picture of the boy. It broke my heart. Their lawyer kept asking me questions about that night, and I couldn't remember. And then all of a sudden, it just all flooded back. It was like someone raising the curtain on a stage."

"Oh my God, Maggie. That's incredible! Don't you feel relief to have your memory back?"

"What I feel is overwhelming guilt."

"Guilt? Because you lived and George didn't?"

"No. Because I'm responsible for that boy's death. For George's death," she said, her voice breaking. Even though she couldn't remember the accident, her mind had created an image of the scene. She saw George, bloodied and broken, slumped behind the wheel. She saw Jason Foster, thrown from the jeep, body crumpled, his clear blue eyes vacant in the moonlight.

"Maggie, Maggie, hold on there," said Ceci. "Why do you think that?"

"I could have stopped him Ceci," she wailed. "I could have stopped George from driving, and I didn't. I didn't want to deal with his anger, so I did the cowardly thing and let him drive, and I *knew* he shouldn't be driving. I *knew!* And now Jason Foster is dead, and George is dead, and it's my fault."

"Whoa, whoa!" said Ceci. "Why do you think you could have stopped him?"

"I told him I wanted to drive and he held out the keys to me. He said, 'Here, take the keys,' but he was mad, and I didn't want to live with his anger, so I didn't stand up to him. I didn't take the keys!"

The last five words came out as a wail, punctuated by a sob.

"Okay, I get why you feel guilty. But we all have things we would do differently if we had known how they were going to turn out. But we don't know. We do our best in the moment. It was George who chose to drink. It was George who chose to drive, not you. You can't blame yourself for this Maggie."

"How can I not?" she sobbed. "I couldn't stand up to him and my cowardice led to this. I'm a coward Ceci. A damn coward! I don't see how I can live with this!"

"You can, honey, and you will. You don't know what would have happened if you'd driven home. Maybe that lawyer is right. Toby told me that those boys were probably speeding, and that George may have swerved to avoid a pothole. Maybe you would have done the same thing, and the accident would have happened anyway. Maybe you would have been the one killed."

"That would have been better. I wish it had been me," said Maggie.

"Maggie, I'm going to come spend a couple of days with you and talk this through. I can't come until day after tomorrow though. Have you told Toby about this?"

"No, I haven't told anyone but you."

"I'm going to call him. I don't want you there alone tonight. This is too much to deal with all at once."

"Toby has his work and his family. He already took yesterday off for the deposition."

"Don't argue with me on this."

When Toby arrived 30 minutes later, he found her striding from room to room. He walked across the room and blocked her path, catching her by the shoulders. Her small frame was stretched taught, ready to burst.

"Why didn't you tell me?" he implored, holding her in place like a struggling child.

When she looked up at him, pools of moisture overflowed her eyelids and made rivers down her cheeks. He gripped her until her shoulders slackened.

"I couldn't," she said. "I'm so ashamed."

He folded her in his arms, and she wept.

When she quieted, he led her to the brown leather sofa where she had read to him as a child and sat her beside him.

"Tell me everything," he said.

She described the scene at the Patterson's and the argument with George, ending with, "It was my fault, Toby!"

"Do you really think you could have stopped him from driving?" he asked.

"Yes," she said. "He would have been mad, and I would have had to live with that for a while, but he would have let me drive if I'd taken the keys. Now look at the price I've paid for my spinelessness."

"I know how he could be when someone challenged him, especially if he'd had a drink or two. And this was clearly more than one or two."

"No excuse," she said.

"I think you're being too hard on yourself. If you'd left ten seconds earlier or later, the accident wouldn't have happened. It was bad luck. And what can you do at this point anyway?"

"I don't know. I can't imagine every day of my life having to wake up knowing this. Ceci says it will get better, but I don't believe her."

"You should believe her. She knows. Besides, what choice do you have."

"What I do know is that I'm done helping Zach Sanderson and the insurance company he represents. I'm not going to testify anymore. He'll have to settle it the best he can."

Toby nodded.

"Will you come stay with us tonight? I don't think you should be alone. This is too much."

"Toby, this is going to sound awful, but I don't think I could stand to be around Eric and Amy right now. To think about that poor boy, dead because of me, and then to see my own beautiful, healthy grandchildren…it's just too painful."

"Mom, you're going to have to get past blaming yourself in this way."

"How?"

"I think you're still in shock from the memories coming back. I'll stay here tonight. I know Ceci is coming the day after tomorrow, so let's just take it a day at a time."

October 20

"Ceci," said Maggie three hours after her sister arrived, "I know you're trying to help me, but talking about this is wearing me out. It's like you're on a mission to expunge my guilt whatever it takes."

"I am, sort of," said Ceci. "Guilt is perfectly normal in your situation. George died and you survived. A boy was killed. But you can't take all that on yourself. It's not healthy. There's a point where you just have to accept that it happened and move on with life."

Maggie thought about the night of the accident. What twisted her gut was the feeling she had as she walked away from those dangling keys and got into the passenger seat. She had felt it was wrong, known it was wrong, but she did it.

"Maybe there are some things from which one shouldn't move on," she said. "Maybe some things make getting on with life impossible, or at least unconscionable if one is an honorable person. Do you think the boy's parents have moved on with life?"

"Have you considered contacting them and asking for their forgiveness? It could be healing for both of you."

Maggie looked at her sister with incredulity. "First of all, the attorney told me I'm not allowed to contact them. Besides, I'm the last person they want to hear from! If you could have seen how they looked at me in that deposition room. It was a look of hatred." Tears stung her eyes. "Please don't push me on this. I could never ask for forgiveness for the unforgivable."

October 23

Maggie was perched on a barstool staring into a cup of tepid tea when Toby called three days later.

"I'm just checking to see how you're doing. Is Ceci still there?"

"She just left."

"Did the two of you have a good couple of days together?"

"You mean did she straighten me out?"

"If anyone can straighten you out, it's her."

"She."

"She what?"

"It's 'she', you mean, not it's 'her'. Aren't you tutoring students in English?"

"She, whatever. You know what I mean. And I'm not tutoring anyone right now, I'm trying to have a conversation with you. Anyway, I just want you to quit tormenting yourself about the accident."

"We talked for two days. It wore me out. Like I told her, I just need some time, so I want you to quit worrying about me."

"I'm hoping you'll start getting out more,' said Toby. "It's not good to spend all of your time in that house."

"There's no place I want to go," she replied. "One doesn't go out just for the sake of going out."

"What about the YMCA. You used to volunteer and go three times a week to swim and work out."

"I'm through with them," she said.

"*Through* with them? Why?"

"If they can't be bothered to proofread the newsletter that they distribute to however many thousands of people in this city, I can't be bothered with them."

"You're kidding," Toby said. "You're throwing over a whole organization because someone made a minor mistake in a newsletter?"

"It wasn't so minor. It's a sign of disrespect for their readers."

"So this is a reason to no longer exercise?"

"It's all the reason I need," she said. "Besides, I didn't like the way they behaved toward me the last time I went there."

"And how was that?"

"All simpering and sad. Those pained and sympathetically knowing looks, as if they knew what I've been through. All that 'We're so glad to have you back with us Maggie' stuff. I couldn't take it."

"Aren't you being a bit harsh?"

She blushed a deep red and held back her initial response. "I don't know, but frankly I don't particularly care. Like I said, I'm through with them."

"What about seeing the kids? They're asking about you."

"Not yet. Ceci thought it might be good for me to have a change of scenery. I'm thinking maybe I'll go to the coast for a few days."

"Great idea," said Toby. "Where will you go?"

"Our usual place in Lincoln City of course."

"Won't that remind you of Dad too much?"

Maggie pictured their last visit. George was dozing in the green, overstuffed chair facing the ocean, University of Oregon baseball cap on his head, book open on his lap. She was standing at the window watching the children and dogs cavorting on the sandy beach. Kites were spinning and dipping above. *How blissfully blind we were to what was ahead,* she thought.

"Everything reminds me of your dad," she said. "And the owners are like family. They sent me a card after the accident and encouraged me to come spend some time. They're good people."

"That sounds good then. When will you go?"

"Day after tomorrow. I have a few things to take care of here."

"Is one of them the lawsuit?"

"I've told Zach that I'm not testifying or helping him pursue it any further. I want him to settle it."

"What did he say?"

"He wasn't happy. You know how lawyers are. They'll march you right into the abyss if they think it means victory. I didn't give him a choice so he's talking to the Fosters about a settlement."

"So, your mind's made up on this."

"My mind is made up."

"End of story then," said Toby.

Maggie had always loved life, and she had thought those who took their own lives were cowards. *How little I understood,* she now thought. She had thought she was tough. She had thought she could withstand pain. And she could when it came to physical pain. But this was pain that gnawed away at her very soul, at her sense of who she was in the world. The need to escape this unbearable guilt and shame trumped everything.

She had been over it hundreds of times in her mind. She told herself that suicide wasn't just escaping. It was restoring some kind of balance. A life for a life. She knew of no other way to tell that family, to tell the world, how sorry she was, how she knew that she didn't deserve to live when this boy had died.

Of course she knew it really wasn't balanced. A seventy-six-year-old life, already lived, already filled with memories of all that happens in a human lifespan is in no way equivalent to a sixteen-year-old life, poised to experience all that the world has to offer.

In the end, perhaps it wasn't about balance at all, only escape.

Then her thoughts would turn to her grandchildren, to Toby, to Ceci. How was this fair to them, leaving them to wonder if they were responsible in some way, if they could have done something to change her mind? But how many years did she have left to live in any case? They would lose her anyway. At least this way her death could be a statement, could mean something.

She had never been one to sit idle, especially when confronted with a problem. She had to act, to do what was in her power to improve the situation. This was the one thing totally within her power to do.

October 25

Maggie walked from room to room with a dust cloth, inspecting each piece of furniture and straightening pictures. She took two manila folders from the kitchen desk and set them in plain sight on the countertop.

In her bedroom she opened each dresser drawer and refolded the clothes into neat stacks. She wiped down the bathroom counter, eliminating water spots and polishing the fixtures. Then she sat on her bed and picked up the two framed photos from her nightstand.

George. Standing at the overlook by Pittock Mansion with Mt. Hood and the Portland skyline behind him, abundant flowers blooming in the foreground. It was one of those crystal-clear spring days when they had hiked the trail through Forest Park. He was smiling her favorite smile. She loved how he smiled with his eyes as much as with his mouth.

The second photo was of Toby, Heather, Eric, and Amy when the kids were in middle school. The family was on a camping trip in the woods, and they were all perched like a row of birds atop a picnic table. How much Eric looked like George!

She closed her eyes and dabbed the corners with a tissue, and then gently replaced the photos.

Walking through the kitchen, she tossed her dust rag into the kitchen garbage can and then took the plastic trash bag to the outdoor can. She stood in the doorway between the kitchen and garage surveying the house a final time. Then she picked up her small overnight bag and jacket and took them to her blue Toyota Camry. It looked lonely in the spacious garage. The dark tracks from George's Acura tires still marked the floor.

It was a fine fall Oregon day. The fog hung in wisps around the coastal mountains, and then as she neared Highway 101 it gave way to blue sky and puffy clouds. The highway ran the length of Oregon's coastline hugging the cliffs above the ocean and passing through a series of small coastal towns. Lincoln City was strung along ten miles of the highway with the typical beach town offerings of motels, restaurants, souvenir shops, art galleries, and salt-water taffy. Lowering the car window to breathe in the salt air, Maggie felt herself grow lighter, as though a heavy fog inside her was lifting.

When she walked into office at the Seagulls Nest Cottages, Rob hurried from behind the counter and wrapped her in a long hug. He was a bear of a man, at least 6' 3" and broad through the chest. He had gray unruly hair and beard, and eyes that sparkled.

"It's about time we saw you over here. Katie was so glad to get your call. We're all ready for you. Say, are you sure you want your usual cottage? We've got two others open."

"Thanks Rob. I thought about that, but I think that even though nothing's the same for me, I'd still like the comfort of familiarity."

"Of course," he replied.

"By the way, I see that you still haven't put an apostrophe on your sign."

"You bring that up every time you're here, and you're the *only* customer who does.

"Common ignorance, or tolerance, whichever it is, doesn't excuse bad grammar. Really, it should be Seagull's Nest, or Seagulls' Nest, but not Seagulls Nest, unless you're trying to make a statement about the brooding habits of seagulls. What do you want it to be, one seagull or many? You tell me and I may just get a ladder and insert the missing punctuation my-self."

"I want it to be just what it is so that you'll keep coming back here to set me straight."

"Hmph," she said. "Well if that's how it is, I think I'd like to settle in if you've got a key for me."

"Here you go," he said handing her a key attached to a small piece of driftwood. "Can I carry your luggage for you?"

"No need. I packed light."

"Okay Maggie, you get settled and then come back and say hello to Katie. She's off to get her hair cut but she'll be back in an hour."

"I'll do that," said Maggie as she slipped the key into her jacket pocket.

She took her small bag from the back seat, locked her car, and started down the gravel path to cottage number seven. As she unlocked the front door, she had an overwhelming sensation that she would find George lounging in the big green chair by the window.

The smell inside the rustic cottage was the same as always; the moist sea air, a bit smoky from the wood-burning fireplace, and lemon from the cleaning solution. After the door swung open there was an instant when she actually *saw* him, sitting in his chair and wearing the green flannel shirt that he always took to the beach, and his U of O baseball cap.

And then the chair was empty.

She walked around it, then sighed and sank into its puffy cushions, holding her overnight bag on her lap. She could barely catch the scent of his aftershave. *If only I could just lose myself in this lovely place,* she thought.

Finally, she got up and unzipped her bag. It contained a nightgown, a single change of clothing, a copy of Joseph Conrad's *Lord Jim,* toothbrush, toothpaste, hairbrush, cosmetic bag, and the one-month supply of pain pills she had brought home from the hospital, only four of them gone. She took out her nightgown and laid it on the bed, put the book on the nightstand, and then took the toothpaste, toothbrush, and pills into the bathroom. Unpacking done, she headed back up to the office to greet Katie.

"Maggie sweetheart, you've been on our minds so much," said Katie, duplicating her husband's long embrace. "I'm so glad you've come. Sorry I missed your arrival. I couldn't stand another day of my hair! You know how that is."

Maggie nodded, noting that Katie's unruly mop of graying red frizz was momentarily tamed.

"Will you have dinner with us tonight? It's nothing special, just some soup, salad, and bread with Rob and me, or is it Rob and I?" she rambled. "I never know, but I get flummoxed about it when it's you I'm talking to."

Maggie hesitated, then smiled and said "Rob and me is correct, and I'd love to have dinner with you as long as it's not late. I'm not much of a night owl. Can I bring a bottle of wine?"

"Wine would be lovely. Come up to our cottage at 6."

Maggie was grateful for the diversion of buying wine and having dinner with two of the nicest people she knew. True to form, Rob and Katie surrounded her with their unique blend of Katie's chatter and Rob's good-natured teasing. They didn't pry into her life or state of mind. They just took her in, as they did all the traveling souls who landed on their doorstep. She found herself laughing for the first time in weeks. The idea seeped into her mind that perhaps things could be normal again. Maybe in this setting—if she could move here, start over with the friendship of these good people, let the ocean and sea air wash her soul clean—her life wouldn't have to end.

She could get a dog. A dog wouldn't care about the past.

Heartened by these thoughts and the pleasure of Katie's potato soup and Rob's parting hug, she followed the path to her cottage. She went out on the deck and let the sound wash over her, willing the waves to wash away all the pain and sorrow of the past six months. She thought back over her life, flashes of memory playing like scenes from a movie. She saw her mother, reading to Maggie and Ceci in the big rocking chair. Her father, striding into the house in his business suit, dropping his brief-case on the bench by the door. She saw Ceci, riding beside her as they bicycled to the park. She saw newborn Toby, dark hair still wet and plastered to his head, wrapped in a blanket in her arms, George at her side with tears in his eyes. She saw legions of animated teenagers, parading into and out of her classroom, hour after hour, year after year. She saw Eric and Amy, laughing and racing up and down the stairs like two puppies.

The pulsing sound of the waves surged and retreated. After a time, the sound took on a voice. "Your fault," it repeated with each arriving breaker. "Your fault, your fault, your fault."

She put her hands over her ears, but the sound only echoed louder. "No escape," she said out loud, the ache of her reality surging back with the ocean waves.

October 26

Maggie awoke before dawn, surprised that she had slept at all. Within a few hours she would no longer be tormented by guilt and shame. She thought about how having the courage to pay the ultimate price would in some small way atone for her earlier weakness, and this idea gave her peace.

She showered and dressed carefully in her one change of clothes and tried not to think about everything she would miss: birthdays, graduations, weddings. She had chosen her favorite blue, hand knit sweater and gray corduroy pants; soft and comfortable, but not frumpy. She styled her hair and added some color to her cheeks. She didn't want to look frumpy or too pale when they found her. "How silly," she said to the mirror. "It won't matter. I'll look dead."

But somehow it did matter.

Then she packed everything neatly into her small bag, reserving the bottle of pills. She tucked the bottle of pills in her purse and went out into the dark morning, silently closing and locking the door and tucking the key under the mat as she and George had always done when they left early. She carried her overnight bag and purse to her car through the wet, sandy grass along the side of the gravel driveway, putting each foot down silently. She closed the car door gently and turned the key, wincing at the roar of the engine and crunch of tires on the gravel. The windows of Katie's and Rob's cottage remained dark. Entering the main highway, she resisted the overwhelming urge to speed through the empty streets. The local traffic cop would have time on his hands at this hour and she didn't want to have to explain herself.

There was no moon, but a few stars still winked in her windshield. To the west, the first hint of dawn gave a phosphorescent glow to the breakers. She put down her window to fill her soul with the sounds and smells of the ocean. Heading east on Highway 18, she was soon away from the ocean and the lights of town and could see large fir trees starting to take shape in the pre-dawn glow. At the Otis turnoff, she went north, and soon found what she wanted—a small dirt road that disappeared into the trees. Maggie turned down the road, holding tight to the steering wheel as her tires bumped over the uneven surface. The surrounding brush and trees gave a sense of driving into a cocoon. After a few hundred yards, she found a wide spot and pulled off the road, turning off the engine.

The world around her car was silent and still, fir trees looming like giant sentries. *My witnesses*, she thought. This was her favorite time of day, light just beginning to play on the dew-laden branches, birds calling and darting from tree to tree. She got out of the car and stood, eyes closed, inhaling deeply, savoring the fragrance of fir and damp earth, so sweet. She had always loved the smell of the woods. To never smell the woods again…

Reflected light from something hidden under the sword ferns beside the car caught her eye, ending her reverie. Two beer cans, bent and folded in on themselves, lay facing each other on the ground. "Why do people do this?" she said aloud, reaching under the wet foliage to pick them up, shaking out any residual liquid. As she moved to drop them into the litter bag in the car, she halted, thinking of how this would look, how people would think she'd been drinking. She pulled them back out of the litter bag and tossed them back into the woods where they wouldn't be seen—something she had never done in her life. It seemed that nothing was ever straightforward.

Back to business, she thought as she got back in the car, looking at her image in the rearview mirror, surprised to see tears in her eyes. "Well, this is it old girl," she said aloud. "It's time to go." Her voice was grating and out of place in the quiet. She took out the bottle of pills and stared at the label. 1-2 tablets every 4-6 hours as needed for pain. "How about 30 tablets in 5 minutes to end the pain?" she said. How many could she swallow at once? Five? Six? Not ten.

She stared and hit her hand on the steering wheel. She had

no water. She planned to swallow 30 tablets, and had no water. She got out of the car and opened the back door to search under the seats, already knowing that this was fruitless. She hadn't brought water.

"For being such a planner, you sure screwed this one up," she said. "How stupid can one woman be? Proof that the world will be better off without you."

With a sigh of frustration, she got back in the driver's seat and shoved the pill bottle into her purse. Then she got out again and waded through the tangle of undergrowth where she had tossed the two beer cans. She pulled them out of the damp foliage, dropped them on the passenger side floor and started the engine, jockeying the car back and forth several times to turn around and head back to the main highway.

A few miles down the road was a small market, the Open sign flickering in the window. Maggie was relieved to see a pickup and camper in the parking lot. Maybe the clerk would be focused on other customers and wouldn't recall selling her two bottles of water. She remembered a news clip she had seen about a sporting goods store clerk who was tormented because he had sold shotgun shells to a man who then shot himself in the head. The clerk felt responsible somehow, as though he should have noticed something. Would he have felt the same way about selling water to an older woman who planned to kill herself swallowing pills? Maggie knew that if she were the clerk, she would feel responsible.

There seemed no end of things to feel guilty about.

She picked up the two beer cans and carried them to the store, setting them on top of the waste can outside the store in hopes that they would get recycled. Inside, a man in white coveralls was talking intently with the clerk who couldn't have been older than eighteen. Maggie pulled two large bottles of water from the cooler and set them on the counter. The young man punched some keys on the register and said, "That'll be three-fifty."

"Three-fifty!" Maggie said, incredulous. She had never bought bottled water and the outrageousness of this price for something she could get out of a tap was almost more than she could tolerate. She opened her mouth to protest, but then she pictured the clerk being interviewed by the police. *Oh yes, I remember her. She went off on me over the price of the water. Can you believe that? She's going to "off" herself and she has a fit over $3.50 worth of water.* Maggie pressed her lips together and handed the clerk a five-dollar bill.

"Do you have a restroom?" she asked as he counted out her change. It occurred to her that she should not swallow the pills with a full bladder. She had read that the body lets loose at the time of death. It would be humiliating for them to find her a sodden mess.

The man in the white coveralls turned to her. She saw that the name "Billy" was embroidered in red across his breast pocket. "It's at the back of the building," he said. "After you exit the building go eight paces and turn left, and then take twenty paces more to the end of the building and turn left again. At that point you'll see a sign that says Women." He held up his hand, looking at her intently. "Actually, given your stature it's most likely nine paces and then twenty-two paces."

"Well, that's very precise." Maggie appreciated precision. "Thank you," she said as she picked up her bottles. She saw

Billy take a small notebook from his breast pocket and begin to write.

It was indeed nine paces to the side of the building and twenty-two paces to the back. She moved toward the toilet and then startled as she heard a sniffling sound from the corner behind the door.

"Oh, I didn't realize anyone was in here," she said to the dark-haired girl huddled in the corner.

"Sorry," said the girl, wiping her nose and eyes on her sweatshirt sleeve.

"What's the matter?" asked Maggie. "Why are you crying in here? Are you sick?"

"Sort of. Actually, I think I may be dying," said the girl.

"You don't look like you're dying," said Maggie, realizing that she didn't look like she was dying either, but she most certainly was—at least as soon as she could get back to the task at hand. "What makes you think you're dying?"

"I'm bleeding to death."

"Where? I don't see blood."

"It's coming out of my insides, down here," she said pointing to her crotch. "I'm bleeding from my privates."

"Oh my dear," said Maggie, taking in the girl's size and age. "Hasn't your mother told you about menstrual periods?"

"I don't live with my mother. What are menstrual periods?"

"You know, women's monthly cycle, periods."

"I've read about that. It's what the machines and waste cans in bathrooms are for," she said.

"That's right."

"But I never knew it was about blood."

"Oh yes, it's about blood. How old are you?"

"Twelve and a half."

"Well, it's time. In fact, it's even younger than that for some girls. What's your name?"

"Minnow. Minnow Marsh."

"Minnow. Now that's unique."

"So there's not something wrong with me?" asked Minnow. "I'm not bleeding to death?"

"No, you're perfectly normal."

"But I don't know what to do about it. How do I keep from getting blood all over? How long does it go on?"

"Well, they make things to take care of the blood. As far as how long it goes on, usually four or five days a month."

"Every month?"

"Every month."

"For the rest of my life?"

"Not quite, but it will seem like it. Until you're too old to have children—sometime around age 50."

Minnow looked stricken. "That's as good as the rest of my life," she said.

"It *is* a bit depressing," said Maggie. "Goodness knows I was glad to be done with all that, although the stopping is worse than the starting in some ways. I'm not sure who designed the female plumbing system. Most certainly not a woman. But in any case, it's the price we pay for being able to have babies."

"I don't even know if I want to have babies," said Minnow.

"Nor should you know at your age, and you certainly shouldn't want to have them anytime soon. It's good to keep your options open, however. Now, you say you don't live with your mother. Who takes care of you?"

"My Uncle Billy," said Minnow.

"And your uncle has never talked with you about this?"

"No. He's kind of uncomfortable talking about personal things. Especially girl things."

"Billy…would that be the man I saw in the store wearing white coveralls? Very precise in his explanations of things."

"Yep, that's him."

"Well, you stay right here Minnow," Maggie directed. "I'm going to get you some supplies, and have a little talk with your uncle while I'm at it."

"Thank you," said Minnow. "But please don't be mad at Uncle Billy. He can't help it. He just doesn't know how to talk about certain things."

"Well, he needs to find someone who does know how then," said Maggie as she exited the restroom. Despite herself she counted the paces back to the store entrance—only twenty and eight this time.

As she was about to enter the store, Maggie caught a glimpse of white coveralls next to the camper in the parking lot. She turned and shouted, "Billy?"

Billy jerked around, his hand frozen on the camper door handle. She walked toward him.

"I'm Maggie Berry," she said as she approached. "You told me how to find the restroom a bit ago."

"Was I right about the number of paces?" Billy asked.

"Precisely," she replied. "But I wanted to talk with you about your niece."

"Minnow?" he asked, alarmed now. "Did something happen to her?"

"Nothing that couldn't have been predicted," said Maggie.

Billy started to move toward the building and Maggie held up her hands. "She's fine, nothing bad has occurred. I happened upon her in the restroom. She was very distraught because she had started her first menstrual period, and it was very frightening to her, as you could imagine, to be bleeding and not know why."

Billy backed up against the camper, looking at the ground now.

"Anyway, she said that you care for her and that she doesn't have a mother at home. Is that true?"

"Yes," said Billy, barely audible, still taking quick, shallow breaths. He raked his hair back with his fingers, letting it flop back over his dark-rimmed glasses.

"How had you planned to handle this when she reached puberty?"

Billy shook his head, still looking down. "I didn't...I don't know...I thought maybe her grandmother had discussed it when she was alive..."

"Apparently not," said Maggie. "I'm surprised she didn't have a sex education class in school."

"She's homeschooled," said Billy. He pulled out his notebook and wrote *Maggie Berry— Minnow—menstruation!*

"I see. Well, in any case, she is going to need some supplies. I told her I would get some to start her off, but you'll need to be sure she has them on an ongoing basis. And then she's going to need someone to talk with her and tell her how things work. Not just menstruation, but what it means. She needs to know that she could become pregnant if she isn't careful. You can't just ignore this. If you're her guardian, you have to take responsibility for educating her."

Billy shook his head and scratched at his neck. With eyes still focused on the gravel parking lot he said, "I don't think I can do this. I don't know how to talk to her about these things, about female anatomy and sexual relations." He looked up. "Would you talk to her?" he implored.

"I don't even know her," said Maggie. "I just met her in a convenience store restroom. That's not where one should seek proper education about these things!"

"But you told her some of it already."

"Well, that was necessary. The poor girl thought she was dying."

Billy stared, silent, desperate.

"Oh for heavens sake," said Maggie. "I'll talk with her, but not because you asked me. I'll do it because that poor child needs someone to prepare her for what's ahead and I don't have any confidence that you're going to do it. You need to ask yourself if you're the right person to care for a young girl as she becomes a young woman," Maggie's piercing blue eyes fixed him in place.

He dropped his head. "Thank you," he said, letting out a long breath.

Maggie stomped toward the store, letting the screen door bang as she entered. After purchasing the needed supplies, she strode back to the restroom—eight and twenty again. She found Minnow on her feet, washing her face in the sink.

"You need to know how to use these," said Maggie. "And there's some other information you need as well. Your uncle asked if I would talk to you about this. Are you okay with that?"

"Sure," said Minnow. "You're a very kind person. I don't even know your name."

"My name is Maggie. And as for kindness, I just try to do what's right—which is more than I can say for your uncle right now. Does he take good care of you? He said you're home-schooled."

"Uncle Billy's good to me. It's not his fault that he's not like other people. He has Asperger's. Do you know what that is?"

"I see," said Maggie. "Well, that explains some things."

She looked around the restroom. "If we're going to talk, I'd rather not do it in here."

Minnow nodded. "Me either. Hey I know. Why don't you come to the camper? Then you can meet Bonkers. He's my best friend, even though he's a dog. Some people say 'just a dog' but I don't think like that. I think dogs are better than people lots of times. And you can have some oatmeal with us. Have you had any breakfast today?"

"Well, no," said Maggie. "As it so happens, I wasn't planning on having any."

"You should. Uncle Billy says breakfast is the most important meal of the day. He says if you want to live a long and healthy life you should eat oatmeal every morning."

"Just so," said Maggie.

"So will you come? Please? You'll love Bonkers. He's the best dog ever." Maggie was amazed at the transformation of the girl from the despondent, tragic figure huddled in the corner to this sunny, chatty being. *The resilience of youth*, she thought.

"Yes, I'll come, but first let me give you some instruction on these things. And then you must let me use the restroom, since that is why I came in here in the first place."

Minnow giggled, a contagious sound. After Maggie explained the workings of feminine hygiene products, Minnow said, "Thanks for telling me. But are you sure this is going to happen to me every month from now on? Unless I get pregnant—which I won't."

"Quite sure," said Maggie.

"Gross! I think guys get off easy." Minnow looked at herself in the mirror, smiled and continued, "I'll go to the camper and start the oatmeal while you use the restroom. Just knock on the door at the rear of the pickup."

Alone in the restroom Maggie considered how her plans for the morning had been derailed. *Oh well,* she thought. *It can't be a bad thing to do one last good deed before I go.*

Maggie could hear Minnow humming through the screened window of the narrow camper door. She saw Billy with a wrench in his hand, busy under the hood. He didn't look up. Before she had a chance to knock, the door flew open and a brown and white bundle of fur sprang to the ground and began to race in circles around her feet. Minnow laughed.

"That's Bonkers," she said.

"So I guessed," said Maggie studying the small dog who was now sniffing her shoes. "Aptly named. He's unusual."

"Billy says he's asymmetrical. That means that his two sides don't match. But I like him that way."

"Well, as long as his legs are all the same length, I guess it doesn't matter," said Maggie.

"That's what I think too. Come on inside and I'll show you the camper."

Climbing through the door, Maggie was immediately

struck by the orderliness of the tiny space. There was a small refrigerator, a two-burner stove on which a pot of oatmeal was bubbling, a narrow table with upholstered bench seats on two sides, and a bed over the cab. Cabinets under and above the sink and under the bench seats were of nicely finished golden oak. There was a row of library books held in place by an elastic cord along the wall behind the table. The small patch of floor was shiny and clean. Minnow had laid out three bowls and spoons on the table.

"This is it," she said. "That's where I sleep, me and Bonkers," she pointed to the bed over the cab. "Uncle Billy sleeps where the table is. It makes into a twin bed."

"Bonkers and I," said Maggie.

"Bonkers and you what?" asked Minnow.

"You said 'Me and Bonkers.' That's incorrect. You should say Bonkers and I."

"Oh," said Minnow. "You and Uncle Billy are kind of alike, you know? He's always correcting me about stuff like that."

"I'm glad to know that he's trying to educate you about *some* things at least. Where do you and your uncle travel in this camper?"

"All over around Oregon. He sells metal sculptures and fixes toilets at stores and gas stations like this one, so we travel around to all the different places. We have a utility trailer we bring sometimes to carry his sculptures."

"Do you live in this camper full time? What about your schooling?"

"Uncle Billy homeschools me so it's okay when we're on the road. But we just go for one week at a time and then we're home for two weeks at our house outside of Boring. It was actually my Grandma's house. She took care of me after I couldn't live with my mom anymore, so that's where I've lived almost all of my life that I can remember. But then she had a heart attack and died so it's just Uncle Billy and me. I mean Uncle Billy and *I* living there now—and Bonkers of course." The small dog wagged his tail at the sound of his name.

"How does your uncle homeschool you?"

"I went to school until my Grandma died. But Uncle Billy is a genius about lots of stuff, so he teaches me about it while we drive and at home when we're there. He makes up games and puzzles to test me. He teaches me mostly about grammar, math, and science and geology and geography and history. I do literature and writing myself mostly, because I love to read. Whenever we're back at home we go to the library and I get a new bunch of books."

"What about other kids. Don't you miss being around other kids?"

"Well, yeah, sort of." A hint of wistfulness crossed Minnow's face. "When I went to school it was fun to play with other kids, but sometimes they were mean because I didn't have a regular family like they did. One friend's mom wouldn't let her come over to my house on account of she thought it was weird that I lived with my grandma and uncle. I did have a best friend in school named Amanda, and we hung out together all the time. We liked the same stuff, but then she went on to middle school, and I went with Uncle Billy, so she got other friends. Anyway, I do still have friends. When I go to the library and use the computer we talk on Instagram."

"Instagram. Do you ever actually see them?"

"Not really. Except their pictures. But it's still good. You can learn so much about people. Only I wish I had a smart phone so that I could talk to people or text them in real time, not just in the library. And if I had a phone, I could take pictures of Bonkers and other stuff and post them. Uncle Billy says it's a waste of money and he won't buy one for me. When I'm old enough to have a job, a phone is the first thing I'm going to get."

"Your uncle has a point. So tell me," said Maggie, easing into the topic, "what do you know about how babies are made?"

"Oh, I know all that stuff," said Minnow, "from books I've read. I just didn't know about the blood part."

As Maggie probed further, it turned out she did know most of what was necessary, minus a few important details. Maggie added some specifics and precautions.

"Since your uncle won't discuss these things, do you have someone you can ask if you have questions or worries?"

"I could ask Sam. She's our friend who owns a store in Connor. She has a thing for Uncle Billy. It's Sam who gave me Bonkers. I could ask her anything. Or I could probably ask Jenny who I met a few months ago. She's kind of like a mom to me in some ways, even though I haven't known her very long."

"Well, I guess that will have to do. Just be sure to ask someone trustworthy, and not just another kid. They act like they know, but lots of times they don't."

"Okay. Can we have our oatmeal now?"

"By all means. You can tell your uncle that it's safe to come in now."

Pulling back onto the highway heading east this time, Maggie noted a section of thick woods just a few hundred yards from the parking lot. "That will do," she said, nosing the car onto a narrow gravel shoulder under an overhanging alder tree. She put the two bottles of water into her bag along with the pills, got out and locked the car, and made her way down a short embankment. She waded through a carpet of bracken ferns and Oregon grape, the dew-covered foliage wetting her clothes and shoes. *I should have brought an extra sweater*, she thought, and then chuckled at the absurdity. Even when planning to die one continued to prepare for living.

Spotting a mossy tree stump, she brushed off the fir needles and sat. She took the two water bottles and the pill container and set them on the stump beside her along with her bag. The sun filtered through the maple leaves, setting them ablaze with color.

Somehow the brief interlude with Minnow and Billy, the innocence of the girl, the way it felt to be needed, made this harder. *If I could just start over, truly lose the past, I'd keep going,* she thought.

But of course that was ludicrous. The past lived inside her. There was no escape. She let herself cry freely now, tears mingling with the dew. She cried until she was spent. Then she broke the seal on one of the water bottles, picked up the pill bottle and shook the first six pills into her palm.

Minnow finished cleaning up the breakfast dishes and wiped the table. She secured everything into the latched cupboards, hung the dishcloth and towel on their rack, and settled onto the bench seat with a book. She heard tires of an approaching car and, peering out of the window, saw a dented, mud-splattered brown van pull in next to the camper. A large, stocky man with curly black hair and a scraggly beard got out of the driver's side. A small girl's face peered out of the rear side window. The passenger side opened with a protesting squeak. A familiar, husky voice said, "You stay put. Scoot over and make room for your sister." Then Minnow's mother appeared from around the back of the van.

Katrina Marsh's double hoop earrings framed what could have been delicate features had they not been hardened by years of hard living.

"Well, hello big brother," Katrina said. "We've been running all over the country looking for you. It's good of you to have a regular route so we can track you down."

Billy turned to face her. "What do you want?" he asked.

"That's no way to greet family. I want you to meet Dirk."

Billy looked at the stocky man wearing a faded orange t-shirt and baggy jeans.

"Dirk and I are building a new life together. We're living like a real family. Dirk, this is my big brother Billy."

Dirk stuck out a thick hand. Billy ignored it. "What do you want?" he asked again.

Dropping the congenial tone she said, "I just want what's mine."

"I don't have anything that's yours."

"You have my kid. I want to put my family back together and to do that I need Minnow. I want to give her a regular home and family."

"I take care of Minnow," he said, fists clenched at his sides.

"What makes you think you know anything about raising a kid? Especially a girl? If I leave her with you, you'll probably turn her into a freak just like you. Mom never meant for you to have her."

"You can't take Minnow," said Billy.

"Oh yeah?" she said.

Minnow couldn't take it. She threw the camper door open and leaped to the ground. She and Bonkers ran.

"Fuck!" shouted Katrina. "See how you've poisoned her against me! C'mon Dirk. Let's go get her."

Minnow disappeared from view around a curve, running at full speed. The van starter labored and the engine coughed but died. Finally it sputtered to life. With gravel flying from the tires, it sped after her. Katrina saw Billy starting to run behind the van, then stopping as the van rounded the curve.

When the van turned, the small girl in the back seat slid hard against the door and started to cry. Minnow was no longer in sight.

"Hurry up!" said Katrina. "Get to that next curve." She turned to the child behind her. "Sit back down and shut up Sadie," she screamed, reaching back and giving a shove to the crying child. "You won't get thrown around like that if you stay on the seat."

At the next curve the road was empty.

"Son-of-a-bitch!" said Katrina. "Stop the van, let me think." After a few minutes she said, "Okay, if she's not gonna come with us the easy way, we'll do it the hard way. Fuck Billy, fuck that bastard, turning her against her own mother like that. Let's head home. I've got some people to call."

As Maggie contemplated the six pills in her hand, she heard a thrashing in the brush nearby. She instinctively clutched her handbag to her chest. Then she saw glimpses of brown and white fur through the undergrowth and suddenly a lopsided dog emerged in the clearing where she sat.

"Bonkers?" she said. The dog ran to her and jumped up at her legs, wagging his tail. She thought for a moment that she must be dreaming. She checked her hand to make sure she hadn't yet swallowed the pills.

Then she heard a louder thrashing and Minnow appeared in the clearing, breathing hard, scratched from the thick brush. Maggie put the pills back in the bottle.

"What has happened?" she asked Minnow. "Did you follow me here?"

Minnow looked at her, disoriented, gasping for breath. "No, I didn't know you were here. How did you get here?"

"Never mind that. Where are you going? Why are you running?"

"It's my mom," said Minnow. "She showed up at the camper. She wants to take me away from Uncle Billy."

"So you're running off through the woods? To do what?"

Minnow shook her head, still panting. "I don't know. I just knew I couldn't go with her."

"Come sit down," said Maggie, patting the mossy stump next to her, sliding the pill bottle back into her bag.

Minnow sat. Bonkers jumped into her lap and she hugged him to her chest. She was wearing only the t-shirt and jeans that she'd had on at breakfast, both now wet from the forest undergrowth.

Maggie jumped into action, a lifetime of caring for others unwilling to be suppressed. "You must be cold. Why don't you come back to my car and we'll figure out something to do."

"Okay," Minnow said. They scrabbled through the brush back to the road. Maggie pulled a towel from the trunk and wrapped the muddy Bonkers in it and placed him on Minnow's lap.

"Let's go see if your mother is still at the store."

"No!" said Minnow. "I don't want to go with her."

"We won't stop," said Maggie. "We'll just see if she's still looking for you. What was she driving?"

"A van. A brown van."

Maggie started the car and reversed course back to the store. When they passed the store, Minnow ducked down below the dashboard, but the brown van was gone. Billy's camper was gone too.

Maggie pulled the car to the side of the highway and pondered what to do. The morning had not in any way gone as planned. She thought of all the times as a teacher when she would become aware of the struggles in kids' lives and how she had yearned to step in and help. But the rules of the profession were to separate oneself from the messy problems in kids' families. Refer them to other professionals, but don't engage. All that pent up desire to do something that really mattered surfaced now. Her willingness to let go of life had somehow unbound her from all these strictures that had shaped her decisions for so many years.

"Well, perhaps you can come with me back to the cottage where I've been staying and get warmed up. Do you know where your uncle would have gone?"

"No," said Minnow. "But what about the stuff for, you know, my period? I left everything in the camper."

"We can stop at a store on our way to get what you need."

As they made the drive to the cottage, they were silent, lost in their own thoughts. Maggie was thinking about how she had tried and now failed twice to do what she had thought would be simple.

At the cottage Minnow looked around. "You're staying here? Where's your stuff?"

"Actually, I thought I was leaving, but that was before this morning. So how about if you hop in the shower and warm up. I'll toss your clothes into the washer here. I should put this dog in with them, but we'll have to use the sink for him. Are you okay if I borrow a robe from my friends in the office for you to wear until they're dry?"

"I guess so, but is it okay to shower with…you know…the period thing?"

"Yes, it's perfectly fine."

Minnow gratefully headed for the bathroom, Bonkers at her heels. In a moment she opened the door and tossed out her sodden clothes. Maggie took care of the clothes, then went to borrow a robe from Katie.

"You came without a robe?" Katie said.

"Actually, it's not for me. I have a young guest," said Maggie.

Katie raised her eyebrows.

"It's a long story. I'll tell you about it later," she said taking the fuzzy purple robe.

"Cool!" said Minnow when Maggie handed it through the bathroom door. She emerged pink-faced from the hot shower and curled up in George's chair.

"What about Bonkers?" Maggie asked. "Will he let me bathe him?"

"Oh sure. He likes baths. Just be sure to get the towel on him before he has a chance to shake," said Minnow. So Maggie took the muddy canine and went to work in the sink. By the time she was done, she had to change into her other set of clothes and put her now soaked sweater and corduroy pants to be washed. But Bonkers was clean.

Maggie sat on the ottoman by the green chair, just as she had done so many times with George. "Before we talk about your mom, what about your uncle? Isn't he going to be terribly worried about you?"

"Yes," said Minnow. "He's going to go nuts."

"Is there some way you can reach him?"

"He doesn't have a cell phone. But I could call Sam. We have a deal that if we ever get lost from each other while traveling we call Sam to say we're okay and where we are."

"Good plan," said Maggie. "You can use my cell phone."

"Will you take a picture of me and Bonkers with your phone?"

"Yes, but first you need to let your uncle know you're safe."

Minnow punched in the number. She had only used their emergency contact system once before. Once, when Billy had thought she was asleep in the camper, he had moved the truck a few miles down the road to where they would spend the night. But unbeknownst to him she had gone into the store. When she came out, he was gone. Both of them had called Sam and things were soon sorted out. "If we each had our own cell phone," she had told him, "this would have been a lot easier." He had replied, "It is illogical to pay for cell phones every month to address an event that has happened once in two years, and for which our established communication method worked fine."

So much for trying to use logic on him.

Maggie could hear the phone ringing and then a voice on the other end. "Minnow, thank God!" the voice exclaimed.

"I'm okay," Minnow said. "I'm with a friend"

…

"Maggie. I met her today—"

…

"She's nice. She helped me with some stuff this morning."

…

"I know, but I panicked. She was going to take me with her and I didn't know what was going to happen if I went with her."

…

"Tell him to call me at this number. Maggie, what's your number?"

Maggie told her the number and Minnow repeated after her.

…

"Okay. I love you too."

Minnow handed the phone back to Maggie.

"Can we do a picture now?" She picked up Bonkers and smiled while Maggie took a picture.

"Can I post it on Instagram?" Minnow asked.

"Yes, but first I want you to tell me about your mother."

Minnow had sketchy memories from when she was three, before she went to live with her Grandma. She remembered being on the bed and being tickled by her mom and laughing and laughing. It felt like the laughter bubbled up all the way from her toes. She remembered being scared in the night and trying to climb in bed with her mom. There was a man she didn't know in the bed and her mom yelled at her to get out. She remembered finding her mom asleep in the chair in the middle of the day and climbing on her lap and shaking her but she wouldn't wake up.

When she was six and went to live with her mom and Brett, she remembered being excited to have a mom and a dad like other kids, even though Brett wasn't her real dad.

She remembered losing her first tooth and she got a dollar under her pillow from the tooth fairy. But then when the second tooth was loose, Brett got mad at her for wiggling it all the time. He said it was disgusting. When she didn't stop wiggling it, he grabbed her and reached in her mouth with his big fingers that tasted like cigarettes and yanked it out, and then he threw it in the garbage.

Then the hitting started. Mostly Brett hit her mom, but sometimes her.

After a neighbor called the authorities, she went back to her grandma's.

"My mom's had a lot of problems," she told Maggie. "It's mostly drugs and drinking, but I think a lot of it is that she has had bad luck with guys."

"So what is going on with your mom now? Why did she come find you?"

"I think she's trying to get me back with her. There was this lady that came from Multnomah County a couple weeks ago and she asked all kinds of questions about Uncle Billy and why I wasn't in school and stuff. Uncle Billy thinks it was my mom who sent her there."

"Do you definitely not want to live with your mom?"

Minnow picked at the purple fuzz on the robe. "I *do* want to live with her. I've always wanted a real mom. But I tried living with her before when I was six and it didn't work out, so I'm just scared that it will be bad again. She has another boyfriend. I guess his name's Dirk. I guess she got Sadie back. Sadie's my half-sister. She's five. Mom was pregnant with her before I went back to my grandma's. I've only seen her a few times, but if I lived with my mom I could babysit and take her places and she could play with Bonkers."

"Dirk isn't Sadie's dad?"

"No, Brett is Sadie's dad. Sadie got taken away when she was a baby and put into foster care because Granny Vi was getting sick and couldn't take another kid. I hated Brett. He used to beat up my Mom and he did drugs and stuff. He hated me too. So I know that my Mom finally kicked him out last year. She says she wants us to be a family again. If she quit doing drugs and would stay away from stupid men, maybe we could be a family, although I don't know about the "again" part since we've never really been a family."

"Sometimes people turn their lives around. Do you think that's possible with your mom?"

"I don't know. Maybe. I hope so. Sometimes my mom is really nice, and smart and funny. But other times she's hard to be around."

"What about your dad?"

"I don't know my dad. He left before I was born. But he did give me my name. My Mom said that when she was pregnant with me he used to laugh at her and say she had a little minnow swimming around inside her belly. She told him that if he didn't quit saying that she'd show him and name the baby

Minnow when it was born. I guess he didn't quit saying it, so that's what she did and that's how I got my name."

"But he wasn't married to my mom, and she said he couldn't handle the idea of being a father, so he took off right before I was born. I don't know if he even knows that she named me Minnow. I'd like to meet him sometime. I think maybe once he saw me, he might think that it wouldn't be so terrible to be a dad. But maybe he'd still think it is and that would make me feel bad. My mom says that I have his laugh, and he loved animals like I do, so I'd like to hear him laugh and to show him Bonkers." Minnow plowed forward. "I have one picture with him and my mom in it, but it's kind of blurry and I can't really tell what he looks like other than he has a mustache and he's tall and thin. He's wearing a baseball cap so I can't really see his hair. At least I don't have his mustache," she laughed.

"Well, you've had a complicated life for someone so young," said Maggie.

Minnow shrugged.

What tugged at Maggie was Minnow's resilient spirit; the way the girl seemed to find ways to be happy despite the lousy hand she'd been dealt. Maggie knew she had no business getting involved here. And yet, to her own amazement, she wanted to make something good happen for this sweet girl more than she'd wanted anything in the last five months. More even than she wanted to escape her own life.

"I'm thinking," said Maggie, "that my sister knows a number of caseworkers who work with Multnomah County. She used to work as a counselor with families in the area. Would you like it if I contacted her to try to find out what's going on with your mom?"

"I don't know," said Minnow. "Would it mean that they'd take me away from Uncle Billy?"

"No, I'm just talking about seeing if I can learn anything about what the situation is. They might not be willing to share anything due to confidentiality, but I'm offering to help gather some information for you, nothing else."

"Yes, I guess I would like that. Uncle Billy gets so freaked out when they talk to him that I think he makes it worse sometimes."

"I can imagine that," said Maggie. Her cell chirped. "Hello?" she said to the unknown number.

It was Billy. The two chatted for a brief moment.

"He's just down highway 101," Maggie said. "He'll be here in fifteen minutes."

Minnow changed into her newly dried clothes and by then the green pickup was pulling into the Seagulls Nest Cottages parking lot. Bonkers started whining as soon as he heard the engine and Minnow sprang to answer the door.

"Where did you go?" Billy said by way of greeting.

"I'm sorry. I just ran into the woods. I was scared she was going to take me."

"Yes, that was what she wanted. But that was a foolish thing you did. You could have gotten lost or hurt. I didn't know how to find you."

"I know, but I ran into Maggie and it all worked out." She turned to Maggie. "You never told me why you were in the woods."

"How did you find her?" Billy asked.

"Bonkers found Maggie," said Minnow.

Billy pulled his notebook from his pocket and jotted "Maggie Berry, Seagulls Nest Cottages, picked up Minnow."

"You have helped us two times in one day," said Billy. "I am grateful."

"And she's going to find out what's going on with Mom," said Minnow.

Billy's expression changed to wariness. "How can you do that?"

"Don't worry," said Maggie. "I may not be able to help at all. My sister knows people in the court system. I told Minnow I could ask her to see if she can find out the status of things, just so you can have some information."

"I already know what's going on," said Billy. "My sister is up to no good."

"Well, perhaps," said Maggie. "But it can be useful to know how the authorities view the situation and what triggered the visit from a caseworker. Do you think it's possible that your sister has turned her life around and is trying to put her family back together?"

"Possible?" said Billy. "If you're talking possibility, of course, anything is possible. Probability is another thing. Based on her life so far, the likelihood is remote."

"In any case, is it all right with you if I ask my sister to see what she can learn?"

Billy hesitated, scratching at his ear. "Just don't get tricked."

"I'm pretty good at knowing when I'm being manipulated. I did teach high school for thirty years."

"You don't know Katrina."

"Fair enough," she said. "How do I get in touch with you?"

"We have a phone at our Boring house. We'll be there next week." He tore a blank slip of paper from his notebook and wrote the number. Then he wrote another number. "This is Sam's number. She can usually find us if we're on the road."

Maggie walked with Billy and Minnow to the camper. Bonkers raced ahead and stood with his front paws on the passenger side running board ready to spring into the truck. Minnow gave Maggie a hug.

"Thank you once again." Billy started to get into the truck, then turned to Maggie and said, "You should tell the owners of this place that they need an apostrophe in their sign."

Maggie laughed for the first time that day. "That's a good idea!" she said.

"Now let me get this straight," Ceci said on the phone later that day. "You met this girl and her uncle at a service station at the coast and now you want to try to straighten out their lives?"

"I know it sounds strange," said Maggie, "and it's really not quite the way you put it. But yes, I want to see if I can be of some help. She's an extraordinary girl Ceci, and she's got no one to advocate for her. I think the uncle has her best interests at heart, but he's ill-equipped to deal with bureaucracy."

"Well, I think it's risky to get yourself mixed up in someone's domestic mess. On the other hand, I'm thrilled to see you taking an interest in something."

"So you'll see what you can find out?"

"Yes, I'll call some people and see what I can learn, but it's all off the record."

"Understood," said Maggie. "Thank you, Sis."

October 27

Entering her house from the garage, Maggie had a strange sense of disorientation. She wasn't supposed to walk in on this scene; she had prepared it for others to find.

The files were on the counter just as she had left them. Everything was orderly and ready to be dealt with by her family. Now, she was deflated. The anticlimax of an ending that didn't happen.

At least no one knows. I'm glad of that, she thought. *I couldn't tolerate all that attention. Besides, this doesn't really change anything. It's just a temporary piece of business prior to the final act. A way to make a positive difference before exiting the scene.*

She picked up the file folders and put them in her kitchen desk file drawer. Then she unpacked her small bag and took the pills from her purse, returning them to the medicine cabinet. When she opened the refrigerator, she remembered that in her efficient manner she had emptied it before leaving. It was pristine, and bare. She pulled a can of soup from the pantry and emptied it into a bowl to microwave for lunch.

So now she would need to go to the supermarket and restock the kitchen. She had been done with all of that. With a sigh she sat at the kitchen counter with her bowl of soup and contemplated how things had gone awry.

November 2

Minnow was in the bedroom when the brown van turned in the driveway. She heard Bonkers barking and peered out the window, momentarily frozen in place. Then she regained motion. She shoved her feet into her shoes and tied them with shaking hands. She called Bonkers and slipped out of the back door. Skirting the back of the house, she found the gap in the hedge and crawled through the hole in the fence on the other side. She stood to run and slammed hard into her mother's arms. She looked for a way around, but Katrina held her shoulders.

"You forget, I used to live in this house too. And believe me, I know *all* the escape routes."

"Let me go!" screamed Minnow. Bonkers growled by her feet.

"Why are you running from me?" Katrina asked. "I'm not going to hurt you. I'm your mother. I just want to talk to you."

"I'm not going with you," said Minnow.

"I'm not trying to take you. Can't we just sit down and talk like civilized people? Is it going to hurt you to talk to your mother for a few minutes?"

Minnow looked around as though seeking help, but no one was coming. She quit straining against Katrina's grasp. "I guess not," she said. Katrina released her shoulders.

"Can we go in the house? Where's Billy?"

"He's welding stuff in the shop."

"We don't have to bother him," said Katrina. "I just want to have a little mother-daughter chat."

She gestured for Minnow to lead the way and followed close behind. Minnow was wary but drawn in at the same time. The words mother-daughter took her to a place of longing that had always been with her. She didn't know what it would be like to be part of a mother-daughter pair, but she knew she yearned for it. When she saw other girls with their mothers, doing things as simple as buying groceries, or laughing in the car as they drove down the road, it touched a spot so deep and primal within her that she had to look away lest she start to cry.

Once inside, Katrina surveyed the rooms, picking up objects from the shelves and then replacing them as Minnow watched. She went into Minnow's bedroom; it had been her bedroom once. The twin bed and quilt, the small oak dresser with mirror, even the lamp with the ceramic lamb base and pink shade were the same. The room was tidy with books lined up on top of the dresser and pairs of shoes lined up in the closet.

When Katrina had lived here it was not tidy. There had been clothes strewn on top of the dresser and piled on the chair in the corner, magazines on the floor, and nail polish and makeup on the dresser.

"What happened to my chair that was in the corner?" she asked.

"I think Billy has it in his room," said Minnow. She followed Katrina into Billy's room. This had been her grandma's room. "Go sit in the front room," Katrina said. "I'm just seeing what Billy's done with the place. I'm gonna use the bathroom. Then I'll be right there."

When she came out of the bathroom a few minutes later she was holding a box of tampons.

"So what's this?" she asked. "Has my little girl reached womanhood?"

Minnow shrugged. "I just started my periods, that's all."

"That's *all*? That's a big deal. My little girl a full-fledged woman. I can't think that Billy would have a clue how to deal with that, bloody mess and all."

"There's a lady friend that helped me," said Minnow.

"A lady friend? Billy has a lady friend?"

"No, she's more my friend. I met her at the coast. She's older. She used to be a teacher. She's really nice."

"What's her name?" asked Katrina.

"Maggie."

"Just Maggie? No last name?"

"Maggie Berry. She lives in Portland."

"Well that just makes me so sad," said Katrina, tears welling in her eyes. "That my girl started her periods and I wasn't there to help her. It's not right."

"It worked out OK," said Minnow. "And I made a new friend in the process."

"So, you and this Maggie Berry are all tight now, after going through this bonding experience?"

"No," said Minnow. "It wasn't like that. She was just nice to me, that's all."

"Look," said Katrina. "I know I haven't been a good mother to you. I had a really hard time growing up too. My dad was a mean S.O.B., and all my mom cared about was protecting her special-needs son. I had to make it on my own, and I've had some bad luck in my life and things have been pretty messed up. But that's all different now. I want to have a fresh start and to be a good mother to you. I want us to be a real family, you, me, and Sadie."

"Just us three?" asked Minnow.

"And Dirk. You don't know Dirk yet," said Katrina, "but he wants to be a father to you. Not like that no-good bastard who got me pregnant and then took off for Alaska."

"Or Brett?"

"Or that bastard either," said Katrina.

"I have Uncle Billy," said Minnow.

"You and I both know that he's not like other people. I grew up with the weirdo. If you were with me, you could get back in school, make friends with other kids, and have a normal life. It's not right him hauling you all over the state, hanging out with convenience store people."

"I have friends," said Minnow.

"Where?" asked Katrina. "When do you see them?"

"Mostly I talk to them on Instagram. I use the computer at the library to talk to them. When I get old enough to get a job, I'm going to save my money and get a smartphone so I can text or call people whenever I want. Uncle Billy thinks cell phones are a waste of money, but I don't think so and it's what I want more than anything."

"He thinks that because there's no one he wants to talk to or who wants to talk to him. If you lived with me, I'd get you a phone just like mine." Katrina pulled the iPhone from her bag and handed it to Minnow. Minnow stared at the shiny black screen, feeling the weight of the phone in her hand, then pushed the button and watched it come to life.

"Really?" she asked.

"Yep. You're about to be a teenager. You should have your own phone."

"Billy says they're too much money."

"Some things you just gotta have, even if they cost money," Katrina said. "Dirk earns good money at his cousin's car repair place."

Minnow jumped when the back door banged open and quickly handed the phone back to Katrina.

Billy stood in the doorway as if braced against an ill wind.

"Why are you here?" he said.

"What kind of question is that?" Katrina smirked. "Shouldn't a mother spend time with her daughter?"

"You shouldn't be here."

Katrina strolled casually around the room, letting her hand brush the furniture. She plucked an apple from the bowl on the kitchen table and studied it. Then she snapped out a large chunk with her teeth and chewed.

"This is my childhood home too you know," she said, the words muddled by the juicy chunks of apple in her mouth. "My home, my kid."

Billy began to pace.

"Ha!" she said, following him with her eyes. "Same old Billy."

"Dammit Katrina, get out of here and leave us alone!"

"Chill out, I'm going." She opened the front door, then turned back toward Minnow and held up the phone. She smiled and waved it back and forth. Then she was gone.

"Why was she here?" Billy asked Minnow.

"I don't know. She said she just wanted to talk."

"It's never just to talk," he replied. "I don't like it."

Maggie felt like everything in her life was unfinished business. Her failure at the coast, the encounter with the girl, her relationship with her family. She tried music, reading, television. Nothing held her attention. She jumped for the phone when its ringtone broke the silence.

"Hey sis," said Ceci. "I know I said it was good that you were engaged with something, but how about your own grandkids? Situations like this are usually tragic and rarely fixable despite well-intentioned interventions. I hate to see you get in the middle of this."

"I know, I know," said Maggie. "I'm not thinking I can fix everything. Just maybe help sort things out for this one girl. She's been through a great deal, but she's still innocent and sweet. She doesn't appear to have anyone to help her."

"Still the Peace Corps volunteer at heart," said Ceci. "Okay, here's what I found out. The parental evaluation specialist is named Helen Lafferty. She has an office in Gresham. As it turns out, I know her a litttle. She's been doing this work for a long time, used to work for Child Protective Servies - CPS. Not brilliant, but a decent person and she tries to do what's right. I talked to her."

"And?"

"She wasn't willing to share much, and it's all off the record. But my take is she's struggling with what to do on this one. The girl's mother is making a play to have the girl placed back with her. But there's a negative history there. That's why the girl was taken out of the home originally. The uncle's got problems. So there's some question about his suitability. And the mother is hinting that there may be something more with him. The court didn't know that the grandmother had died and left the girl in her uncle's care, so there's never really been an evaluation of him as guardian. That's about all I know."

"Would the caseworker talk with me about the situation if I called her?" asked Maggie.

"In general terms, but she won't share anything confidential. She'd welcome any insights you might have into what's really going on with the uncle and with the mom."

"Well, I don't know the mom, but perhaps I can find a

way to meet her. I know her name."

"Just be careful Maggie. There's always stuff going on un-der the surface in these situations. You really shouldn't get involved."

"Don't worry. I'm a big girl," said Maggie.

"A big girl with a bruised heart. Don't lay it out there to get trampled again. I can guarantee that this is a quagmire."

"Thanks Ceci. You're always there for me."

Maggie spent the next half hour at her computer searching for Katrina Marsh. She found one entry from 2006 regarding a claim filed against a Katrina Diane Marsh by U.S. Bancorp—probably for nonpayment of credit card bills. Other than that, nothing. Apparently it was possible to fly that completely under the radar in the 21st century.

In the end, she needn't have bothered searching. When her home phone rang an hour later the husky voice on the other end said, "Is this Maggie Berry? My name is Katrina Marsh. I think you know my daughter Minnow."

Nearly speechless, Maggie said, "Well yes, I know her slightly. Why?"

"Minnow and I just had a wonderful chat and she told me what a help you'd been to her, with her periods and all, and as her mother I just had to call to say thank you."

"Well, that's very thoughtful of you," said Maggie, in-stantly on guard. "It was really no trouble. She's a remarkable girl you know."

"I know. That's why it's just killing me that I'm not there to take care of her. It's just not right, my not being there at a time like that."

"No, it's not," said Maggie, "but I understand there are

some reasons for that."

"Yeah, well I admit I've screwed things up in my life big time. I don't know what you've heard, but it's probably not all true if it came from my brother. I admit I'm no angel. But if you could have seen what I had to live with growing up, you'd understand. I cry every day thinking about what a mess I've made of things. But isn't there any such thing as forgiveness in this world? Don't you think it's possible for a person to change?"

"I think so," said Maggie. "But change is hard work and just claiming to have changed is no guarantee that it has happened."

"That's the other reason I called," said Katrina. "Besides to say thank you. I'm hoping that if I can convince someone Minnow trusts, and who is a respectable person, that I've got my life together now, then maybe I have half a chance. Billy won't never be on my side."

"Won't ever," said Maggie.

"That's what I said. He's hated me all my life, the little sister who took his mama's attention away from him."

"You said 'won't never,' which is a double negative," said Maggie. "The correct thing to say is 'won't ever.'"

Katrina breathed deep on the other end of the line and said, "See how helpful that is? To have someone who knows the right way to use English. Minnow said you used to be a teacher. I woulda done better if I'd had someone like you when I was in school."

"How do you propose to convince me that you 'have your life together,' as you put it?" Maggie asked.

"I think if you were to meet me in person, you'd see that I'm not some kind of a monster. I thought maybe I could buy you a cup of coffee and you can ask me anything you want."

"I guess there'd be no harm in that," said Maggie. "Although I really don't think I have much influence. I've only just met Minnow."

"I'm grasping at straws here Maggie—can I call you Maggie? I'm just a desperate mother trying to put her family back together. I'll do anything that might help."

"Well as long as we're clear there are no guarantees that it will help you get what you want, I guess there's no harm in meeting."

"Oh thank you so much," said Katrina, her voice breaking. "It at least gives me some hope."

They arranged for a meeting at a Starbucks in two days on Tuesday. Maggie was left with a lingering feeling of unease from the conversation. Was it all the warnings from Ceci? From Billy? Was it the strangeness of Katrina suddenly appearing on the phone after Maggie had tried and failed to find her? Was it that she didn't really know why she was getting involved in all this to begin with?

Whatever the case, she would know more Tuesday.

November 4

Maggie arrived at the Starbucks early and sat with her drink at a small table by the window. She recognized Katrina as she approached the store from her gait and features. She looked like a well-worn version of Minnow.

"Are you Maggie?" she said, her voice sounding like she was on the verge of laryngitis. She extended her hand. Maggie took it—a firm handshake—and nodded.

Katrina bought a cup of coffee and sat across from Maggie.

"I can't tell you how grateful I am to you for meeting me. I know you probably think I'm crazy, calling you out of the blue like that, but I didn't know what else to do. My life is never going to be complete until I can have both of my kids with me."

"How, exactly, are you thinking I can help you?" asked Maggie.

"I could tell that Minnow trusts you," said Katrina. "I can't get through to her because she's got Billy there filling her with poison about me every chance he gets. I just need someone to tell her to give me a chance."

"And why should she give you a chance? I don't know much about the situation, but my understanding is that she had to be removed from your care in the past."

"Well that wasn't really fair. Like I said on the phone, I haven't been perfect. I was too young when I had her, and her father took off and left me with a baby and no way to get by. That's what got me involved with drugs and stuff. I was just trying to survive. That turned the authorities against me, and my own mother too. And then I finally got things straightened out, and I met Brett, and had Sadie, and all that seemed good. But he wasn't good to Minnow, I think on account of she wasn't his, and he got mean when he drank. So then she had to go back with her grandma. It broke my heart." Katrina stared hard at Maggie. "I'm trying, and I just wanna do right by my kids. There's nothing more important to me."

"How do you support yourself?" asked Maggie.

"Well Dirk, he's my boyfriend, has a good job at his cousin's car repair place. We're not rich, but we get by."

"And what does Dirk think about Minnow coming to live

with you?"

"Oh, he loves kids. You should see him with Sadie! Always playing with her and fixing her meals and other stuff. I know he'll love Minnow too. Do you have kids Maggie?"

"Just one. A son."

"What's his name?"

"Toby. He's grown with kids of his own now."

"Oh, grandkids! Lucky you! I wanna be like you someday, close with my kids and grandkids. Anyways, can you imagine how it would have been if they had taken Toby away from you when he was young? It's the worst thing that can happen to a mother. Some days I just don't think I can bear it." Katrina's voice broke. She took the napkin from under her coffee cup and dabbed her eyes, sniffling gently.

She looked at Maggie with watery eyes. "Do you think you can help me? Will you talk to Minnow and ask her to give me a chance?"

"I care about Minnow," said Maggie. "I only want what's best for her, and I'm not sure what that is in this situation."

"Well *I'm* sure," said Katrina, no longer sniffling. "She needs to be in a family like other kids and go to school like other kids and have real friends, not just online people, whatever the hell those are. She needs to get away from Billy and be raised by normal people. By me, her real mother."

"Billy seems to have her interests at heart," said Maggie.

"Billy! He may seem okay to you, but he doesn't feel things like other people. What do you think that does to someone who lives with him? I know what it does 'cuz I had to live with him. It's like living with a robot. Mom always protected him because he was different, so I never had the kind of mom a girl should have either. Everything was about helping and shielding him. It's not fair to a girl to not have a loving mother. And there's other things about Billy that I won't go into, but I think when the authorities find out they're going to figure that he shouldn't be raising a teenage girl. I just want to make sure that if they're gonna put her someplace else, that it's with me, not with some stranger. I want to make up for the years we've missed together."

"Well, I see why you would want that," said Maggie.

"So you'll talk to her?"

"I am happy to talk with her, but ultimately she has to make up her own mind about what she wants."

"That's what people say, but how're you supposed to know what you want when you're twelve, especially when you're living with a freakin' robot who drags you all over the country fixing people's toilets," said Katrina. "You tell me what's weirder 'n that."

"Well, I admit it's different…"

"It's different all right. Tell you what. If you don't already think Minnow'd be better off with me, you spend some time with the two of them and see for yourself. If she doesn't get outta there soon, he's gonna make her just as weird as he is. Just do that for me, will you?" She clutched Maggie's forearms and pinned her gaze with pleading eyes.

"I can't make promises like that," said Maggie, pulling back. "I don't belong in the middle of this situation. It is between you, your brother, and Minnow. I only came today because I care about Minnow."

"But people will listen to you. I can tell just from meeting you that you're a fair person and that you speak your mind. I know I can count on you to do the right thing by me and my Minnow." Katrina rummaged in her purse until she found her phone, then checked the time.

"I need to get home to my other girl, but I appreciate you meeting with me," she said, putting out her hand to shake. When Maggie responded Katrina clamped Maggie's hand in a hard grip and held it a few seconds too long before releasing her. Then she was out the door, leaving behind her half-empty coffee cup, a red smear of lipstick on the rim.

Maggie sat staring at the cup, wondering once again how she had gotten herself involved in this. And was she involved? She could walk away at any time. Perhaps she would just walk away. It was no concern of hers. What did Katrina mean by *other things* about Billy that she wouldn't go into? Was Minnow truly at risk?

Maggie didn't know Billy at all. If Minnow was at risk and Maggie knew it, didn't she have an obligation to intervene if she could? She traveled back in her mind to the morning she'd met them. If only she'd had the sense to bring water with her in the car, none of this would matter to her now.

Sighing, she pulled out her phone and found the entry she'd made for Billy Marsh in her contacts.

"Hello," said the clipped voice on the other end.

"Billy, this is Maggie Berry from the convenience store at the coast. I have some information about your sister and wondered if I could stop by."

Surveying the neighborhood expanding eastward from the city of Gresham, Maggie felt like she was straddling two worlds. Cul de sacs of large, brick-facade houses emerged from the west, each house with its manicured lawn and three-car garage. To the east the lawns became scruffy, the houses tiny with carports or single car garages. Just past an ornamental plant nursery she found the driveway and the crooked house. There was Bonkers, standing at attention on the porch, one ear up and the other down. Somehow the crookedness of the house seemed right.

When Bonkers recognized her, he flew from the porch and circled around her legs, his tail beating against her ankles. She bent to scratch his ears. Then Minnow came out and picked her way barefooted down the walkway to where Maggie stood. She gave Maggie a hug.

"Uncle Billy said you were coming. I was so excited!"

"Where *is* your uncle?"

"He's working in the shop," Minnow said, pointing to the left of the house.

Maggie looked at the path between the house and shop. Every few feet there stood a whirligig, planted in the earth, each a unique twist of metal. These were not simple creations. They had multiple whorls that spun in different directions, some at different speeds. The metal cups that caught the wind changed colors as they reflected the light. The motion was mesmerizing.

"What is all this?" asked Maggie.

"Those are Uncle Billy's metal sculptures. It's what he does when we're here."

"They're beautiful!" said Maggie. "Does he sell them?"

"Yes, at some of the places we visit. It was Sam who talked him into trying to sell them, and now he gets a lot of money for them. C'mon, we'll go tell him you're here."

Maggie followed Minnow toward the shop, Bonkers racing ahead.

Everything in the shop was in order. Each tool hung precisely against the outlined pegboard. The concrete floor was painted glossy gray. The wooden workbench held a partially finished sculpture of leaf-shaped cups and copper metal stems. Billy was bent over a similar piece wearing a welding mask, the torch in his right hand spitting out arcs of white light and sparks. Minnow motioned for Maggie to stay by the door. She waited for Billy to stand and then tapped him on the shoulder. He flipped up his hood. "I will meet you up at the house."

The two tromped back up the spinning walkway and entered the sparsely furnished house. Maggie noted that it was equally neat and clean.

"Come see my room," said Minnow.

The twin bed, with its faded pink chenille bedspread, was carefully made. Maggie picked up one of the library books from the dresser, examining the title.

"*The Book Thief*," she said. "What do you think of that one?"

"I haven't finished it yet," said Minnow, "but I think it's really good. I've never read a book before where Death told the story, and it makes Death seem not so scary. And I think that Leisel feels the same way about books as me. Even though she steals them, I don't think it's wrong for her to steal them because she's not doing it for bad reasons—just to read. And she shares them with other people. And I like that even though she doesn't have her regular family anymore, she still has a home where people love her."

"I liked all those things about it too," said Maggie. "And I thought it showed how resilient and courageous people can be in really tough situations. I actually met the author when I was in Australia. That's where he lives."

"Wow!" said Minnow. "I've never met an author. That would be so awesome!"

They heard Billy come in and joined him in the living room. He was running his long fingers through his hair where the welding hood had ruffled it.

"What did you find out about Katrina?" he asked without preamble.

"I'll tell you all about it," said Maggie. "Could we sit down?"

Billy nodded and motioned to the sofa. He pulled his notebook and pen from his pocket. Minnow leaned toward Maggie from her perch on the front of the recliner seat. Billy chose a straight-backed wooden chair from the kitchen table. Bonkers joined Maggie on the sofa and put his head on her lap.

"Well, I actually spoke with her."

Billy jumped up from his chair. "You talked to her? I thought you were just going to get your sister to ask someone she knew at Multnomah County what she was doing."

"And I did," said Maggie. "But in the process, *your* sister contacted *me* and asked if we could meet."

Billy paced.

"Why did she want to meet with you? How did she even know to contact you?"

Minnow jumped in. "I mentioned Maggie to her when she was here. I told her about how she helped me and all."

"She said she wanted to thank me for helping Minnow. But the real reason I think is she was hoping I might influence

Minnow to want to go live with her."

Billy stopped pacing and turned, his fists clenched into balls.

"I knew it," he said.

"In any case, your suspicions are correct," said Maggie. "She wants to have Minnow returned to her."

"Returned," Billy scoffed. "How could she call it returned when Minnow has lived here 70.6% of her life?"

"What she said is that she wants to put her family together, Minnow and her other daughter. She says she's made mistakes in her life, but that she's turned it around and wants another chance."

"That's what she told me too," said Minnow.

"And you believe her?" Billy asked, stationary now, looking at Maggie.

"I don't know what to believe," said Maggie. "I don't know your sister. But I don't know you either. I know that it's natural for a mother to want to have her children with her. And I know that it's possible for people to straighten out their lives. Katrina also implied that she had information about you that would affect the authorities' decision about Minnow's placement with you."

Billy had been pacing again, head down. He stopped again and looked at Maggie.

"Did she say what information?"

"No, only that it could influence whether you should be caring for a teenage girl."

Billy paced again, more quickly now. "Did you tell her you'd help her?"

"No," said Maggie. "I told her that it's none of my affair,

and that all I would do is share my perceptions with you and Minnow."

"And what are those perceptions?"

"That's just it," said Maggie. "I really don't know. Like I said, I don't know either of you enough to know what to believe."

"I can tell you what to believe," said Billy. "But that probably won't do any good. You need to see for yourself."

"I have an idea!" said Minnow. "We should go see Sam. She always knows what to do. And Maggie could come with us. Then she'd be able to get to know us better. Would you come Maggie?"

"Well I don't think I …"

"Pl-e-e-ease!" said Minnow. "You'll love Sam. She's who gave me Bonkers. We could go tomorrow. Just for the day. Can't we do that Uncle Billy?"

"Tomorrow's not our day to go to Connor," said Billy.

"I know," said Minnow. "But this is kind of an emergency situation. Sam always helps us in emergency situations."

Billy shrugged. "I guess we could talk to Sam," he said. "She knows how Katrina operates, and she gets me."

"And can Maggie come?"

"We don't travel with other people."

"I know," said Minnow. "But we could do it, just this once couldn't we? It'll be okay, it's just Maggie and there's room for three in the pickup."

Billy was silent, thinking. "I guess this once," he said. He flipped open his notebook and scribbled, frowning.

"So will you come Maggie?" Minnow implored.

Maggie found that she couldn't resist Minnow any more

than Billy could. "Well, I guess I could meet your friend and get her take on things. But I'll be glad to drive myself. Can you give me directions?

"Sam lives in Connor," said Billy. "You could follow us."

"I guess that will work. When should I be here?"

"Nine a.m.," said Billy. "We always leave exactly at nine."

Driving home, Maggie was plagued by the realization that she was no longer in control of her life. She had always believed that with the proper planning she could manage any situation.

Since her memories of the accident had returned, things had been spinning out of control. Now she found herself making decisions and doing things beyond her own understanding. Was she really following these two people she barely knew thirty some miles to Connor to meet with someone she didn't know at all? She couldn't believe she had agreed to this, but having given up on her life, she realized that she had no other plans, so why not?

She saw the potential in Minnow. So bright. So unspoiled, despite what the girl had been through. As a teacher, she couldn't resist potential. Yet, there was still something more. Maggie just genuinely *liked* the girl and wanted to know her more, to be a positive influence in her life, and maybe balance out some of the bad people who had preceded her.

She couldn't really explain it, even to herself. She had known hundreds of young people during her career, had cared about them and, she hoped, been a positive part of their education. But this was deeper, not professional but personal.

This was friendship.

November 5

Minnow was up early cutting letters out of old wrapping paper and gluing them onto white poster board. The result was a large sign declaring "Happy Birthday!" in cheerful colors and patterns. Billy spooned oatmeal into a bowl, setting it on the table with a clatter. He sat on the edge of the chair across from Minnow, then sprang up and paced the room, scratching at his cheek.

An unplanned trip to Connor would mean that he'd need to buy gas sooner, making it nine times this month instead of eight. On top of it all, the thought of losing Minnow, especially to Katrina, was unbearable. And yet it could happen. Other people might forget your past, but not your sister. Especially not this sister. He scratched nervously at his ear, grabbed up the bowl and ate a couple of bites before setting it in the kitchen sink.

"It's going to be okay today," Minnow said. "It's just Maggie, and we both like her."

"We don't normally go to Samantha's on this day," he said.

"I know, but we need her advice. Also, I'm hoping you'll stop on Winter Hill Road on our way back. It's his birthday today. I want to leave a sign."

"That's three things today that we don't usually do."

"Sometimes we do stop there," said Minnow. "And a birthday only comes once a year. Please Uncle Billy? I'll bring the card and you can decide on the way home."

"I'd rather decide now. I don't like sudden changes in plans."

"Okay, then decide to stop. Pretty please?"

"All right. I will stop. But no more changes for today. Three is enough."

"No more changes," she said. "We'll do our usual routine for Connor—Algebra and Literary Endings."

Billy nodded.

Maggie arrived sharply at 8:45. Minnow threw the door open before Maggie could knock and Bonkers bounded out, spinning in circles at Maggie's ankles.

"I'm so excited that you're coming!" said Minnow, jumping up and down.

Walking toward the pickup two minutes before nine, Billy stopped and knelt along the right side of Maggie's car. "Your tire's going flat," he said, pointing to the right front tire.

"Oh no," said Maggie, surveying the tire. "I see what you mean. I can't drive it like that. I'll need to call Triple A. I'm afraid you two will have to go without me."

"Our whole purpose in going was for you to meet Sam and tell her about what you found out," said Billy.

"Can't she just ride with us?" asked Minnow. "Uncle Billy can fix your tire when we get back."

"I guess we could do that," said Billy, "if Maggie is willing."

"Well I don't want to obligate you. I do have roadside service."

"The tire is no problem," said Billy. "This way we can keep to our schedule, and I'll repair your tire when we get back."

"In that case," said Maggie, "I'll be glad to come with you."

Minnow clapped her hands. "I've never had anyone ride with us, except Bonkers of course, but he doesn't count."

The brown and white dog cocked his head and whined at

the sound of his name.

"Sorry, Bonkers," said Minnow. "Of course you count, just not as another person. Although you're better than a lot of people," she added, scratching his ears. He wagged his tail and raced back and forth on the porch.

Getting into the pickup truck promptly at 9, Maggie noted the dust-free dashboard, shiny chrome trim and comfortable upholstered bench seat. Minnow sat in the middle with Bonkers settled at Maggie's feet.

Minnow explained, "We always do algebra and literature on trips to Connor, so that's what we're doing today. You can help."

"I might be of some help with literature, but algebra was a long time ago for me."

"You can help Uncle Billy with literature. I get to test him on that since I teach myself literature."

"That sounds fun," said Maggie, surprised to realize that this was a true statement.

Minnow pulled a spiral notebook and pencil from the glove box.

"Okay Uncle Billy, make it a good one."

Billy said, "Let's say you found eighty dollars in fives and ones on the sidewalk and decided to share it among the three of us, but not equally. You decide that I get half as much as you, and Maggie gets five dollars less than you. Figure out how much each of us gets."

"Hmm," said Minnow, pencil poised over the notebook.

"Okay," she said, "if the amount you get is x, then the amount I get is 2x, because you get half as much as I do. And the amount Maggie gets is 2x - 5." She wrote.

"So x + 2x + (2x - 5) = 80." She stared at the page for a few moments, then started to write again.

"So if I add 5 to each side of the equation, then I get x + 2x + 2x = 85, or 5x = 85. So that means x = 17. So you get $17, I get $34, and Maggie gets $29. Right?"

"Very good," said Billy. "Five points for that one."

"Yes!" said Minnow. "Give me another one."

"All right," said Billy. "A group of 532 persons consists of men, women, and children. There are four times as many men as children, and twice as many women as children. How many of each are there?"

"Okay. x = the number of children. 2x = the number of women, and 4x = the number of men. So x + 2x + 4x = 532. So 7x = 532, so that means x = 76. So there are 76 children, 152 women, and 304 men."

"Right again," said Billy. "Five more points."

"These are too easy. Give me a ten pointer," Minnow said.

"Try this: You have six times as many dimes as quarters in your piggy bank. You have 21 coins in your piggy bank totaling $2.55. How many of each type of coin do you have?"

Minnow was silent for a full minute. Then she started to write.

"Okay, if x is the number of quarters, then 6x is the number of dimes. Since one quarter equals 25 cents, x quarters equals x times 25 cents or 25x cents. Since one dime equals 10 cents, 6x dimes equals 6x times 10 cents or 60x cents. And 2.55 equals 255 cents. So the equation is 25x cents + 60x cents = 255 cents. 85x cents = 255 cents. 85x cents divided by 85 cents = 255 cents divided by 85 cents. x = 3, so 6x = 6 × 3 = 18. So I have 3 quarters and 18 dimes, at least I wish I had 3 quarters and 18 dimes. I don't even have a piggy bank!"

"But you are getting good at equations," said Billy. "Ten points for that one. Maybe we should skip the hamburger and milkshake when you hit 500 and buy you a piggy bank instead."

"No way!" said Minnow.

"We'll take a break for a few minutes," Billy said.

"I noticed that Minnow uses pencil and paper," said Maggie, "but you seem to just carry these mathematical equations in your head Billy."

"Yes," he said. "In my head it's the same as if they were on paper. I can just see them."

"Quite a gift," said Maggie.

The trio sat in silence enjoying the beautiful morning.

Billy drove exactly two miles under the speed limit, both hands on the wheel. Yellow and brown leaves drifted past the windshield in front of a pale blue sky. Being on the road with these two unusual people gave Maggie a sense of adventure and relief. She felt somehow untethered from her own life and problems.

"Do you have a favorite color Maggie?" Minnow asked.

"Definitely blue," said Maggie.

"Just any blue?"

"What do you mean?"

"I mean, like my favorite color is green, but not just any green. It's that green you see when you lay down under a tree and look up through the leaves on a sunny, summer day. When I see that color, it makes me feel like the world is good, and anything is possible."

Lie. When you lie under the tree, Maggie thought. "I see,"

Maggie mused. "That is a lovely green indeed. Well, in that case, mine is the blue of the sea along the Cote d'Azur."

"I know where that is," says Minnow. "It's in France along the Mediterranean Coast. But I don't know what the name means."

"It literally means the blue coast and that part of the coast is called the French Riviera."

"You've been there?"

"Oh yes," said Maggie with a distant look in her eyes. "Two years ago, my husband and I spent a week in St. Tropez."

"I would love to do that!" said Minnow. "Describe the blue to me."

"It's translucent and deep at the same time—electric and alive. There are hints of green, but mostly it's full of light."

"That sounds beautiful!"

"It is," said Maggie. "More beautiful than I can describe."

"It's the light in the tree leaves that I love too. Uncle Billy, what's your favorite color?"

"White," said Billy without hesitation.

"White? That's not a color," said Minnow.

"To the contrary. Technically speaking, white is made up of all the colors combined. The fact that our eyes can't perceive them doesn't alter the beauty of it. Sunlight is white light that is composed of all the colors of the spectrum. We just can't see them until something bends the light rays and then we see the rainbow. What's more beautiful than a rainbow?"

"Wow," said Minnow.

"Indeed," said Maggie.

When they turned into the parking lot at Maverick's store, Bonkers started whining and scrabbled to Maggie's lap, his front paws and nose pressed to the window. As soon as she opened the door he flew from the truck and raced for the entrance.

Maggie noted the rustic but neat appearance of the place. The single-story rectangular building was covered in vertical rough-sawn cedar planks. Magenta ornamental cabbages and golden chrysanthemums sprang from half-barrels placed at intervals across the front of the store. Under the overhanging roof bracketing the front door, four wooden rockers beckoned. A hand-painted sign in the window said:

Maverick's General Store

We welcome:	We ignore:
Hugs	Whining
Laughter	Griping
Straight Talk	BS
Dancing	Gossiping
Singing	Proselytizing
Dogs	Scowling
Quirky People	Grumpy People

As they emerged from the truck, Donovan wrapped Minnow in a bear hug, then shook hands with Billy.

"Donovan, this is my friend Maggie," said Minnow.

"Well, that was right nice of you to finally bring along a lady friend from my generation," said Donovan, winking at Maggie. "Usually you just show up with that scruffy dog."

"You love Bonkers and you know it," said Minnow, "or you wouldn't have rescued him."

"I just did it in hopes he might get hisself straightened out, but look at him. Just as lopsided as ever."

"He's perfect," said Minnow.

"That he is," agreed Donovan.

Just then the door swung open and a woman in her mid-thirties with honey blond, curly hair came out. Bonkers leaped vertically into her arms and began licking her face.

"I love you too," she laughed.

She walked to Billy and Minnow.

"Well this is a pleasant surprise!" She looked with concern at Billy while pulling Minnow into an embrace, Bonkers happily sandwiched between them.

She held out her hand to Maggie.

"I'm Samantha Maverick, but my friends call me Sam. Billy's never brought a friend with him before. And he's never come on the first Wednesday of the month."

"I'm Maggie Berry," said Maggie.

"She's my friend I met at the coast," said Minnow. "Maggie's who I was with when I called you."

Billy paced in front of the pickup.

"What's wrong?" said Sam.

"Katrina," said Billy.

"I suppose I could have guessed that. You all come inside the store where it's warm and fill me in. Donovan, would you take care of any customers for a few minutes?"

They followed her into the store. On a braided rug in the corner were four wicker chairs with gingham-checked cushions arranged around a small wood stove. They settled around the warm stove and told her their story, including how Maggie came to be involved. She listened intently, stroking Bonkers' ears while he was curled up on her lap.

"What do you think, Billy? Does Katrina have information that could cause them to take Minnow away from you?"

Billy stood and paced.

"Maybe," he said. "It's not something I want to talk about right now. But it's possible."

"So Minnow, if that should happen, what do you want to do? Do you want to go live with your mom?"

"I don't know," said Minnow, tears gathering in her eyes. "I've always wished I could live with my mom, but it was bad last time. If I knew it wasn't going to be like that, then maybe yes. I'd like to have a little sister. But Bonkers would have to come with me." Then she looked at her uncle who had not stopped his pacing.

"But I don't want to leave Uncle Billy either. I wish things could just stay like they are."

Sam turned to Maggie. "What do you think?"

"I only met Katrina once, and then only briefly," said Maggie, "so my thoughts aren't worth much."

"Perhaps, but I'd like to hear them anyway."

"Well," said Maggie, "I thought Katrina made a reasonable case for wanting to put her family back together. She did admit that she'd made mistakes that had led to the current situation. And she begged me to believe that it's possible for someone to change. All of that seemed like it could be legitimate. But there was something that I didn't quite trust."

"I know what you mean," said Sam.

"She's not trustworthy," said Billy.

"So what to do," mused Sam. "I really think you're going to have to wait for her to play her hand, unless there's something you can do to preempt her. Can you think of anything?"

"No," Billy groaned.

"But Minnow, ultimately it may come down to what you want. If they do decide you can't stay with Billy, which I hope is not the case, then you may be faced with either living with your mom or going into a foster situation. How do you feel about that?"

"I don't want to be a foster child," said Minnow, tears now trickling down her cheeks. She swiped at them with her sweater sleeve. "Maybe I could come stay with you. What about that?"

"Well, that's a thought," said Sam. "I'd love it, but that would be totally up to the State. Let's hold that thought and hope it's an option if it comes to that."

"I don't know why we can't just keep things the way they are," said Minnow, brushing away more tears.

Sam set Bonkers down and squeezed into the chair beside Minnow, folding her into a hug.

"I know love," she said, using her fingers to comb Minnow's hair back from her face. "I know."

The morning progressed as people went about their day. Maggie followed Sam into the back room. "I was hoping to catch you alone for a few minutes to fill you in a bit more on the circumstances of my meeting Minnow."

She then described the scene in the restroom at the coast.

"Poor kid," said Sam. "Billy wouldn't know what to do with all that. I love the guy, he's really a gem you know, but he has some flat sides."

"I've noticed that," said Maggie. "Anyway, he said you

were the person to whom Minnow could talk if she needs more help or information. Having met you, I can see why. It seems you truly love her."

"I love them both. Donovan gives me a hard time about it. He says, 'Do you really want to get involved with a guy who's short on emotions like that?' and I say, 'I've had enough of guys and their emotions to last two lifetimes. Give me someone who's predictable and steady. Emotions are just the leaves dancing in the wind. What I care about is the part that's rooted in the earth.' When I first met Billy at college, I liked him immediately. I could tell he was brilliant, and I sensed there was so much more beneath the surface that he didn't know how to show, or maybe just didn't feel safe showing. But it was when I saw him with Minnow that I started to love him. I could see his tenderness, his innate goodness, in how he cared for her. It's so difficult for him to disrupt the routines in his life, but he will do it for her. It's clear he would do anything for her."

The mood was noticeably brighter on the way back. Sam hadn't really solved anything, but being with her made things better. And whatever happened, she would be in their corner.

"On the way back from Sam's is when we usually do Literary Endings. What's great about it is I get to test Uncle Billy. You see, he's not into literature like I am, and he hasn't read most of the books I've read. So I give him a summary of the story up to the ending, and he has to guess how it ends."

"And do you get points for this one too?" asked Maggie.

"Yeah, but I get ten points just for reading and summarizing a book, whether Billy gets it right or not. It's kind of like a book report in school, only more fun. He's pretty good with stories that are like math formulas where there's just a good guy and bad guy and the good guy wins in the end. But when the people in the stories do weird things, sometimes he's way off."

"That seems to be more a problem with the author creating flawed characters than with my analysis," said Billy.

"So are you ready Uncle Billy?"

"Go ahead," he said.

"My book this time is *To Kill a Mockingbird* by Harper Lee. It's about a six-year-old girl named Scout, and her older brother Jem, and their friend Dill. I love the names in this book, especially Dill. It's like a pickle. Scout and Jem live with their Dad Atticus Finch. He's a lawyer and they live in Alabama in the nineteen-thirties when people were really poor, and they were also really prejudiced against black people. They use the N word in the book, but I'm not using it because I don't like to say it."

"Anyway, there's a guy named Boo Radley who's their neighbor, but they've never seen him, and everyone's scared of him. He's like some kind of scary monster. But someone leaves gifts for the kids in a tree outside Boo Radley's place, although they never see who does it. It's really Boo who does it, and he does other things to help them, even though no one ever sees him do it."

"There's a Black guy named Tom Robinson who's accused of raping a young white woman named Mayella Ewell, and Atticus ends up being Tom's lawyer. That makes people mad at Atticus because they just want to believe that Tom Robinson is guilty since he's Black. Atticus proves that Mayella and her father Bob Ewell are lying and Tom is innocent, but that doesn't matter. The jury's all white people and they convict Tom anyway and he goes to jail. Then later when he tries to escape, he gets shot and killed."

"Bob Ewell is a really bad man and he's out to get Atticus because he thinks his reputation is ruined, even though he's the town drunk and doesn't have a good reputation to begin with. He attacks Jem and Scout when they're walking home from a Halloween party, but Boo Radley saves them, and he stabs Bob Ewell to death. Jem gets hurt and Boo carries him home. Then he disappears back to his own house again."

"So here's the question Uncle Billy. When the sheriff comes because Boo Radley killed Bob Ewell, what does he do?"

Billy said, "That's easy. He arrests Boo Radley for murder. Obviously he broke the law."

Minnow giggled. "Nope. Boo broke the law, but that's not what happens. The sheriff makes up a story that Bob Ewell tripped over a tree root and died, so no one gets arrested because the death was an accident."

Billy frowned. "So the sheriff lied and he didn't do his job to uphold the law, so then he broke the law too. Did he get fired?"

"Well no, but that's not the point," said Minnow.

Maggie couldn't keep silent. "What do you think is the point Minnow?"

Minnow was quiet for a moment, looking off in the distance.

"I think it's that people and things aren't always the way they seem at first," she said. "Like Boo Radley seems really scary, but it turns out he's good. And the town seems like a nice friendly and quiet place, but there's all these bad things that happen and people end up being really mean and unfair. And the sheriff seems like he's like the other white people in town, but he knows that Bob Ewell is really a bad guy, and Boo is really a good guy, so he protects Boo."

"Who killed the mockingbird?" Billy interjected.

"There wasn't really a mockingbird in the story," said Minnow.

"That's another irrational thing. If there's no mockingbird, then why call it that?"

"That's a good question Billy," said Maggie. "Minnow, why do you think the author gave it that title?"

"I don't know," said Minnow. "I think they talk about mockingbirds in the story a couple of times."

"Right," said Maggie. "Do you still have the book at home?"

"Yes."

"I think you should go back to it and see if you can figure out the significance of the title."

"Okay. Can I call to tell you what I think after I do that?"

"I'd like that," said Maggie.

Minnow looked up as signs for the I-205 Freeway came into view.

"Don't get on the freeway Uncle Billy," she said. "Remember, it's his birthday. You promised we could stop."

"I remember," said Billy.

"Is it one of your friends who's having a birthday?" asked Maggie.

"Yes," said Minnow. She reached for her backpack and pulled out a spiral notebook.

"See," she said. "I have all my friends listed here with

their birthdays, and their ages and other stuff about them. This is my newest friend, Carrie. She's the same age as me. She liked to play soccer, which is something I've never done except in P.E. when I went to school."

"That's very organized," said Maggie. "So will you see your friend who's having a birthday today?"

"Not exactly," said Minnow. "This is sad, but actually he died. So I just made a birthday sign in his honor. I don't know if he can see it, but I know his mom, dad, and sister will. He would have been seventeen."

"So young," said Maggie, an unwelcome sense of foreboding beginning to shift her mood. There was a long silence except for the truck noise.

"Tell me," said Maggie, "are your other friends in the notebook also people who've died?"

"Yes," said Minnow. "I hope you don't think that makes me weird or something. It's just that I see their memorials along the road, and I want to know about them. I think if people go to all the trouble to put up a memorial, it's because the person who died was important to them and they want others to know about them. So I figure it's the least I can do."

"I don't think it makes you weird. Lonely maybe, but not weird. How do you find out about them?"

"I ask people. And I go online and find them and make friends with their friends."

"Do you ever meet their actual friends?"

"Sometimes, or their families. Like Jason whose birthday it is. I met his mom and sister when I was at his roadside memorial, and she invited me to their house. She said that most people are afraid to talk about her son around her, and that hurts her feelings because it's like he didn't ever exist. But I'm not afraid to talk about him. I asked her lots of questions about him, and she said that helped her. She told me I could come visit any time."

They turned the corner and started up a steep incline. Maggie's dull sense of foreboding shifted to full-blown panic. She hadn't been on this road since the accident, and then it had been dark. She saw the oak trees lining the road beyond the gravel shoulder, just bare branches now. There was the street sign. Winter Hill Road.

The double yellow line stretched up to the crest of the hill. On the left side of the road, halfway up the hill, there was a bit of color. Flowers, a skateboard, a photo encased in plastic.

"Please stop!" said Maggie, breathing rapidly. "I need to get out."

"Are you ill?" asked Billy, slowing the truck.

"Yes. I'm not feeling well. Just let me out here. You go on. I'll just get some air." She had the door open and was halfway out before the truck had stopped. She dropped to the ground and shut the truck door, waving them on.

Billy hesitated for a moment, then urged the truck up the hill. Maggie stepped off the road and leaned against an oak tree, hands on her knees, head down. She did feel quite ill.

When she looked up, she saw Minnow jump out of the truck with a handmade sign that she placed amidst the flowers. Then Maggie realized that there was someone else at the memorial. A woman. The woman walked toward Minnow and embraced her in a lengthy hug. When they separated, they stood talking quietly. Even at this distance, Maggie recognized her—the large frame, the flyaway hair.

Jason Foster's mother.

Suddenly Maggie was back in the deposition room facing a photo of a blue-eyed teenage boy.

She pushed herself away from the tree and began to stumble down the hill, her only thought was getting off of this particular stretch of road. She was four blocks away when she heard the panting of a small dog racing toward her. He ran in circles around her legs as she walked. The pickup and camper came next. Billy stopped the truck and Minnow ran to Maggie's side.

"Maggie, where are you going? What's wrong?"

Maggie stopped, but did not speak. She realized she was crying.

"What is it?" Minnow demanded. "Did we do something wrong? Are you sick?"

"No," Maggie managed to say. "It's not you."

"Then what?" Minnow grabbed her hand. "We are friends. You can tell me."

"It just brought back memories," said Maggie. "My husband… My husband was killed in an accident several months ago. It's still difficult…"

She imagined how Minnow would look at her when she found out that Maggie was the person responsible for Jason's death. Innocent affection shattered. Loving eyes becoming accusatory and angry. She couldn't bear it. Not yet.

"Oh," said Minnow. "I didn't know."

She continued to hold Maggie's hand, thinking. "I'm sorry," she said. "I shouldn't have talked about my friends who died in accidents."

"It's all right," said Maggie. "It was just the shock."

Minnow pulled her back toward the truck. When they were inside, Billy asked, "Where were you going? We're nowhere close to the location of your car."

"I wasn't thinking about it I'm afraid," said Maggie. "I was just going."

"Maggie's husband was killed in a car accident," said Minnow. "She got upset because talking about my roadside memorial friends reminded her."

"I know it wasn't rational," said Maggie. "It just came over me."

"I know what that's like," said Minnow. "You know how I said that it was bad living with my mom and Brett and that's why I'm not sure about going back with her?"

"Yes," said Maggie.

"Well, Brett was really mean, and when I get around other mean people or something happens that reminds me of living with him, sometimes I just freak out. Like that time when I ran into the woods. I didn't think about it. I don't even know Dirk. He may be really nice like she said. But it just reminded me of Brett."

"You said Brett beat your mom," said Maggie. "Did he hit you too?"

"Yes, he hit me sometimes when he was really mad, like when I changed the channel on the TV to something he didn't want to watch. Or when I didn't want to eat all my food."

"Did your mom know he hit you?"

"Of course she knew," interjected Billy.

"She knew," said Minnow. "At least some of the times, 'cuz she was right there."

"And she stayed with him anyway?" asked Maggie.

"I think it was because they were doing drugs, so she was pretty spaced out a lot of the time. I think it's probably better now if she's really off drugs like she said."

"She is not trustworthy," said Billy.

Maggie was quiet. After a while she said, "I'm sorry you had to go through all of that Minnow."

"It's okay," said Minnow. "Once I got back with Granny Vi, and then with Uncle Billy, everything's been all right."

They spent the rest of the drive back in silence. When they arrived, she stood by as Billy efficiently jacked up her car and replaced the tire, now completely flat, with the spare.

"You should get that one repaired immediately so you're not stranded," said Billy.

"That I will," said Maggie, offering a thank you and a quick goodbye as she got in her car.

Driving home, Maggie was plagued by images. Jenny Foster on the hill next to Jason's memorial. Her anger at the deposition. The tears at George's memorial service.

How was it possible that this crazy entanglement with Minnow and Billy would land her here, in the abyss of her deepest shame? Why was it that every time she tried to bury the memory of this unpardonable moment, it reared back to life like a zombie from the graveyard?

Then she saw six-year-old Minnow suffering blows from a brute because she didn't eat everything on her plate. She saw Katrina sitting nearby watching, drugged out, passive. Maggie thought of the Katrina she had met a day earlier. Now the nagging doubts about Katrina's motives, about her willingness to protect her daughter, began to dominate Maggie's thoughts. She heard Billy's voice. "She's not trustworthy."

"But what am I doing?" she asked herself. "Why am I even involved in all of this?"

Ten days ago she hadn't even known these people, not Billy, or Katrina, or Minnow. Ten days ago she was clear on what she needed to do to put things right, or as right as she possibly could.

Seeing Jason's mother, being at the very scene of the tragedy she could have prevented, revived her thoughts of escape. But walking away from this child who had somehow dropped into her life, and who she could possibly help, felt like another wrong that she couldn't live with, and more importantly, didn't want to die with. Maybe if she could make a difference here it would go a short distance toward making up for the other unbearable wrong.

Later that evening she called Ceci.

"What are the chances," she asked, "of a mother changing and becoming a protector of that child, a mother who would watch her child be beaten and not act?"

"It's not impossible," said Ceci. "Particularly if, as you say, drugs were a factor and the mom's no longer involved with drugs. On the other hand, I'd say it's iffy. If there's a basic lack of empathy on the part of the mom, if she's truly narcissistic, then that's probably something that remains with or without drugs."

"That's what I fear," said Maggie.

"So you're still pursuing this domestic soap opera," said Ceci.

"Oh, Ceci, if you could see this girl. She's so bright and engaging, and so alone. She's created imaginary friends based on roadside memorials of accident victims. She researches them, and records everything about them, and then befriends their friends and family online."

"That's really very creative on her part, but also pretty strange. It speaks to her resilience and her loneliness. She's a survivor. I see the reason for the heart tug," said Ceci.

"Her uncle's doing the best he can," said Maggie, "He's brilliant, but he's not capable of being emotionally present for her."

"So what are you going to do? Are you planning to foster her?"

"Oh no, I just think I need to try to discourage the authorities from placing her back with the mom."

"Just be careful of your own emotions in the process," said Ceci. "These things get complicated. And you're a stranger."

"Understood," said Maggie.

She sat quietly after the call, scenes of the day spinning through her mind like the frames of a movie.

November 6

Maggie slept poorly. She knew this was none of her business, but then whose business was it? Who is there to protect kids like Minnow if the adults who know them don't act?

"Are you going to have another situation in your life where someone is hurt because you didn't have the courage to act?" she asked herself aloud.

Maggie found the number for Helen Lafferty, Parental Evaluation Specialist located in Gresham, and dialed.

"This is Helen Lafferty."

"Uh, hello Mrs. Lafferty. My name is Maggie Berry. I'm

calling about Minnow Marsh. I understand you're her case-worker."

"Hello Mrs. Berry. I do parental evaluations for the court system," said Helen.

Maggie heard a shuffling of papers.

"May I ask your relationship to Minnow?"

"I'm just a friend who's gotten to know her recently. I've also gotten to know her uncle, and have met her mother, although I can't say that I know her."

"I see," said the caseworker. "I had someone call a few days ago about this case. A social worker from Eugene. Is she related to you in some way?"

"Uh yes," said Maggie. "Yes she is. She's my sister."

"I see. Well before we talk about Minnow, I need some more information from you, such as the reason for your involvement. I also need basic contact information."

Maggie provided these, fighting back doubts about inserting herself directly into Minnow's situation.

"You know I can't share any confidential information with you," Helen Lafferty said.

"I understand," said Maggie. "I'm not calling to get information. Like I said, I just wanted to share some information that I learned from Minnow when I last saw her that may be important for you to know."

"Do you mind if I record this call?" asked Helen.

Maggie hesitated; the doubts stronger now. "I don't know. How will the recording be used?"

"Just to keep my memory accurate, and so I don't have to take notes."

"In that case, I guess it's all right," said Maggie.

"Okay," said the caseworker. "This is Helen Lafferty in conversation with Maggie Berry at 10:30 a.m. on November 6, 2014 in the case of Minnow Marsh, number 8635902. Go ahead Mrs. Berry."

"Minnow's mother told me that she is seeking to have Minnow returned to her. When I was with Minnow yesterday, she shared some information with me that made me concerned about her safety if she is returned to her mother."

"What was that information?"

"Apparently, she had been with her mother for a short time when she was six and then had been removed from the home and returned to her grandmother. She talked about Brett, her mother's boyfriend, and his violence against the mother, and also against her."

"We're aware of that situation," said Helen Lafferty. "My understanding is that Brett is no longer in the picture."

"Yes, I think that's right," said Maggie. "But the thing that was disturbing to me was that when Minnow described being mistreated by Brett, she said that her mother had been present and did not intervene. I think drugs were involved. But nevertheless, it has just been bothering me that a mother would allow this to happen and would not at least try to protect her child. And that she would stay with a man like that, and even have another child with him. I would hate to see this happen to Minnow again."

"Yes, there is a risk there," said the caseworker. "We do see people turn themselves around in these situations, however. Particularly if they can keep off the drugs."

"I'd like to think that would be the case," said Maggie. "I just had too many nagging doubts to let it ride. I used to teach school, you see, and saw my share of domestic problems, and I guess I still have the mindset of a mandatory reporter. Plus, I'm very fond of Minnow."

"Yes, well we encourage people to come forward with concerns like this. So far we don't have any reason to believe that the same kinds of problems exist in the mother's home. Do you have any additional information that would shed light on the matter?"

"Nothing more about the mother. But I did spend time with both Minnow and her uncle, and actually observed him in action with his home schooling. I must admit, I was impressed. He seems to be doing a good job with her, and she's very bright."

"Thank you for that insight. As a teacher yourself, that's a valuable observation. I can't predict what the court will decide in this case, but I assure you we'll take the information you shared into consideration should we make a recommendation regarding a different placement."

"That's all I can ask," said Maggie.

"Thank you for your call, Mrs. Berry."

Maggie set her phone down and tried to decide if she felt better for making the call. She had made an attempt. Surely that was better than nothing. Yet she felt she had not adequately conveyed the seriousness of the situation. She realized that her sense of danger for Minnow was based more on gut feelings than facts. A judge wasn't going to act on an old woman's gut feelings.

Helen Lafferty was troubled by her own gut feelings. In this case, as in so many of her cases, she didn't like any of the options for this kid. The mom was manipulative, with a bad history. The uncle had Asperger's syndrome. And then there were the mom's veiled comments about the uncle. Was there really something of concern, or was Katrina just lying?

Normally Helen didn't take reports like Maggie Berry's too seriously, but she couldn't write it off entirely this time. She wished there was another family member, or even a close friend, as a back-up placement option if necessary. Perhaps an unannounced home visit would shed more light on the mom's situation.

November 8

Katrina was having a bad morning. Sadie had a cold and was moping around in her pajamas whining about one thing or another. The landlord had been by to hassle them about the rent, which was two days late. And Dirk's cousin had just called with some bullshit excuse about why he couldn't pay Dirk until next week for their last job. She stood next to Dirk, who was sitting on the couch with his feet propped up on the coffee table amidst beer bottles, two full ashtrays, and a roach clip, when she saw Helen Lafferty drive up.

"Shit!" she said. "It's that Helen Lafferty from the court!"

"What's she want?" asked Dirk.

"She wants to check us out!" shouted Katrina. "Look at this mess!"

"So?"

"What do you mean 'so'? Get the fuck off the couch and clean up this shit! If she doesn't like what she sees, we're screwed. I'll never get Minnow back."

Dirk lurched to his feet and started picking up beer bottles. Meanwhile Katrina began sweeping dishes off the counters into the sink and stuffing wrappers and the remains of past meals into the garbage can.

"What's wrong Mama?" whined Sadie.

"Just shut up Sadie," said Katrina. "Quit being a pain in the ass for a change."

Sadie began to cry just as Helen Lafferty knocked on the door.

"Fuck!" said Katrina. "Knock it off Sadie," she hissed as she walked to the door. She stood still, took a deep breath and opened the door enough to peer outside.

"Oh, hello Mrs. Lafferty!" she said with feigned surprise, smiling. "We weren't expecting you."

"I was in the area," said Helen Lafferty, "so I thought I'd drop by for the home visit I mentioned. I hoped that since it's Saturday you would be home. Could I come in?"

"Of course," said Katrina. "Like I said, we weren't expecting company, so I hope you'll excuse the mess."

"No problem," said Helen Lafferty. "I prefer to see things as they are on a normal day, not when you're expecting someone."

"Well, this is it then," said Katrina. "This is where we live right now, but we expect to be able to move to a better place real soon."

Helen turned to look around and Katrina pushed some debris under the sofa with her foot.

"This is Dirk." Katrina gestured toward Dirk who stood barefoot with his back to the television. He nodded. "And my younger daughter Sadie," she reached behind her and pulled the sniffling child forward to face the caseworker.

"What's the matter Sadie?" asked Helen Lafferty. "You look like you've been crying."

"She has a cold, poor thing," said Katrina. "Don't you sweetheart?" She picked up Sadie and caressed her tangled hair.

"May I sit down?" asked the caseworker.

"Oh, of course. Pardon my manners." Katrina gestured toward the couch. Helen Lafferty hesitated, then chose the wooden kitchen chair facing the couch.

"I thought we could chat for a few minutes," she said, nodding toward the couch. "All of us."

Katrina and Dirk sank onto the couch. Katrina tried to sit Sadie between them, but Sadie scrambled back onto her mother's lap, away from Dirk.

"They always seem to want their mamas when they don't feel good," laughed Katrina. "Now, what is it you want to talk to us about?"

Helen Lafferty asked a series of questions about their source of income and Dirk's employment situation. Then she said, "Dirk, how do you feel about the idea of Minnow living with you?"

"It's okay," he said. Feeling Katrina's stare he added, "I mean it's good. I want her to come."

"Have you lived with children before? Do you have any of your own?" asked Helen.

"I don't have any kids," he said. "But I take care of Sadie here when Katrina's out, and we get along real good, don't we Sadie." He fixed Sadie with his eyes. She was sucking her thumb and now she buried her face in her mother's bosom.

"Sadie," said Katrina, pulling the thumb from her mouth.

"Doesn't Dirk take good care of you when I'm gone?"

Sadie looked at her mother, then at Dirk who still held his gaze on her. She nodded and then re-buried her head.

"She's just not herself today," said Katrina.

"I understand," said the caseworker. "I can see that she's a bit shy."

"There's one last thing I wanted to ask you about," she said to Katrina. "About your former boyfriend Brett."

"Yeah, Brett was Sadie's dad," said Katrina. "He's history, so don't worry about him."

"These questions may be uncomfortable for Sadie. Would it be possible for us to talk privately?"

"Uh, I guess, sure. Dirk, could you take Sadie to her room for a few minutes?"

"C'mon," said Dirk, prying Sadie from her mother's lap. She squirmed and started to cry harder as he carried her from the room.

"I understand that Brett was physically violent with you," said Helen.

"Right, well that's why he's history. He started out real nice but turned out to be a real bastard, pardon my language," said Katrina.

"I also understand that he was violent in front of Minnow when she lived with you at age six, and that he may have been violent toward her as well," said Helen.

"Who said that?" asked Katrina. "Was it Minnow?"

"What's important is whether it's true or not. I'm especially interested in whether you personally witnessed him committing violence against your daughter or were at least aware that it had occurred."

"I don't remember that. Who said that? But I don't know everything he might have done," said Katrina. "It was a really hard time for me, dealing with that S.O.B. I tried to make it work for Sadie's sake, him being her father and all, but finally I'd just had enough. And good riddance."

"Were drugs a factor at that time of your life?" asked Helen.

"Yeah, well, that was all because of Brett too," said Katrina. "He was a druggie, and he got me into it. It's taken until now to straighten myself out after all of that. But I'm good now—clean and sober. And I've got Dirk, and he's nothing like Brett. I just want us to be a normal family, but I need my other girl back. Like I told you, it tortures me not to be able to do my job as a mother. Do you know that she started her periods and I wasn't even there to help her and tell her what's what?"

Helen made a few more notes and then asked for a tour of the little house.

"This is where Sadie sleeps," Katrina explained, showing her the tiny bedroom where Sadie was curled up on the bed with Dirk standing guard. "Minnow will have to share with her, but when we move to a bigger place, she can have her own room. I know I wanted my own room when I was a teen-ager. And I'll get her back in school so she can have friends. She's going to turn out as weird as Billy if she doesn't get away from him soon."

"Speaking of Billy," said the caseworker, "what was it you were going to tell me when you were last in my office?"

"I don't know if I should share it," said Katrina. "I don't want to mess up his life or anything. If you would just let me have Minnow back, I could let the past stay buried. What do think, Mrs. Lafferty. Will you give her back to me?"

"It's not my decision. I can only recommend, and I'm still gathering information," said Helen. "You need to understand that at age 12, what Minnow wants is also a major consideration. The court will let you know the next steps in making a determination."

"Couldn't you at least give me a chance to prove myself? Couldn't I have visitation rights? My brother's poisoned her against me, but I know if I could spend some time with her, be a mom to her, she'd see that things are different now. If she never sees me, how can she know what she wants?"

"That's a possibility," said Helen. "Let me give it some thought."

With that, she took her leave.

As soon as Helen was in her car, Katrina turned on Dirk.

"Jesus Christ! Couldn't you at least have acted like you *wanted* her to live with us? 'I'm okay with it.' That's the best you could do? Plus, your shit's strewn everywhere around here so the place looks like a dump."

She looked at Sadie. "And you, little miss thumb sucker. Would it have been so hard to say 'I like Dirk. He takes good care of me'? But no. Just hiding your face and sucking on your damn thumb the whole time. Don't you want your sister to live with us?"

"Chill out Katrina," said Dirk. "She'll probably give you what you want."

"She will," said Katrina. "But no thanks to the two of you. She's going to do it because she won't have any choice once she finds out what a pervert Billy really is." With that, she went into the bathroom, slamming the door behind her.

As soon as she was gone, Dirk grabbed Sadie's pajama top and pulled her next to his face. "I'm warning you," he said. "Don't you go telling anyone about our little games. Not your mom. And not that nosey caseworker. You tell them that I take good care of you. You got it?"

She nodded, pulling back against his grip.

"Don't try to get away from me," he said, jerking her closer.

She quit struggling and then he relaxed his grip. "Good girl," he said, reaching under her pajama top and rubbing her tummy.

Helen Lafferty drove slowly back toward her office, thinking that the home visit hadn't added the clarity she had hoped it would. The mother said all the right things, but the boyfriend was a concern. Was the little girl's behavior shyness, or perhaps fear, or was she just not feeling well as the mother had said? And what was the revelation about the uncle that Katrina kept dangling and not revealing? Maybe recommending visitation was a way to get a better picture of what was going on.

Minnow was studying at the kitchen table when the phone rang.

"Is Billy there with you?" her mother's voice said without preamble.

"No, he's out in the shop," said Minnow.

"Good. Did you call that Lafferty woman on me?"

"What? No," said Minnow. "What do you mean?"

"Did Billy?"

"No, he hates to talk to anyone on the phone. He would never call. What happened?"

"Your caseworker came by asking questions about Brett and how he treated you. Now why would she be doing that if you didn't talk to her?"

"I don't know," said Minnow. "But honest, Mom, I didn't talk to her."

"Did you talk to anyone else?"

Silence.

"Well, did you?" asked Katrina again.

"Um, well, I did say something to Maggie, you know, my friend from the coast. I did tell her about Brett. Maybe I shouldn't have. I'm sorry. I was just trying to explain how I understood what it's like to go through something hard because she was going through a hard thing."

"Maggie huh?"

"Really Mom, I didn't mean for her to do anything. I'm really sorry."

"Don't worry about it," said Katrina. "I'll take care of it. Just don't go saying anything more to that caseworker, okay?"

"Okay," said Minnow.

Ten minutes later, Maggie's cell phone showed an incoming call from Katrina Marsh. *What now?* she thought.

"Hello, this is Maggie," she said.

"Maggie, this is Katrina. Did you call Minnow's caseworker on me?"

"What do you mean?" said Maggie, instantly on guard.

"I mean, did you tell that Helen Lafferty woman that Brett beat Minnow up? She was at my house asking questions this morning."

"I did share some concerns with her," said Maggie. "As I told you when we met, I only want what's best for Minnow."

"As if I don't?" said Katrina. "Look, you don't know anything about me or about Brett or what happened with him. He was a bastard, no question, but I got rid of him. I came to you asking for your help, and now you've stuck your nose in and messed things up. It's time for you to butt out of our business."

"I understand your feeling upset," said Maggie, "but I won't stop doing what I think is right for Minnow just because it makes you unhappy."

"What gives you the right? You don't know anything about Minnow either. She's my kid and I know what's best for her. You got that?"

"I hear you," said Maggie.

"So are you going to butt out?"

"No promises," said Maggie, now feeling less inclined than ever to do so.

"Bitch."

Katrina hung up.

Katrina sat for a moment lost in thought. Then she pulled up Google on her phone and typed in *Maggie Berry Portland, Oregon*. Five minutes later a smile spread across her face. "Bingo," she said. "You stick your nose where it doesn't belong one more time you old hag and we'll see if you don't just change your mind about messing with my family."

November 10

The phone rang so rarely that the sound was like an alarm bell. Billy startled, some of his cereal splashing onto the table.

Minnow picked up the receiver and listened briefly. "Uncle Billy, it's Mrs. Lafferty for you."

His anxious expression did not ease as he listened to the caseworker. Then he said, "So that means I have no choice?...I heard you. Wednesday at 10."

He hung up and looked a Minnow, scratching at his cheek.

"Your mother has gotten the court to agree that she can have visitations with you. She's going to pick you up day after tomorrow at 10 and bring you back by 2."

"What happens in a visitation? What am I supposed to do with her?" Minnow asked.

"I was not made privy to that," snapped Billy. He grabbed his jacket off the coat rack and started for the shop.

Maggie sat on the bed surrounded by stacks of folded clothes. George's clothes.

She had avoided dealing with his things for six months, in fact had thought she would avoid it entirely by exiting the scene. But for some reason, when she got up this morning, she felt ready. She wanted to make the bedroom her space, to move forward.

Now, in the midst of it, she wasn't so sure. The clothes still carried his scent. They carried memories. They carried him.

She brought them to her face one at a time and inhaled deeply, each item bringing a scene from their life together.

George playing with the grandkids.

George working in the yard.

George going fishing with his best friend Mark.

George at the backyard grill.

As she put each piece of clothing into the cardboard boxes

at her feet, she felt as though she was packing him away as well.

When she finished with the clothes, she moved on to his desk. She sat frozen in place after picking up the first of the file folders with his handwriting on the tab. He had a neat hand, bold and strongly forward slanting. The form of each letter, each word, was uniquely his. She shut the file drawer, deciding that she would ask Toby to deal with the desk.

Then there was his wallet. They had sent it home from the hospital with her and she had put it in the desk drawer without opening it. Now when she looked inside, she was shocked to find nearly two hundred dollars cash. She had the sensation of having discovered someone's lost wallet and feeling responsible to get the money back to its rightful owner. To remove it and put it in her own purse felt like stealing. George's photo stared at her from his driver's license. She was grateful that it didn't really look like him. They had made him remove his eyeglasses and caught him with a sterner-than-normal expression.

"I'm sorry love," she said aloud. "I know you can't use this anymore, but I always felt like your wallet was your personal territory. I'll spend it on Eric and Amy. I know you'd like that."

She removed the money and lightly kissed the driver's license photo. Then she folded the wallet and caressed the leather before putting it back in the desk drawer. She called Toby's cell.

"I've been going through your dad's things," she said when he answered.

"That's good mom. That's very good. Do you need any help?"

"Actually," said Maggie, "that's part of the reason I called, that and to see how you are of course. I could use some help hauling clothes to the Goodwill. And I'm hoping you'll go through the desk and deal with what's there."

"Right," said Toby. "Well sure, I can take care of that, no problem. Since you're on the phone, we were talking about Thanksgiving. We want you to have dinner with us. Will you come?"

"Ceci also asked," said Maggie. "I haven't said yes or no to her yet."

"Have her come too," Toby said. "Please Mom. The kids really miss you. They don't get it why you've just disappeared from their lives. Heather and I miss you too."

Maggie had been missing them as well. The time spent with Minnow had reawakened her need to be a part of their lives, especially sweet Amy. She still didn't know if she could be around Eric without overwhelming guilt over the other boy whose family would be spending their first Thanksgiving without him.

"I can give it a try," she said. "But I may not stay long. I'll ask Ceci if she can come up. And tell Heather I'll bring pies."

"Great!" said Toby. "Just stay as long as you're comfortable."

November 12

Minnow was dressed in her usual jeans, t-shirt, and sneakers as she waited for Katrina. She held Bonkers, stroking his ears, the book on her lap unopened.

She didn't know how to think of her mother. She wondered

if it there was something wrong with her, if other people had these contradictory feelings. Is it possible to long for something you've never known? From her earliest memories, Minnow had a sense of something missing, an empty place she could not fill. She didn't always know it was there. It wasn't there as much when Granny Vi was alive and she'd think sometimes she was over it. But then she would be walking down the street and would see the simplest thing, a mother with her arm around her child, and the feeling would wash over her like a wave, pulling at her insides.

She couldn't talk with Billy about it. He would just be angry. As it was, he had barely spoken to her since Helen Lafferty's call two days ago. Did he think she was abandoning him? She hadn't asked for this visit with her mother, but it had always been this way with him. Any mention of her mother and he became angry and sullen.

Bonkers sprang from her lap and jumped on the couch to peer out of the window at the sound of tires on the gravel driveway. Minnow watched Katrina emerge from the van, dressed in a tight red skirt, knee-high boots, and clingy knit shirt. She stood on the porch, talking on her phone and gesticulating for five minutes while Minnow peered out the window, standing against the wall where her mother couldn't see her. Katrina stowed the phone in her large shoulder bag and walked in the front door without knocking.

"There's my Minnow girl," she said. "Are you ready for some fun?"

Bonkers stood at attention on the couch, guarding Minnow and letting out low, guttural growls.

Minnow shrugged. "I guess so," she said. "What are we

going to do?"

"Something I'll bet you never get to do with Billy. We're going shopping, and to lunch. Some real girl time."

"Can Bonkers come?" Minnow picked him up and hugged him to her chest.

"That's his name? Bonkers? Of course he can come. Only he'll have to stay in the car while we shop."

Katrina reached out to pat Bonkers' head but drew back when he snarled.

"Not very friendly I see."

"He's friendly, but he doesn't know you."

"Well, that's about to change," said Katrina. "You better get used to me little Mister Bonkers, 'cuz you're going to be seeing a lot more of me."

Turning to Minnow she said, "I'm surprised Billy let you have a dog."

"Sam rescued him," said Minnow, "and talked Billy into letting me keep him."

"Oh, Samantha," scoffed Katrina. "That explains it. She probably taught him to growl at me too. That woman's got a burr up her butt about me, and I don't know why. Billy's doing, I suspect. Well never mind that. Bring your dog and let's get you out in the real world for a change. Do you have a purse or anything?"

"I don't have a purse," said Minnow.

"Where do you carry your stuff?" asked Katrina.

"The only thing I have to carry is my library card, and sometimes some money, so I just put that in my pocket."

"Well, that's proof that you need your mother," Katrina said. "C'mon."

The trio drove through southeast Portland to a cluster of stores that included Ross and T.J. Maxx. The last time Minnow went to a store to try on clothes Granny Vi was still alive, and then it was just Walmart.

Inside the store, Katrina held her at arm's length, hands on shoulders, and studied her build.

"You're lucky, you got my body. I can tell just by looking at you what size you'll wear. We could even share clothes."

With that, she started down the racks, flipping through the hangers, pulling things out, putting some back. Eventually she had an armful of clothes and hangers and gestured for Minnow to follow her to the dressing room. The attendant counted their items and gave them a tag with a number. Once inside, Katrina pulled two more items that hadn't been counted from her bag and winked at Minnow.

"Don't just stand there. Take off your clothes."

Minnow realized that while she wasn't self-conscious getting undressed in the camper with Billy five feet away, she was apprehensive about undressing in front of this woman, her mother who felt like a stranger.

"Go on," said Katrina. "I won't bite."

Minnow stepped out of her jeans and pulled the t-shirt over her head.

"Where's your bra?" asked Katrina.

"I don't have one," said Minnow, shivering as the air hit her bare skin.

"Well, we'll fix that," said her mother. "You stay here. I'll be right back."

With Katrina gone, Minnow stood in her cotton underpants and examined her body. She couldn't reconcile the body in the mirror, the beginnings of a woman's body, with her image of herself. She lifted her arms over her head and looked at the springy hair sprouting in her armpits. She quickly put them down when Katrina turned the handle on the dressing room door and entered holding four bras of varying sizes and two pair of bikini underpants.

Starting in on the pile of garments, Minnow had the sense that she was not so much trying them on as being dressed by Katrina. It was strange and somewhat uncomfortable, but on some level, she liked it. When they were finished, Katrina had rejected all but a pair of leggings, a tiny skirt, a long-sleeved striped top, a pair of body-hugging jeans, two bras, and the bikini panties. She went back to the pile of rejects and held up two of the tops to her own shoulders.

"These are good colors on me," she said. She then took a small screwdriver out of her purse and pried off the inventory control tags before stuffing the garments into the bottom of her bag.

"They overprice things here, so I figure they owe me a couple. Okay, let's go see about some boots for you."

After the clothes, they went to the drug store where Katrina picked out eye makeup, blush and lipstick. Then she picked through all the bags, selecting a complete outfit, and led Minnow into the shopping center restroom.

"Use that big stall on the end and put this on."

When Minnow came out, Katrina examined her and nodded. Then she beckoned Minnow to the mirror and applied the makeup.

"Nice!" said Katrina. "All but the hair. Let's do something about that."

Next they drove to the Shear Happiness salon displaying a "Walk-ins Welcome" sign where Katrina described what she had in mind to the stylist.

"Okay with you?" the stylist asked Minnow.

"I don't want it too short," said Minnow.

"Don't worry. I'm just going to shape the ends so they frame your face, and cut some bangs. Your hair is such a beautiful color. You'll look stunning."

Minnow nodded and the stylist went to work. When she finished, the face looking back at her was older and attractive in a whole different way.

Minnow giggled. "Wow, I can't believe that's me!"

Katrina squatted beside the chair so that they were the same level in the mirror. "That's my girl," she said.

"Oh my God," said the stylist. "You two could be twins!"

It was true, Minnow realized with a shock. Except for the lines around Katrina's eyes and mouth, they could at least be sisters. This new awareness was both unsettling and appealing. Minnow had never thought of herself as looking like anyone else, especially not her mother. Feeling different had bred strength, but also loneliness. *What else*, she wondered, *do I have in common with this woman I barely know?*

"Lunch!" Katrina said, breaking Minnow's musing. She led the way back to the car.

Minnow thought the clomp of her new boots on the pavement must be drawing attention from all quarters, but no one seemed to notice. She had worn only sneakers for as long as she could recall. In the van, Bonkers climbed onto Minnow's lap and carefully explored the new clothes and hair smells with his nose. When Katrina reached out to pet him, he backed off of Minnow's lap toward the passenger door with an uneasy whine.

In the restaurant, Katrina ordered a chicken salad and Minnow ordered a grilled cheese sandwich. After the waitress delivered their order, Katrina rummaged in her bag and brought out a tiny prescription pill bottle.

"Watch this," she said to Minnow. "I call this my prescription for a free lunch."

She twisted the top off the bottle, looked around to make sure no one was watching their booth, and then tapped the bottom gently until a dead cockroach slid out into the palm of her hand. She grasped it with the tips of her thumb and forefinger and slipped it onto her salad plate so that it was partly obscured by a lettuce leaf. She dropped the pill bottle back into her bag and winked at Minnow.

"Go ahead and eat," she said. "Just watch. This is magic."

When the waitress next walked by, Katrina beckoned to her. "Excuse me," she said in a hushed tone. "I don't think this was supposed to be in my salad." She pointed to the cockroach.

"Oh my goodness!" said the waitress. "I am so sorry! Let me get you a replacement right now."

She whisked away the salad.

"Now watch what happens next," said Katrina.

In less than a minute, a short, balding man in dark slacks and a vest arrived at their table. He spoke to Katrina in a half-whisper.

"I'm Vincent, the manager. I want to personally apologize for the little problem with your salad. We've *never* had that happen here before. We use the strictest cleaning and food preparation protocols, so I don't know how it occurred, but I promise you we're going to make sure it doesn't happen again. Of course, we'll replace the salad, but I'm also going to take care of the bill for both of your lunches, just so you know how committed we are to the highest standards of customer service. I also want you and your daughter to each have a dessert on the house."

"Why, thank you," said Katrina, her hand to her chest in surprise. "I didn't want to make a fuss, but it did kind of upset me. That's so kind of you. I'll be sure to let my friends know how well we were treated here."

"That would be most appreciated," said the manager. "Thank you for being so understanding."

He shook Katrina's hand and bustled away.

"Wow," said Minnow.

Katrina smiled. "You see, *I* can do homeschooling too."

Minnow pushed aside her half-eaten scoop of chocolate ice cream, watching silently as Katrina ate the last bite of her complimentary lunch. Then Katrina brought her phone over to Minnow's side of the booth and took a few selfies of the two of them. They sat side-by-side looking at the photos.

"Oooh, can I use your phone to post that on Instagram?" asked Minnow. "I never have any pictures to post."

"Sure thing," said Katrina. She handed the phone to Minnow who labeled the photo "My mom and me."

"Do you have an Instagram account?" asked Minnow.

"No," said Katrina.

"If you had an account, we could follow each other."

"Well," said Katrina, "if you were to come live with me and Dirk and Sadie, you could show me how to do that, on your own phone. Think about how cool that would be."

"I could really get my own phone?" said Minnow.

"Damn straight you could. And you could make some real friends, not just Internet people and old ladies."

"Can we take a picture of Bonkers with your phone too, so I can put him on my Instagram page?"

Back at the car, Minnow held Bonkers while Katrina took the picture. Minnow was laughing into the camera while Bonkers licked her face.

On the way back to the crooked house, Katrina veered off the main road onto a narrow lane that eventually turned to gravel and ended next to a barn in a field of hay.

"Why are we going here?" asked Minnow.

"I need to get some gas," said Katrina.

"Shouldn't we be at a gas station then?"

"You see that tank up there?" said Katrina.

She pointed to a large steel drum mounted six feet up on a wooden stand. It had a long hose and nozzle at one end.

"That tank is full of gas, and the best thing about it is that it doesn't cost me a cent,"

"But how did you find out about it?"

"I used to date the son of the guy that owns it. He showed it to me. His dad keeps it for his farm trucks and his car, but he's never around. I've been coming here for years."

With that, she jumped down from the van, unhooked the nozzle and squeezed the handle to start the flow of gasoline into the van's gas tank. When it was full, she replaced the nozzle and they proceeded on their way.

"So the guy doesn't mind you using his gas?"

"He hasn't so far," her mother said.

As they approached the driveway Katrina said, "Didn't

we have a good time today?"

"Yes," said Minnow. "Thank you for all the clothes and everything."

"It's only right that I take my daughter shopping. Now that you're about to be a teenager, you need someone to show you how things are done. Remember this. Billy's never gonna take care of you the way your mother will."

"He can't help how he is," said Minnow.

"Just don't forget what a good time we can have together when you have a decision to make about where to live."

"Are you trying to get them to take me away from Uncle Billy?"

"When they find out the truth about your Uncle Billy, they're going to have to do what's right."

"What truth?" asked Minnow.

"Now look, I'm not going to go into all of that with you. All you need to know is that there's some things in Billy's past that someone should have thought about when they put you with him."

"But where would I live if I can't stay with him?"

"That's what I'm talking about," said Katrina. "If you let that caseworker know that you want to be with me, you can stay in the same house where you live now, only it will be with me and Sadie and Dirk."

"But then where will Uncle Billy live?"

"Don't you worry about that," said Katrina. "He's happiest when he's driving around from one podunk town to another in that camper. You know he only stays home because of you. Just be sure to tell them that you want to be with me so that you don't end up with some creepy foster parents in some crappy house a hundred miles from here."

It was ten past two when they drove up to the house. They could see Billy watching out the front window.

"I'm not gonna come in," said Katrina. "But listen, don't let him make you feel bad about being with me or about showing your stuff. You're a beautiful girl and it's time the rest of the world see's that."

"Okay," said Minnow, glancing at her image in the side mirror as she stepped from the van holding the bag with her clothes.

When she walked into the house Billy gaped at her.

"Why are you looking at me like that?" she asked.

He continued to stare.

"Uncle Billy? It's just some new clothes and a haircut. Do you like it?"

"No," said Billy.

"Why not?"

"You look like her. Is that what you want? To be like her?"

"No, but is there anything wrong with looking good? I'm about to be a teenager, you know," said Minnow.

Billy paced.

"I don't like you spending time with her," he said. "She's up to no good."

"Maybe she just wants to do the stuff mothers do with daughters. Stuff you never do with me. Maybe she understands what girls need."

Billy stopped pacing, staring again. Then he stomped from the house, slamming the front door.

Minnow went into the bathroom and studied her face in the mirror. Her mother's face. She felt the silkiness of her hair, brushing the newly trimmed ends with the backs of her fingers. She shook her head back and forth and watched the hair swing. Tears began to flow, running the dark mascara in streaks down each cheek. She couldn't remember feeling this confused before, except maybe during the times with her mother and Brett.

She took off the new clothes and arranged them in her bedroom closet, then pulled her old jeans and t-shirt from the shopping bag and put them on. They felt worn and sloppy.

November 14

Billy was installing a new sculpture in the yard when Helen Lafferty turned in the driveway. He looked up briefly when he heard the car before returning to his work with renewed concentration. Helen stood silently in front of him for a full minute, waiting for him to look up. Finally she said, "Hello Mr. Marsh. Do you remember me? Helen Lafferty, parental evaluation specialist with Multnomah County."

"Yes," he said, continuing to adjust the sculpture on its pole.

"That's quite a remarkable piece of art," she said.

"You shouldn't have let my sister take Minnow," he said in reply.

"Why is that? Did something happen?" asked the caseworker.

"She's trying to make Minnow just like her. She's not a good person. Minnow is a good person," said Billy.

"Mr. Marsh, I need to talk with your niece again for a few minutes. Is she at home?"

"She's inside," he tipped his head toward the house.

"Will you come in with me?" she asked.

He finally looked up. "Yes."

Bonkers was on the back of the sofa with his nose pressed to the window when they reached the porch. Once inside, they found Minnow in the recliner with a copy of *To Kill a Mockingbird*.

"Oh, that's one of my favorite books," said the caseworker. "Are you enjoying it?"

"I already finished it," said Minnow. "I'm just trying to understand what the title means."

"I must admit that I never really got that myself," said Helen. "Will you tell me if you figure it out?"

"Okay," said Minnow.

"I wanted to talk to you for a few minutes about your mother. How was your visit with her?"

"It was good," said Minnow, glancing at Billy. "She took me shopping and bought me some clothes." Minnow stood up and turned in a circle, modeling the new jeans. "And we got my hair cut and went out to lunch."

"Very nice," said Helen. "The haircut looks good on you. I didn't realize before how much you look like your mother."

"I know," said Minnow. "Me either!"

"What I wanted to ask you about has to do with the time you lived with your mom when you were six. Our records show that you were there with her and her boyfriend Brett for five months before returning to your grandmother. Is that right?"

"I guess so," said Minnow. "I was pretty little, so I don't remember too much about it."

"Do you remember why you had to leave your mom and move back in with your grandma?" asked Helen.

"Not exactly," said Minnow. "I know my mom was having a hard time. She and Brett fought a lot."

"Did Brett get physically violent when you were there?"

"I remember that he got mad easy," said Minnow.

"Did he hurt you or your mom?"

"I don't remember exactly, except I know he got mad when I wouldn't eat my dinner," she said.

Billy, who was pacing, stopped and said, "I remember. He was a brute who beat people up."

"Did you observe him engaging in violent behavior?"

"No," said Billy. "But I know he did it."

"That may be," said Helen. "But I'm trying to get Minnow's recollection at this point since she was actually in the situation."

"I just think that he was into drugs and stuff, and he got my mom into that stuff too, so she couldn't really take good care of me."

"Do you worry about the same thing happening if you were to go to live with your mother again?" asked Helen.

"Sometimes," said Minnow. "But I think she really wants it to be different now. She says she's done with drugs, and she wants to have a normal family. She seems different to me now."

"She seems however she wants to seem," said Billy. "That doesn't mean she's different."

"Mr. Marsh, could I speak privately with your niece for a moment?" said Helen.

Billy opened his mouth to speak, then closed it and stomped out the front door to the porch.

"I need to know," said Helen, "how you really feel about the possibility of living with your mother."

"I don't know how I feel," said Minnow, her voice breaking. "I love Uncle Billy and he's really good to me. And I don't want to hurt his feelings."

She was silent for a moment. Then she said, almost in a wail, "But I want to have a mom." Tears slid down her cheeks.

"Of course you do sweetheart," said Helen, feeling the depth of the pain in this last statement. "Of course you do."

November 17

Back on the road things seemed almost normal to Minnow for the first time in two weeks. Billy was talking to her again. They were doing their home-schooling routine. She had a fresh stack of library books awaiting her attention in the camper. Bonkers slept blissfully between them, head on Minnow's lap and hind feet against Billy.

Their first stop was Maverick's store, and she was anxious to see Sam and Donovan.

"Look at you!" Sam said when Minnow entered the store. "Cute haircut!"

"Thanks," said Minnow. "My mom took me to get it cut."

"Did she?" said Sam, holding the ecstatic Bonkers as he licked her face. "So she has visiting rights now?"

"Yeah, it was a trial sort of thing last week. She bought me some clothes and makeup too. Billy was mad about it."

"I'll bet he was," said Sam. "How about you. How did you feel about it?"

"It was pretty much okay. Fun really. Mom was super nice

to me and everything. But I felt bad because I think it hurt Uncle Billy's feelings. And he really hates it that I look like my mom with my haircut and new clothes."

"You *do* look like her," said Sam. "You did even before the haircut. But that's not such a bad thing. Your mom's a good-looking woman. She just hasn't always been a good-acting one. And *looking* like her doesn't mean you have to *be* like her."

"I know," said Minnow. "But she seems to be different now, at least I hope she is."

"Say," said Sam, "Are the two of you doing anything for Thanksgiving? My brother and his family have invited me down to Grants Pass and I was thinking maybe you and Billy could come along. We'd spend the night since it's a long drive, especially after turkey and pumpkin pie, but you could bring the camper if Billy would prefer his own bed. Donovan and his boys are watching the store and the Critter Spa."

"That would be really fun," said Minnow. "Jenny, she's Jason's mom, invited us, but I didn't think Uncle Billy would be comfortable so I told her we had other plans. Now maybe we really do!"

The bell dinged as Billy and Donovan came through the door engaged in conversation about the merits of Ford versus Chevy pickups.

"Uncle Billy," said Minnow, unwilling to wait for the discussion to end. "Sam invited us to have Thanksgiving with her brother's family in Grants Pass! Can we do it? Pl-e-e-ease? We haven't had a regular family Thanksgiving since Granny Vi died."

"Really?" Bill asked.

"Sorry," said Sam to Billy. "I was going to issue a more

proper invitation, but we'd love to have you come."

"I don't know your brother or his family," said Billy, looking out the window as if he might spot them there. "I've never gone to someone's house for Thanksgiving."

"I know," said Sam. "But you will like them. They're just good-hearted folks. And my brother is a welder. You've got to see his shop."

"That would be interesting," said Billy, shifting his gaze to Sam. "Maybe it would be all right. I need to think about it for a couple of days, if that's okay with you."

"Of course it's okay," said Sam.

Minnow hopped from foot to foot with her hands clasped together in hopeful anticipation.

Billy said, "I have something for you in the trailer Sam. Can you come outside?"

"I guess so," she said, "if Donovan minds the store. What is it?"

"It's a gift. Kind of a surprise."

"Really?" Sam blushed. "I've never known you to give gifts before. Well by all means, lead the way."

Billy held the door open, looking down at the floor, and Minnow walked through first, tugging Sam by the hand. Sensing the excitement of the moment, Bonkers raced in circles around the parking lot. A moment later, Billy wrestled a tangle of metal pieces mounted on a six-foot pole from the back of the trailer. He hoisted it in the air, bracing the bottom of the pole against his feet, and the metal pieces caught the wind. The apparatus oriented itself, and as it began to spin it transformed into a copper-colored solar system, with sun, planets, moons, and outside that a ring of stars. Sam stared, mouth open, transfixed.

"Oh my God Billy, that's the most beautiful thing I've ever seen! You made that for me?"

"Yes," he said. "Because you said you liked me with a capital L. I call it Cosmic Spin."

"That's the sweetest thing anyone's ever done for me." Tears flowed down her cheeks.

"Are you sad then?" he asked, alarmed.

"No, not sad at all. These are tears of happiness. The good kind," she said. "You must like me a little bit as well to have made such a wonderful gift for me."

"Of course I like you. You are my best friend," he said. "You understand me. Most people don't understand me."

"Most people don't take the time to try," said Sam. "Bring it over here. I know the perfect place for it in front of the store."

He carried it to the spot where she pointed.

"Minnow," she said, "can you hold this in place so Billy and I can stand back and look at it?" Minnow held the spinning sculpture while Billy and Sam stepped back from it.

"Don't you think that's perfect?" she said.

"Yes."

She turned her head toward him and said, "Billy, would it be okay if I gave you a hug?"

He glanced at her sideways, reddening.

"Yes, it would be okay."

She stepped toward him and gently embraced him. For a moment he stood stiff, unmoving. Then in a jerky move he raised his arms and gave a quick squeeze in return. Sam smiled and pecked his cheek before releasing him.

"Thank you, Billy. It's a wonderful gift."

Billy looked at the ground, but he was smiling, and blushing.

Katrina handed Dirk a cup of coffee and switched off the television.

"Hey!" he said. "I was watching that."

"You watch it twelve hours a day. We need to talk for a minute."

"What about?"

"About moving," she said. "I'm going to fill that Lafferty woman in on the truth about my big brother, and once that happens, they're going to have to give Minnow to me. That means we get the house, and the money that should have been coming to me all along."

"You seem mighty sure of yourself."

"You just watch."

"So the only way to get the house and money is to have another brat running around?"

"She's no brat. She's twelve years old," said Katrina. "Almost thirteen. Here, look." She turned on her phone and found the photo of Minnow and herself at the hair salon.

"Whoa! I see what you mean. She's hot. She looks just like you," he said.

"I know. So don't you go getting any ideas in that nasty mind of yours. She has a dog too, so that's part of the package."

"Great, just what we need. Another kid and a dog to feed," said Dirk.

"You're really not getting this," said Katrina. "When we get the kid and the dog, we get a house, and we get money. A-a-a-and, she's old enough to babysit Sadie, so that gives us time to do adult stuff. So don't give me shit about the dog or moving or anything. Got it?" Katrina tapped her foot until Dirk nodded. "Speaking of money, aren't you supposed to be working today?"

"Yeah. I'm going in at 10."

"Well, tell that bastard to pay you on time this week. We're late on the electric bill, and we need food."

"I did tell him. Probably didn't do any good. He's got no money until people pay him."

"Well, that's not our problem is it?"

"Yeah, it is our problem if he owes us money."

"Well, just get some balls when you talk to him. Just because he's your cousin doesn't mean he can screw us. Anyway, I'm going into town to see Minnow's caseworker as soon as Sadie leaves for school."

"Maybe you're the one who needs the balls, to get them to give you your own kid back."

"Not a matter of balls," said Katrina, "although that's never been my problem. This is about smarts. Mom always thought Billy was so smart, but we'll see about that."

Katrina drummed her painted nails on the chair arm, waiting for Helen Lafferty to finish with her appointment. She threw down the tattered, year-old magazine she'd been reading and looked around the room.

"I hate this place," she said to no one in particular, picking up her phone and scrolling through the screens.

A plump, middle-aged woman with stringy blonde hair and doughy skin said, "We all hate this place, hon. But that don't really make any difference does it?"

Just then the receptionist called Katrina's name and directed her back to Helen's office. Katrina grabbed her handbag and strode from the waiting area.

"Hello Miss Marsh," said Helen. "I only have a few minutes today, so let's get right to it. You said you had information for me."

"This won't take long," said Katrina. "Do you remember that I said there were problems with my brother you should know about?"

"Yes, of course," said Helen.

"I've been wrestling with what's the right thing to do. A person shouldn't have to make choices like this between her brother and her kid. But I decided that I've got to protect Minnow, so I came in to show you this."

She pulled from her handbag a yellowed newspaper clipping and stared at it as if still conflicted about showing it to the caseworker. Then she took a dramatic deep breath and handed it to Helen.

"This is about your brother?" asked Helen, seeing the headline.

"Yes, from when he was nineteen. It nearly killed my mom, she was so ashamed. And I couldn't even look people in the eye at school, it was so embarrassing."

"It says here that he was arrested for Invasion of Personal Privacy, that he was caught peering through the window at a neighbor girl while she was undressing."

"That's right. She was only sixteen. One of my classmates. I'd always thought he was a secret pervert, but my mom never could see it. Then this happened. It gave me the creeps to live in the same house with him after this. So you can see why

I'm worried about Minnow, especially now that she's got her periods and all. And the two of them driving around in that camper. It's just not right."

"This is quite concerning I agree," said Helen. "Did your brother do any jail time? Did he get treatment of any kind?"

"My mom got a lawyer who got him out of doing jail time, and she talked the girl's mother out of pressing charges. She said it was just because of his Asperger's, like he couldn't help it. He just had to go see a counselor a few times. But he's still got Asperger's doesn't he? And now there he is with my daughter. I mean if Asperger's made him a pervert then, why would that be any different now?"

"Well, this is an important piece of information," said Helen. "Can I make a copy of this article?"

"Yes of course," said Katrina. "But please, I don't want anything bad to happen to my brother, even if he *is* a pervert. I just want Minnow safe."

"I understand," said Helen. "Nothing will happen to him as long as he hasn't behaved inappropriately toward your daughter."

"Please, just get her away from him before he does."

After Katrina left, Helen Lafferty sat thinking. Minnow's woeful words still rang in her ears, "I want to have a mom!"

"All right sweet girl," she said, deciding. "I hope she can be the mom you need."

November 22

The letter from the court was waiting for them on Saturday when Billy and Minnow returned home from their week-long rounds. It was dated November 19 and addressed to Billy, informing him of a custody hearing on November 24 at 10 a.m. before Judge Simon Kilgore. Both he and Minnow were ordered to attend.

"Shit!" said Billy handing her the letter. "That's Monday! This is your mother's doing."

"What's going to happen?" asked Minnow.

"That's not something I can know," said Billy, pacing, "but if your mother is behind it, it will be bad."

He paced in silence for a while, then stopped and turned to Minnow. "They may ask you if you want to live with your mother. What will you say then?"

"I don't know, Uncle Billy," she said, starting to cry. "How am I supposed to choose?" The words came out in a sob. Bonkers jumped onto her lap and started licking her face. She hugged him close.

Later that day, after dropping Minnow at the library, Billy returned home and picked up the phone. He found face-to-face communication rife with confusion and misunderstanding and telephones nearly impossible, but fear about losing Minnow was pushing him beyond what was comfortable.

When Maggie answered, he said without preamble, "This is Billy Marsh."

"Well, hello Billy. This is a surprise," said Maggie. "Is Minnow all right?"

"She's all right," said Billy. "But there's a custody hearing Monday and I think her mother's going to try to take her away from me."

"Oh my," said Maggie. "I was afraid of that. Is there something I can do? I'm afraid I didn't make things better with your sister last time I saw her."

"I'm worried that Minnow will agree to go with her. Katrina's been trying to influence her. She's been buying her stuff and filling her head with lies about how they can be a family again. Minnow listens to you, more than to me right now. I thought you could talk to her and make her see that it's a bad idea."

"I agree that living with her mother is probably a bad idea, and I had thought about talking with her," said Maggie. "But I don't know if I should try to dissuade her if she's wanting to give it a try."

"Katrina doesn't care about her," Billy spat out the words. "Katrina only cares about herself."

"Yes, well I'm sure that's a distinct possibility. All right, why don't you put Minnow on the phone, and we'll at least chat about it."

"I can't," said Billy. "She's at the library, but you could call her this evening."

"I'm afraid I can't this evening," said Maggie. "There's an event at my granddaughter's school and I've promised to attend. When and where is the hearing on Monday?"

"10 a.m. at the Juvenile Justice Center in NE Portland. Do you know where it is?"

"Hmmm, well, yes I do know. I'd prefer to see Minnow in person anyway, so how about if I meet you there at 9:30 and we can talk before you go in?"

"Yes, okay, yes please. I think that would work. I would be grateful," said Billy. His hands shook as he hung up the phone.

November 24

Maggie arrived with time to spare and stopped at the driveup window of a nearby coffee shop. The skies were steely gray and a steady drizzle wet the pavement.. Holding the warm paper cup with one gloved hand and her umbrella with the other, she walked from the parking lot into the lobby of the courthouse and settled on a bench to wait for Billy and Minnow, rehearsing in her mind what she would say to Minnow.

She felt Katrina's approach before she saw her, like a chill wind.

Katrina was dressed in a short, burnt orange skirt, a black and orange striped turtleneck, knee-high boots, and a short leather jacket. She had her usual thick layer of eye makeup. A pale blond girl, Sadie, Maggie assumed, dressed in purple leggings and a pink dress was walking with her, holding her hand. They had been walking toward the elevators when Katrina whirled around and strode toward Maggie, dragging Sadie with her.

"What are *you* doing here?" she demanded.

"It's a public building. I have a right to be here," said Maggie, startled.

"You have your nerve, still meddling in my family business after I told you to butt out."

Maggie didn't respond. Katrina moved in closer and stood over her, arms crossed.

"You, of all people," she said, "shouldn't be in the middle of other people's families after what you did."

"What are you talking about?" Maggie asked.

"Oh, I know about you. I know all about you and your drunk husband running down that car of teenagers and killing that boy. And you're in here like you want to save my kid. Why didn't you save that one? And now, here you are all high and mighty like you have a right to get between me and my kid. Sure, I've made some mistakes in my life, but I've never killed anyone. So why don't you go fix your own life and get out of mine."

The words struck like a dagger. Maggie couldn't move, couldn't breathe, as wounded as if she'd been stabbed in the gut.

"You're disgusting," Katrina said, "c'mon Sadie," and she stomped away toward the elevator.

Maggie sat with her eyes closed, head spinning, taking short breaths. Then she found her feet, and knocking her paper coffee cup to the floor, she ran from the courthouse.

Billy and Minnow arrived three minutes later. Billy wandered around the vacant lobby while Minnow sat on the bench.

"What are you looking for?" she asked.

"Maggie Berry is supposed to meet us here," said Billy.

"Maggie? Why?"

"I asked her to come talk to you," said Billy. "She's smart and I think she can help you decide what to do."

"Oh," said Minnow. "I wonder why she's not here. Traffic maybe." She looked at the overturned coffee cup at her feet.

"Why do people litter like this?" she asked and picked up the cup to discard it. A small puddle of black coffee remained.

They waited until 9:50 when Billy decided they had to get to the hearing room. Minnow and Billy were silent on the elevator ride to the hearing room floor. The elevator doors slid open to a group of people scattered along the hallway, Katrina's orange skirt together with Sadie's pink and purple shouted for attention against a background of subdued blacks and grays.

"I was beginning to wonder if you were coming," she said as they approached. Sadie opened and closed the fingers of her free hand in a tiny wave to Minnow.

"We were waiting for my friend Maggie," said Minnow. "Have you seen her?"

"Maggie?" said Katrina. "Why would she be here? No sign of her as far as I can see. Maybe she's not the friend you thought she was."

Billy avoided eye contact with his sister and beckoned Minnow to a more distant part of the hallway.

"You can run, but you can't hide," Katrina's whisper bounced across the empty space.

Minnow felt her anxiety rise when they were called into the hearing room. The clerk announced that the honorable Simon Kilgore was presiding. It was only 10 a.m. but the judge looked already weary. He surveyed the faces below him as if with a look of recognition. He'd seen them all before, heard their stories, passed judgment. He thumbed through the file on his desk.

"We're here to consider a request to award custody of Minnow Marsh, a minor residing in Multnomah County, to her birth mother Katrina Marsh," he said.

"Is Katrina Marsh in the courtroom?"

"I'm here," said Katrina.

The judge studied her for a few moments.

"What about Minnow Marsh? Is she here?"

Minnow raised her hand as though she were in a classroom. She couldn't believe this was really happening, that she could be awarded like a prize in some contest. Billy clenched and released his fists beside her. Every few minutes he would grab his notebook out of his pocket and write something. Sadie was whispering something to her mother and Katrina was trying to shush her.

"And how about Mrs. Lafferty, the parental evaluation specialist assigned to this case?" asked the judge.

"I'm here your honor," said Helen Lafferty.

"All right, then let's get started."

Helen Lafferty spoke first. She was recommending giving physical custody of Minnow to her mother, Katrina Marsh. She then laid out her case for the recommendation. It came down to a few simple facts. Katrina was Minnow's birth mother. Katrina had made sincere and apparently successful efforts at rehabilitation since her earlier problems with drugs and involvement with an abusive man. Katrina wanted Minnow with her and had been awarded custody of her younger child Sadie. Billy Marsh had never been granted legal custody, but had assumed care of Minnow when her grandmother died. He had been previously arrested for criminal invasion of personal privacy. While there had been no further infractions, there was also no evidence that he had been rehabilitated since this offense. He had not created a normal and healthy environment for her, keeping her out of school and traveling with her in a small camper one week out of every three.

"Is it true Mr. Marsh," the judge asked after putting Billy under oath, "that you were arrested for this offense in 2001?"

"Yes, but I…"

"Just answer the question Mr. Marsh," interrupted the judge. "Did you commit this offense?"

"I did, but I didn't know it was an offense, so that's why I wasn't convicted."

"You didn't know? You were how old?"

"Nineteen," said Billy.

"Have you had other arrests or convictions since that time?"

"Not for that," said Billy.

"For something else?" asked the judge.

"I was arrested once for trespassing," said Billy. "But they dropped the charges."

"What were the circumstances of that arrest?"

"I was in the men's restroom at the library."

"That does not normally lead to a trespassing charge," said the judge. "What were you doing there that caused the arrest?"

"I was fixing the toilet. It had a faulty float valve," said Billy.

"You're not helping me here Mr. Marsh. Why did this toilet repair lead to your arrest?"

"Because I didn't have permission to fix it, so they thought I was tampering with it. But after my mom talked to them, they understood that I was just trying to help and they dropped the charges."

"Hmm...," said the judge. "And do you have any other past arrests or brushes with the law?"

"No," said Billy.

The judge shifted his focus to Minnow. Her hands were damp and clammy where they rested on her lap, her heart racing.

"Minnow, if it turns out that you can no longer live with your uncle, how do you feel about returning to live with your mother?"

"I don't want to leave my uncle," said Minnow.

"That may be the case," said the judge, "but sometimes we must do things other than what we want. If it should turn out that you can no longer be with him, what about living with your mother?"

This question had played in Minnow's thoughts for all of her memory. In her mind, she had answered it one way, then the other, had put conditions on her answers, had gotten angry that it was even a question. And now here it was, demanding a final answer. How could she know? Who would she even be without this unanswered question?

That was the heart of it. She knew how to be the girl without a mother. It had its tragic aspects, the constant reminders of what she was missing, like an amputee with an empty sleeve. But it drew others to her, brought admiration for her resilience. It defined her and gave her freedom to define herself. Did she want to give that up?

And what was she trading it for? Could Minnow ever feel safe with her? Would Katrina love her?

The judge was looking at her.

They were all looking at her.

The question hung in the air, an open door waiting for her to walk through.

"It would be okay, I guess," said Minnow.

"Just okay?" asked the judge.

"Well, it's been a long time since I lived with her, so I don't really know how it will be."

"Do you have any specific concerns. Things that worry you?"

"No, not really, as long as my mom doesn't use drugs anymore."

Now he shifted to Katrina, putting her under oath.

"Miss Marsh, what about drugs. Are you currently clean and sober?"

"Yes."

"How long has it been since you used drugs?"

"Almost two years," said Katrina. "I'm through with drugs. I just want to have a normal family life."

"Who else is in your household currently?"

"My daughter Sadie here," she said, reaching behind her to pull Sadie forward, "and my boyfriend Dirk Rosco."

"Where is your boyfriend today?"

"He had to work this morning."

"And what is his experience with parenting children?"

"He doesn't have children of his own, but he loves being around them. He takes care of Sadie all the time, doesn't he sweetheart?" She squeezed Sadie's hand and looked at her until Sadie nodded.

"And you're prepared to take on the responsibilities of a second child, soon to be a teenager?"

"It's what I want more than anything," said Katrina, a single tear tracing a line down her cheek.

And with a few more questions and procedural instructions, that was it. In the course of forty-five minutes, the judge awarded custody to Katrina, effective immediately. Minnow was handed over like a pet store animal.

Billy stood outside the courtroom, still reeling from the first blow when Katrina delivered the second one.

"I want you out by this afternoon," she said.

He looked at her, not comprehending.

"The house goes to whoever has custody. That's what Mom's will said. It should have been me all along, but now it's officially me. So Dirk and Sadie and I are moving in tonight. I've already talked to the attorney, and when he sees the court order, he'll switch the money to me too. So go find a toilet to fix somewhere. Just be sure you clear all your stuff out of the bedroom, and don't take anything that was Mom's. C'mon Minnow."

"But what about Uncle Billy? You can't just throw him out…" said Minnow.

"Don't worry about him. He can't stand to stay home anyway. You know he only hung around there because of you. He's got his camper. This way, you don't have to move, and he's free to go. Everybody wins. Now I've got a surprise for you, kind of a welcome home gift. So let's go."

She gave Minnow a light push with one hand and pulled Sadie along with the other. Minnow half walked, half stumbled forward, turning back with a pleading look at Billy. Billy stood alone, dumbstruck, watching the three of them disappear into the elevator.

Minnow was struggling to comprehend what had just happened. Once inside the van with Katrina and Sadie she said, "So I live with you now? And Uncle Billy has to move out? And you're moving into our house?"

"That's pretty much it," said Katrina. "It went just the way I'd hoped."

"That lady made Uncle Billy sound like a pervert. He's not a pervert."

"Oh, he's a pervert all right," said Katrina. "Just because

you haven't seen it doesn't mean it's not true. "

"I don't think it's true," said Minnow.

"Well screw Billy anyway," said Katrina. "I don't want to talk about him. Remember I told you I had a surprise for you? Well check this out!"

She reached into the back seat for a small bag that she handed to Minnow.

"Whoa!" said Minnow, peeking inside. "Is this really a phone? My own phone?"

"Yep," said Katrina.

"With my own number? And a camera, and Internet and everything?"

"The whole deal," said Katrina. "Remember, I told you I'd get you one when you came to live with me. Take it out of the box and turn it on. It's already activated and charged up."

Minnow pulled the box from the bag and reverently removed the phone from its packaging. She stroked its shiny face, seeing her reflection in the black screen, marveling at the perfectness of the object. When she pressed the power button the tiny screen came alive.

"Thanks Mom!" said Minnow, her pleasure momentarily overriding the distress she had felt moments before.

"You just be sure you hang onto it. It costs a lot of money."

"Don't worry. It's not leaving my sight! Can I call you on your phone? Just to see if it works?"

"Sure, but I've got to call Dirk first," said Katrina.

Sadie piped up from the back seat. "I want a phone too. Can I have a phone too?"

"Shut up Sadie," said Katrina. "You don't need a phone when you're five."

"Marcie Rogers has a phone at my school. And she's only five. And Olivia has a phone. And Marcus Sherman."

"I don't give a shit who else has a phone. You're not getting one," said her mother.

"No fair!" said Sadie.

Minnow turned around to look at Sadie, this sister who she hardly knew.

"It's okay," she said. "You can use my phone sometimes. Here, I'll take your picture with it."

Katrina pulled away from the curb and started making her way to the freeway toward Gresham. It was raining harder now, the van's windshield wipers setting a monotonous rhythm. She picked up her own phone and called Dirk.

"We're in!" she said when he answered.

Minnow could hear an indistinct male voice on the other end of the line.

"No, I mean we're in! We're moving. Today! Minnow's with me, and we're heading there now. So start getting your shit together. Get your clothes in a box or bag, and the food in the kitchen. I'll get Sadie's and my clothes when we get there."

She heard Dirk say something about furniture.

"No, we're not bringing any of that crap—except the TV. Billy doesn't have a TV. Oh, and Sadie's bed."

She turned to Minnow.

"You and Sadie are going to share a room, just like normal sisters do."

"Oh boy!" said Sadie. "I'm going to have a sister!"

"You already have a sister dummy," said Katrina. "But now you get to live in a new house with her. I always wished I had a sister when I lived in that house, but all I had was a weird brother. When you share a room with a sister you can stay up at night talking and tell her all your secrets."

Sadie frowned, becoming quiet.

"What about Bonkers?" asked Minnow. "We left him in the house. He won't know where I am."

"Relax," said Katrina. "We'll be there before he's even missed you."

"Can he still sleep in my room?"

"Yep."

"You'll like Bonkers," she said to Sadie. "He's the best dog in the world!"

Minnow spent the rest of the drive taking photos with her phone and showing them to Sadie.

When they arrived at the house, Dirk was slumped in front of the television, a black plastic garbage bag full of clothes on the floor beside him.

"What about the food?" said Katrina. "I told you to pack up the food."

"I didn't know what you wanted me to put it in," he said, "so I thought I'd wait for you."

She switched off the television and pulled the plug from the wall.

"You can start by hauling this out to the van," she said, pointing to the door. Then she noticed Minnow still standing by the front door.

"Oh, sorry," she said. "Minnow, this is Dirk. Dirk, this is Minnow."

"Come over here and let me have a look at you," said Dirk.

The house was chilly and smelled of cigarettes and mildew. Dirk held a lit cigarette between the fingers of his left hand and cradled a can of Budweiser in his right. Minnow walked over and stood in front of the blank television. He motioned with the cigarette hand for her to come closer.

"Pretty girl," he said. "Just like your mama, but hopefully more agreeable."

Minnow shrugged.

"C'mon Minnow," said Sadie. "I'll show you my room."

"Here Minnow," said Katrina, handing her an empty garbage bag. "Put Sadie's clothes in this while you're in there."

"All of them?"

"Of course all of them. Everything you see. Look under the bed, behind the door. Everywhere. Put the sheets and blankets in there too."

It was after 4 when they pulled into the driveway of the crooked house. Every inch of the van was filled, with Sadie's mattress tied to the top. Minnow scrambled over piles of black plastic bags to get out of the van and ran to the house. To her relief Bonkers burst onto the porch and jumped into her arms when she unlocked the door.

Billy's absence created an emptiness that tore at her heart. She went into his bedroom. The bed was made as usual, but his closet was empty. She opened the dresser drawers; all empty. She went into the bathroom. His razor and toothbrush were gone. She sank onto his bed, running her hand over the pillow. A single dark hair clung to her fingers. She pulled it between thumb and forefinger, feeling the strength of the strand. Then she tucked it into her jeans pocket.

The remainder of the day was a blur. She was in her own home, but everything around her was different. Her room now held two beds. Sadie followed her everywhere. Bonkers continually whined and panted with anxiety. Katrina's makeup and hairbrush replaced Billy's shaving stuff in the bathroom. Cigarette smoke hung in the air. The television, not yet connected to cable, was where her recliner had been and the recliner now sat in the middle of the room facing the television complete with Dirk, his cigarette and beer back where they belonged.

Katrina made scrambled eggs and toast for dinner. Minnow could hardly eat, the toast dry as sawdust in her mouth. Dirk had no such problem. He finished the uneaten portions on both Minnow's and Sadie's plates. Then he belched loudly, got up from the table and returned to the recliner.

Minnow took her new phone into the bedroom and began programming in numbers of people she knew. The list was short: Maggie Berry, Samantha Maverick, her mom, and Jenny. Then she added the number for the library. She sent the same text message to Maggie and Jenny.

"Hi, this is Minnow. Guess what? I have a cell phone now too! I'm back living with my Mom but at the same house. U can txt me at this number if u want."

Sam didn't have a cell phone, so Minnow called the store. Donovan answered.

"Your uncle was here," he told her, "and he was upset. He said that he can't have any contact with you. I don't know what that's all about, but it don't seem right to me. Anyways, he and Sam took off for the coast early this evening in the camper so it's just me here. Are you all right?"

"I'm okay," Minnow said. "I'm living with my mom now."

"That's what I heard. Is that scruffy dog okay?"

This made Minnow smile. "Yeah, he's okay too."

"Okay, well you take care little lady. I'll tell them you called when they get back, after Thanksgiving weekend. Scratch that mutt behind the ears for me."

"Thanks Donovan," said Minnow, not wanting to end the call. "I'll be back to see you, I just don't know when. Please give Sam and Billy my new phone number."

"Will do," he said and hung up the phone.

She was wired, but exhausted from the events of the day. In all the times she had imagined what it would be like to live in a normal family, it hadn't felt like this. Nothing felt normal. Nothing felt real. She rested her head against the familiar pillow in her now-unfamiliar life and dozed off. Sometime later she was awakened by someone tapping her on the shoulder.

"Minnow?" Sadie said.

"What?" yawned Minnow.

"I'm scared. Can I sleep in your bed with you?"

"I guess so," said Minnow scooting next to the wall and pulling the little girl next to her. She tugged the blankets over them both. Bonkers sighed from the foot of the bed.

It had been nearly dark when Billy pulled the camper into the lot at Maverick's store. The lot was empty except for Donovan who was hosing down the pavement by the pumps. Billy parked the truck and trudged toward the store without looking in Donovan's direction. When Sam saw him walk through the door she broke into a huge grin.

"Early for Thanksgiving?" she said.

Then she saw the devastation on his face.

"Billy? What's happened? Where's Minnow?"

"Katrina," said Billy, tears sliding down his cheeks.

"Oh no!" said Samantha. "Oh God no."

She walked to him and took his hands, pulling him to the soft chairs by the wood stove.

"Tell me," she said.

He spilled out the story of the past two days in a torrent of words. When he was finished, he paced.

"Now that you know about me, you probably don't like with me a capital L anymore," he said.

"I don't think I do know about you," said Samantha. "Why did you peek in that girl's window? What was going on?"

"I was out walking, and her blinds were open and I saw her. She was so beautiful that I stood there and looked," he said miserably. "I didn't know it was wrong."

Why hadn't he known it was wrong? He had asked himself this question thousands of times. He was like a blind person in the world of the sighted. He couldn't see what was right in front of him, what everyone else could see. He didn't know what they knew. He was a person who did unforgivable things without even knowing they were wrong.

"And once you learned it was wrong, you never did it again?"

"No, of course not," said Billy. "But it was too late. I'd already been arrested."

"Did you spend time in prison?" asked Samantha.

"No, just two nights in jail. My mom talked to the girl's mom and she agreed not to press charges."

"Well then, I don't see that there's a problem," she said. "You did something you didn't know was wrong, and when you learned it was wrong you didn't do it again. That happens to all of us. Case closed."

"So you still like me?" he said, stopping his pacing to look at her.

"I don't just like you Billy," Sam said. "I love you."

He looked at her, not comprehending, his face a portrait of shame and misery.

"I love you Billy," she said again.

His expression transformed to bewilderment, and then to relief.

She stood and he let her hold him. This time his tears were of relief.

After running from the courthouse, Maggie had to almost feel her way to the car, tears merging with the rain pelting her face. She sat behind the wheel and closed her eyes, slowing her breathing, wiping the moisture from her cheeks with a tissue. It was as though she had been asleep for the past month and Katrina's outburst had been a glass of water in the face, bringing her back to reality.

"What have I been doing?" she said aloud. She realized that while she had thought she was helping Minnow, she was actually just using this as an excuse to run away from the truth and from her earlier decision. It was like waking from a dream. "The right decision," she said, a flood of sadness and resignation washing over her. She started the car and drove home.

At the house she started a new plan. She was expected at Toby's for Thanksgiving in three days. To do something before then would forever taint the holiday for her family. Plus, she realized that she desperately wanted to see them all one last time. This would be her way to say goodbye. Her chance to show them all how much she loved them.

She retrieved the file folders that she had prepared before her trip to the coast, an event that now seemed years ago. She read the letters to Toby and Ceci like the English teacher she was, editing the language, adding and deleting. Then she pulled up the saved copies on her computer and made the changes before reprinting them. She put each back into its labeled folder and shredded the earlier versions.

She had gotten off track and was back on.

The house needed cleaning. She needed ingredients for pies. She wanted to write a note to each of the grandkids so they would understand why she had to do what she planned to do. She wanted to box up her own clothes, as she had done George's, so that Toby wouldn't have to do it. The clothes wouldn't fit Heather or Ceci, so they might as well go to charity. And she wanted to give something to Eric and Amy, a symbol of their importance to her. After a two-hour search, she found what she thought would be perfect for each. The hours stretching ahead of her that she had struggled to fill now seemed too short. *So much better than too long*, she thought.

Maggie was savoring a bowl of tomato soup when Minnow's text came through on her phone. So it's happened, she thought with a pang of guilt, wondering if it would have made any difference if she had talked with Minnow that morning. "Well," she said aloud, "Katrina was right. It's not my place to get involved when I've got my own mess to clean up. Good luck to you dear Minnow and Billy." For reasons she herself didn't understand, she added Minnow's name and number to the contacts list on her phone. Then she set the phone down without responding to the text. Better to make a clean break. But later that evening she went back to her computer and typed a third letter, putting it in a folder labeled *Billy and Minnow Marsh.*

Sam was quiet on the drive south. The clouds snagged in the tops of the tall cedars and firs in the coastal mountains, giving a mystical feel to the journey. She watched Billy's hands, gripping and releasing the steering wheel, and pictured the events of the past day that must be replaying in his mind. Occasionally he would shake his head, or mutter something under his breath.

"Do you want to talk about it?" she asked.

"Why can't people see what's happening?" he said. "Why does she always get away with fooling people? She even fooled Minnow, and now what's going to happen to her?"

"Let's hope you're wrong about Katrina. Maybe she really has gotten her life together," said Sam.

"I'm not wrong, and it's not right what happened."

"No, I agree. It's not right. But there's nothing we can do about it right now. We just have to let things play out and maybe try to pick up the pieces if what you fear is true."

"I promised my mom I would take care of her. I don't break promises," said Billy.

"I know you don't," said Sam, "and your mom knew that too. That's why she left Minnow in your care. But Billy, you didn't break your promise. Katrina took things out of your hands."

Billy opened his fingers and looked at his hands on the steering wheel as if he could somehow will them to take back control of his life. He blew out a long breath through pursed lips and closed his grip, shaking his head.

At Gold Beach, they cut back inland and found a place to camp along the crystalline Illinois River. The moon peeked through the clouds, reflecting off the fast-running water and made earlier raindrops shimmer in the evergreen branches. Billy made soup in the cozy warmth of the camper, and the tensions of the day lost some of their edge. Sam cracked the windows to listen to the water cascading over rocks and breathed in the earthy forest smell.

Billy pointed to the bed above the cab. You can have Minnow's bed, he said, a new sadness settling on his features. He took down the table and stowed it under the benches to make a platform for his own bed. After stepping outside to relieve himself, and brushing his teeth, he sat on the edge of the bed, his arms wrapped over his chest, and rocked slowly forward and back, eyes closed.

"What am I going to do Sam?" he asked after she came back in from outside. He looked utterly lost.

"I don't know, but we'll figure it out," she said. "It's going to be okay."

She settled next to him, as she would when approaching an injured bird, matching her breath to his, silent but present.

"Billy," she said, "would it be okay if I touched you?"

He looked at her, not comprehending. "Touched me where?" he said.

"I'd like to hold you," said Sam, "but I know that touching is sometimes uncomfortable."

He nodded. "It would be okay," he said, "because it's you."

She slid closer to him and felt him stiffen as she put her

arms around his torso and began to rock with him. He let out a shuddering breath, relaxing into her.

"You could put your arms around me too," she said. Billy sat frozen. Then slowly, he untied the knot of his arms and clasped her in a tremulous embrace.

"Are you doing okay?" asked Sam. "Does it feel okay?"

He worked his mouth as if to speak, but instead just nodded.

After a while his trembling subsided and she said, "I'm wondering, have you ever kissed anyone?" Billy shook his head, looking down. She turned her face toward him and planted a soft kiss on his cheek and then tipped his face up toward her and brushed his tightly compressed lips with hers.

"Try kissing me back," she said.

He breathed rapidly through his nose. Glancing at her, then looking away, he unclenched his jaw and pursed his lips. He moved toward her, taking a few, shuddering breaths, then pressed his lips against hers, before jerking back.

"How was that?" she asked.

"I don't know," said Billy. "It felt electrical."

Sam smiled. "Electrical in a good way?" she asked.

"Not a bad way," said Billy. "Kind of a scary way."

"Have you ever wanted to make love with someone?" asked Sam.

Billy was silent, looking down again and frowning as he considered the question. "I've always been too afraid," he said, "after the thing that happened with the arrest. I've read about it in books, but I don't want anything bad to happen again."

"If you knew nothing bad would happen, would you want to give it a try? If it was with me?"

Billy glanced up at her, then looked down again, his face flushed. "If it was with you," he said, still looking down, "maybe yes."

Sam unbuttoned his shirt and slid it off his arms, taking in his smooth chest and flat stomach. She gently stroked his chest and then his back, feeling him shiver. She talked through each move she made, explaining what she was going to do before she did it. She asked him to pull her own shirt over her head, and then to unfasten her bra, which he did with trembling fingers. She took his hands and guided them to her breasts. When he touched her skin, he jerked back as if burned. She told him how his touch made her feel. He reached with one hand, then the other, and touched her nipples. She felt them harden with his touch. His whole body was trembling, electrified.

One by one, she untied and pulled off his shoes and slowly tugged at his jeans and briefs, letting them slip to the floor.

He gripped the edge of the bed like a coiled spring. She pulled off her own jeans and panties as he stared, open-mouthed, his breath coming in short gasps. She took off his dark-framed glasses, setting them out of the way, and gently pushed him back on the bed, sitting astride him on her knees. Ever so slowly, she guided him inside her, holding very still, feeling his hardness, ready to burst. When she started to move rhythmically, he shuddered almost instantly, crying out, then continuing to moan softly.

She smiled at him, brushing the dark fringe of hair away from his eyes. She stretched out her body to lay lightly on top of him, feeling the tension ebb from his body. His soft moans continued, and then grew louder, turning to painful sobs, and then wails as tears streamed from his eyes, the dam of shame and fear built up over years finally breaking loose. She lay beside him, not speaking, holding him gently. When he quieted, she got up and wetted a washcloth to bathe his face, then covered him with the sleeping bag and watched as he fell into an exhausted sleep.

Sam drifted into sleep, awaking some hours later to find Billy sitting up in bed, hugging his knees. In the pale moonlight coming through the camper window she could see him shaking his head.

"What is it Billy?" she asked.

"I don't understand," he said.

"Don't understand what?"

"I don't understand how the same day can be both the saddest day of my life and the happiest day of my life. It doesn't make sense. Shouldn't one exclude the other?"

"Ah," said Sam. "Sometimes life works in ways that don't make sense. Sometimes instead of going in a straight line from point A to point B, things circle back around on themselves. All we can do is take it as it comes and do our best with what comes our way."

"I never expected …" he stopped, at a loss for words.

"I know," she said. "Did you like it?"

"Yes, I liked it very much. With a capital L."

Sam laughed. "Would you like to do it again?"

Billy smiled. "Yes," he said. "I would like to do it again, with a capital L."

She pulled him to her. This time, they merged with an excitement and joy in each other's bodies, no longer tinged by the fear that had been with Billy his entire adult life. This time was about pleasure for both of them.

Later, after a hearty oatmeal breakfast, they went for a walk along the river. Sam could see Billy was struggling to reconcile feelings of euphoria over his good fortune to be loved by someone, and feelings of despair over everything else.

"I don't know what to do!" he told her. "Where will I live? What about my metal shop? And I can't stop thinking of Minnow with Katrina. I know something bad will happen. And then what will Minnow do? They won't let her be with me. They won't even let me see her!" He walked faster as he talked. Sam lengthened her stride to keep up.

"Billy, would you consider living with me," she asked, "when you aren't out with the camper on your rounds?"

He stopped and looked at her. "You would want that?"

"Yes, I would love that. You could help me with maintenance around the store and station. There's always more than I can do. And there's room for your metal shop in the outbuilding behind the store next to the Critter Spa. It needs some work, but it could be fine. There's already a wood stove in there and electricity. You could still sell your metal sculptures from in front of the store."

"I need to think about it," he said.

"I know you do," she replied. "We can talk more about it later. Just know that the offer is out there when you decide."

"Out where?" he asked.

She laughed. "If I live with you, I'll learn to speak without ambiguity. What I meant was that you can take your time to decide, and I won't rescind my offer while you're thinking about it."

"Oh, okay. Thank you," he said.

"As for Minnow," said Sam, "I'm worried too. I so love

that girl."

"Can we do anything?" asked Billy.

"I don't think so. At least not right now. Katrina's gotten what she wants, and all we can do is hope that there's some mother instinct buried somewhere inside her that will make her do right by Minnow. She's a clever one, your sister. I just wish she'd apply all those smarts to doing good in the world."

"Katrina only cares about Katrina," said Billy.

"I hope you're wrong, but you probably aren't. You've watched her for years."

"I'm not wrong," he said.

November 25

Minnow made oatmeal for Sadie and herself. Katrina and Dirk were still sleeping. She realized that she liked having a sister, even though she wished that Sadie would leave her alone at least some of the time. Maybe she would be less clingy after she got used to living at the new house.

"Do you want to take Bonkers out for a walk with me?" she asked Sadie. "I know some great places to show you."

Bonkers started spinning in circles and leaping at Minnow's legs.

"Yeah!" said Sadie. "Can I hold the leash?"

"Sure, when we use it. Part of the time he doesn't need the leash. Let's get dressed and go before Mom and Dirk are up."

Minnow put on her old jeans and found some jeans for Sadie. Wearing rain jackets and sneakers, they scampered off the porch to the gravel driveway. Bonkers raced ahead, then circled back before rushing off again. When they reached the street, Minnow clipped on his leash and handed it to Sadie who held it with both hands, arms and leash stretched taut by the pulling dog. They skirted the perimeter of an ornamental nursery, went through the parking lot of the old Grange Hall, then entered an abandoned orchard. Some of the trees still had red apples hanging from upper branches and others were smashed and brown among the leaves at the base of the trees.

Minnow let Bonkers off the leash and he raced among the trees, sniffing, chasing critters, chomping on apples, and barking. The girls ran after him, ducking behind trees, then jumping out and scaring each other.

They were like three puppies, sprinting in circles, springing in front of each other, chasing, dashing away. Minnow laughed and Sadie squealed with the pure fun of it. Bonkers made playful growling sounds as he leapt at their ankles, his mouth in a doggy grin. They ran and ran until they collapsed in a heap together, Minnow first, Sadie on top of her, and Bonkers lunging at their jackets, trying to keep the game alive.

"This is fun!" Sadie laughed. "Do you do this all the time?"

"Bonkers and I come here and run around," said Minnow. "But it's more fun with another person."

Sadie took Minnow's right hand in both of hers. "I like having a sister," she sighed.

"Yeah, me too," Minnow said. "Did mom tell you she wanted me to live with her again?"

"Oh yeah," said Sadie. "She talked about it all the time. 'Just wait until we get your sister back. Then we can move out of this dump and have a real house like other families, and money every month.' She was always telling me that I had to be nice to the caseworker and tell her how much I liked living with Dirk so that she could get you back."

Minnow pulled Bonkers to her side and stroked his ears. "Do you like living with Dirk?"

Sadie shrugged her shoulders, looking away.

When they got back to the yard, Bonkers ran into the shop and barked. Minnow followed and found Dirk there rummaging through Billy's tools.

"Can't you shut that dog up?" he said when he saw her.

"Those are Billy's," she said. "You shouldn't mess with them."

"I don't see no Billy living here now," said Dirk.

"It's still his stuff," said Minnow. "He's going to need it."

"Well then he shouldn't have left it behind should he? Now why don't you just mind your own business? Billy's a grownup. He don't need you to protect him."

She left him there and called Bonkers to come to the house. Sadie had started to follow her toward the shop, but had halted outside the door when she'd heard Dirk's voice.

"Is he always mean like that?" Minnow asked her.

The little girl shrugged again and walked toward the house.

Before Minnow reached the door, she was startled by her vibrating pocket. It was the first time her phone had rung since she'd gotten it. She pulled it out and saw Jenny on the screen.

"Hello?" she said.

"Minnow?"

"Yes, hi Jenny. You must have gotten my text."

"Yes I did. So you're back with your mom?"

"Yes," said Minnow. "Just since yesterday. She and her boyfriend and my half-sister Sadie moved into our house."

"What about your uncle?" asked Jenny.

"They said I couldn't stay with him anymore. So he had to leave with the camper. I guess he's at the coast with our friend Sam. But I feel bad about him having to leave. I was supposed to go with him and Sam to her brother's for Thanksgiving, but that's not happening now obviously."

"You know you're still invited here for Thanksgiving. Do you want to come?"

"I do," said Minnow. "But I don't know if that's okay with my mom. Plus, I don't know how I'd get there."

"Rob could come pick you up if you want to come. You just let me know."

"Thanks, I will," said Minnow.

"I actually called for an additional reason," said Jenny. "I noticed that when you sent your text, you also sent it to a Maggie Berry."

"Yeah, she's my friend I met at the coast," said Minnow.

"Is she a friend who's your age?"

"Oh no," laughed Minnow. "She's more like my grandma's age, or the age my grandma was before she died. She's really nice. I feel kind of sorry for her. She told me her husband died in a car wreck."

"I know," said Jenny.

"You do? Do you know her?" Minnow asked.

"Not directly. But I know who she is. Minnow, it was her husband who was driving the car that killed Jason. She was in the accident too."

"Oh my God!" said Minnow, remembering the day they drove up Winter Hill Road when Maggie had bolted from the pickup. "She never told me."

"Did she know that you're a friend of our family?" asked Jenny.

"Yeah, well I told her that day when I saw you at the memorial. On Jason's birthday. She was in the car with us but she got upset and ran away from the car."

"And she didn't tell you why?"

"Only that her husband had died in a car wreck too. She didn't tell me it was the same wreck! No wonder. She must have felt really bad. That's so awful. She's really a good person, and she said her husband was a good person too. They met in the Peace Corps. I know she really misses him."

"You know he was drunk when he caused the accident."

"I didn't know. That just makes me extra sad. When someone messes up like that, and there's no way to fix it, and people's lives are wrecked, and no one can get over it, I think that's the worst thing in the world."

"So it is," said Jenny. The phone was silent for a long pause. Then she said, "Minnow, when you see Maggie Berry again I'd appreciate it if you didn't mention that you and I had talked about her. I think it might make her more upset."

"Okay," said Minnow. "But she already knows I know you, and that Jason is special to me."

"Just the same…"

"Okay. I don't know if I'll see her anyway. She was supposed to meet us at the courthouse yesterday for the hearing with my mom and she didn't show up. And she didn't answer my text. So maybe something's happened. I don't know where she lives or anything."

"All right. Well in any case, I'd appreciate you keeping it between you and me. Meanwhile, let me know about Thanksgiving. We'd love to have you."

"I will," said Minnow. "Thanks for calling me. You're the first phone call I've gotten on my phone!"

"I'm glad I called then. Bye Minnow."

"Bye Jenny."

Minnow stood on the porch for a minute staring at her silent phone and thinking of the strangeness of things. How could it be that her Maggie had been in the car that killed Jason? Why did life always get so complicated? She went into the house where Katrina was also on the phone.

"Yes, I know that Thursday's a holiday," she was saying. "But I want to get those papers signed so that those checks start coming to me. If you can't have them ready tomorrow, when will you have them?

"Okay, Friday then. I can come in Friday morning. I'll be there at 10."

She shut off her phone.

"Fuckin' lawyers," she said to no one in particular.

"Mom?" said Minnow, the word feeling strange as it left her mouth.

"What?" Katrina replied. "Why are you wearing those baggy old jeans instead of the new ones I bought you? You look like a frump."

Minnow looked down at her jeans as if noticing them for the first time.

"I took Bonkers for a walk and I didn't want to get the others dirty. Besides, these are comfortable."

"So's a bathrobe, but that doesn't mean you should wear it out in public."

"Anyway, I had something to ask you," said Minnow. "A

family that I'm friends with invited me to their house for dinner on Thanksgiving. Would it be okay with you if I went?"

"What family?" asked Katrina.

"Just some people I know. Their son Jason died in a car wreck and I got to be friends with his mom and dad and sister. And they asked me to come for Thanksgiving."

"What about your own family? Isn't this a family? What about your own mom?" said Katrina. "We're together one day, and already you want to go spend a holiday with some other family?"

"It's not that," said Minnow. "I just didn't know if we were doing anything for Thanksgiving. I didn't see that we had any food for it or anything."

"Sure we are," said her mother. "I just haven't been to the store yet. We'll make it a regular family holiday. You tell that other family thank you very much, but you already have plans with your own family."

"Okay I will," said Minnow.

November 26

Katrina had never cooked a Thanksgiving dinner and didn't know how to cook a Thanksgiving dinner, but she had told Minnow that they were having a family dinner. She was pondering this problem on her way to the grocery store when the answer providentially appeared on a marquis outside the Salvation Army Community Center. "Thanksgiving Dinner, Thursday, November 27 – All Are Welcome"

She swung the van around into the parking lot and went into the office. "Yes," they told her, "if her family was in need, a free Thanksgiving dinner would be available." And, "Yes, if there were family members unable to come to the center, she could get her meal packaged to go."

Sometimes in life things just work out right, she thought. In the last two days she had gotten her house and her kid back, and in two more days she would have money coming in every month. And now the Salvation Army was cooking her Thanksgiving dinner. Finally things were going her way.

"Bless you," she told the woman in the office. She then continued on to the grocery store where she bought three bottles of wine and a six-pack of cola.

November 27

Maggie arrived at Toby's house at noon. She saw Ceci's red Miata already in the driveway. As she was parking beside it, the front door burst open and Eric and Amy came out. They hugged her and she handed them each a pie to carry while she followed with a paper bag.

"Wow Granny, these look great!" said Eric, inhaling the aroma of the apple pie he carried. "You should teach Mom to make pie like this."

"Hush Eric," she said. "Your mom and dad keep you well-fed. Just look at how tall you are."

In truth, cooking was neither Heather's nor Toby's strong suit. It just didn't particularly interest either of them, but they got by. Judging by the smell of the roasting turkey, today's dinner would be fine. She made a mental note to check it for doneness before it met the carving knife. Details like that sometimes escaped Heather.

Ceci, Toby, and Heather greeted her like a long lost relative. She knew that her refusal to visit over the past months had worried them. She had been to Amy's school choir performance, but had left immediately after. Now she could see that they were watching her for signs of distress. Ironically, she felt none. Her experience with Katrina at the courthouse had somehow freed her from angst. She suddenly had great clarity about what she needed to do. Until then, she would treasure these moments with her family. Thanksgiving had always been her favorite holiday. It had none of the commercialism and buildup of Christmas. It simply brought people together around a meal in a spirit of gratitude. She liked that.

Once all the greeting was over, and she was settled on the sofa with a glass of wine, she opened the top of her paper bag and called Eric and Amy to sit beside her.

"I have something for each of you," she said. "I've been going through stuff at the house, and I found a couple of things that I'd like you to have." She pulled a magazine from the bag and handed it to Eric.

"Whoa! This is Grandpa's autographed Marcus Mariota edition of Sports Illustrated! That's so cool!" Eric held the magazine in both hands like a prayer offering. "Are you sure you don't want to keep it?"

"Your grandpa would have wanted to you have it. And you'll appreciate it far more than I would," said Maggie, smiling at his pleasure.

"And Amy," she said, "I have something autographed for you as well." She pulled a hardback book from the bag. "I know you and I both loved this book."

"*The Book Thief!*" said Amy, opening the book to the flyleaf.

"Signed by Zusak Markus! Wait! It says *To Maggie and Amy.* How did you get this?"

"When Grandpa George and I took our trip to Australia a couple of years ago, I happened to visit a bookstore when Zusak Markus was there doing a book signing. The line was a block long, but I couldn't resist buying a copy and having him sign it. I always knew I'd give it to you someday, so I had him put both our names on it."

"Wow. I love this! Thanks Granny!" She leaned over and gave Maggie a hug.

Maggie noticed Ceci watching her intently.

"You seem to have turned some kind of corner," Ceci said. "Last time we talked you said you just couldn't find the energy to go through things at the house."

"Well," said Maggie, "sometimes you just have to push past your resistance and do it."

"So that's it?" probed Ceci. "You just pushed past your resistance?"

"Pretty much," said Maggie.

"Are you still involved with your domestic soap opera situation?" she probed further.

"Actually, no," said Maggie. "It's kind of resolved itself, though maybe not for the best. The girl is back with her mother. I've decided to take your advice and focus on my own life rather than put my nose where it doesn't belong."

"A wise decision," said Ceci, scrutinizing her sister.

"You can quit examining me like that," said Maggie. "I simply decided that I have the best family that anyone could want, and I want to make sure you all know how grateful I am. That's what Thanksgiving is about, is it not?"

"Thanks Mom," said Toby, bending down to give Maggie a hug. "I'm so glad we're all here together—you, Ceci, Heather and me, and the kids. It means a lot."

"Heather and I," corrected Maggie.

Toby sighed. "Actually mom," he said, a smirk playing at his lips. "It is Heather and me."

Billy scratched at his cheek, as he surveyed the one-story, rambling structure, sprawled across the top of a grassy, oak-covered knoll. Sam jumped from the pickup, eager to stretch her legs after the two-hour drive from the coast, while Billy stood on the running board, clinging to the open door. Suddenly they were corralled by two black dogs the size of bears. The beasts romped around the camper, tails wagging, first nuzzling Sam who was laughing, and then Billy, still clutching the pickup door.

"Don't worry, they're harmless," boomed a voice from a building next to the house. "Rufus, Barney, come back here!" The dogs retreated toward the voice.

Framed in the sliding barn door of the outbuilding was a tall, burly man in overalls with red curly hair and a beard to match.

"My favorite sister!" he said, advancing to wrap Samantha in a hug. "And you must be Billy who I've heard so much about." He gripped Billy's hand in both of his. "I'm Riley," he said.

"C'mon inside. Becky's got the kitchen under control. I was just getting some more wood for the stove. The twins are running wild as usual."

They followed Riley into the house and were immediately

struck by the mixed smells of a wood fire, roasting turkey, and fruit pies. Two, identical four-year-old girls were in the midst of a chase through the house, screaming and laughing. They stopped running and started jumping up and down when they saw Sam.

"Aunty Sam! Aunty Sam!" they said in unison, then ran to her for a hug. She scooped up one in each arm.

"Boy, you two are getting too big for this. I'm going to have to do one at a time from now on!"

She turned to face Billy.

"Gracie and Abby, this is my friend Billy."

The girls each gave a little wave to Billy. He waved back. Then Sam set them down and they spurted off on a new round of chasing and giggling.

"Come into the kitchen," said Sam, "so you can meet Becky."

Billy was already overwhelmed with meeting and greeting but followed obediently.

"Hey Beck," said Sam, "it smells heavenly in here."

A short, stocky woman in her thirties with wavy dark hair turned around from the sink and broke into a grin. "Sam! I didn't hear you come in! Welcome." She dried her hands on a towel and gave Sam a hug. Then she turned toward Billy who had stopped in the doorway.

"You're Billy," she said. "I'm so glad you've come. Welcome to our crazy household."

"Thank you," Billy managed.

"Where's Spencer?" asked Sam.

"He's right there in front of you," said Becky, pointing with a wooden spoon at the kitchen nook to her right. Seated at the table, eyes glued to a book, was a red-haired skinny boy of twelve.

"Hey Spence," said Sam, walking over to him. He glanced up briefly.

"Hello," he said, returning to the book.

"What are you reading?"

"It's about forensic entomology," he said.

"You mean bugs?" asked Sam.

"Specifically, the use of insects to help with criminal investigations. If someone is murdered, the types of insects, their location on the body, and their stage of development can often help determine the time of death."

"Interesting," said Sam. "I'd like to hear more about that. But first, Spencer, I want you to meet my friend Billy."

Spencer again glanced up briefly, this time in Billy's direction.

"Hello," he said.

"Hello," Billy said. He was overcome with the eerie sensation that he was looking at himself at age twelve. Within two minutes he knew exactly how it felt to be this kid surrounded by a world of people who saw and felt things differently than he did. Sam saw the recognition in Billy's face and nodded.

"Spencer, maybe after dinner you'd show us your insect collection," she said. "I know you've added to it since I've been here."

"Okay," said Spencer.

"Meanwhile, Beck can we help with anything for dinner?"

"Not yet," said Becky. "Maybe when we hit the last-minute rush to get it all to the table. Why don't you take Billy out to Riley's shop. I know he can't wait to talk metal working to someone."

They dodged the squealing twins on their way to the front door and headed for the outbuilding where they'd first seen Riley.

On the way, Billy said, "Spencer, he's like me isn't he."

"Yes," said Sam. "Very much so."

"Does he have a hard time at school? I don't mean with the schoolwork, I mean with other kids."

"He did," she said. "A very hard time. Now Becky and Riley homeschool him and it's better. He's a great kid."

"Is that why you understood me when other people didn't?" asked Billy. "Because you knew about him?"

"Maybe in part," said Sam. "Just because it's hard for someone to communicate what they feel or need, that doesn't make their feelings or needs any less real or important. For me, it seems even more important to understand them."

In the welding shop, Riley and Billy were soon in deep discussion about the qualities of different metals and welding techniques. Riley had always been in the more practical end of the trade, fixing farm equipment and building metal structures. Lately, however, he had started to put together random metal parts into whimsical creatures.

"Wow, I didn't know you had such an artistic bent!" said Sam.

"Well, I just started playing around one day. Actually I made a thing for the yard because I thought the twins would like it, and then I kept thinking of other things to make. Maybe someday I'll be a metal sculptor like Billy here."

"I'm not a metal sculptor," said Billy. "It's just something I do when I'm not on the road."

"But you are," said Sam. "Riley, you've got to see the sculpture Billy made for the store."

"I made it for you, not for the store," said Billy.

"Even better," said Sam. "For me. Anyway, it's magical—the solar system and beyond. I can stand there and watch it spin for hours."

Conversation at dinner was wide-ranging, from obscure insect facts, to the history of toilets, to home-schooling techniques, to the wholesale price of gasoline, to dogs, to how to make the best fart sounds (thanks to the twins). Billy was astonished. Except for his conversations with Sam, he had never been part of human interaction that felt natural and comfortable. It was as though he'd come home to a home he'd never known.

During dessert Sam announced, "We have news to share."

"Well please share it! We're all ears," said Riley.

"No you're not Daddy," giggled Gracie. "You've got a nose and eyes and hair and elbows and knees and toes."

"And a bottom!" said Abby, joining in the giggling.

"Bottom!" said Gracie, falling off her chair laughing.

"Oh save us from four-year-old humor," said Becky. "Tell us your news Sam."

Sam laughed too. She reached over to Gracie and tickled her, launching a new round of giggles.

"We've spent the past two days talking about this," she said, "and we've decided that Billy's coming to live with me in Connor, and to help with the store."

"That's great news!" said Riley. "And we're the first to know?"

"Yep."

"Are you giving up the metal work Billy?"

"No," said Billy. "Sam says I can set up my shop in the outbuilding behind the store and keep selling some sculptures in the side yard."

Becky clapped her hands. "I'm so glad for you," she said. "We've worried about you running that place by yourself Sam, not that you aren't capable, but it's a lot to manage. And we didn't want to see you get hooked up with someone who took advantage of you. This calls for a celebration! Riley, bring in some champagne, will you? And sparkling cider for the kids."

Minnow awakened to the unfamiliar sound of music and voices blaring through a small speaker. The cable company had started their television service yesterday and Sadie was sitting on the floor staring at the screen, thumb in mouth. Minnow got a bowl of cold cereal and sat in the recliner, but already it had absorbed the cigarette and perspiration smell of Dirk. She wrinkled her nose and took her cereal and phone to the kitchen table.

"Have you had breakfast Sadie?" she asked.

The little girl shook her head.

"Do you want some?"

Sadie nodded.

Minnow poured a second bowl of cereal and took it to her sister who accepted it without looking away from the television.

When Katrina emerged from the bedroom, Minnow said, "Do you need help with Thanksgiving dinner Mom? I'm a pretty good cook."

"Nope," said Katrina. "It's all done, I just have to go pick it up by noon."

"Done where?" said Minnow. "Who cooked it?"

"Salvation Army," said Katrina. "Free Thanksgiving dinner for deserving folks like us. Brilliant, don't you think?"

"Right, brilliant," said Minnow.

"Was that a sarcastic comment?" asked Katrina. "Because I don't see you out bringing home money to buy food with."

"No, it's fine Mom. Free dinner's good. I just didn't know."

She retreated to her bedroom with her phone and Bonkers. She held Bonkers next to her face and took a selfie that she posted as her new Instagram profile picture. Then she updated her status:

"Regular Thanksgiving – hanging out with the family – can't wait for the big dinner!"

She spent the next two hours catching up on posts from her online friends and adding her own comments. Sadie came in and Minnow took photos of her, and of Bonkers with her and uploaded these, labeling the Sadie pictures as *my sister*.

"Can we take Bonkers for a walk?" Sadie asked. "That was so much fun last time."

"Good idea," said Minnow.

They found Dirk in place in the recliner, and Katrina gone to pick up the food.

"We're taking Bonkers for a walk," Minnow called to Dirk on their way out the door.

It was a drizzly November day, not truly raining, but wet nonetheless. The sky was mottled tones of gray against white, car tires hissing on the wet pavement. The two girls repeated their trek to the orchard to play hide and seek with Bonkers. By the time they tired of the game, they had mud spattered up to their knees, and Bonkers was more brown than white.

"Minnow," Sadie asked, "how does a dog know he's your dog?"

"I don't know," said Minnow, "he just does."

"But I mean, why does he just know? Why doesn't Bonkers just walk off with someone else and become their dog?"

"Well, I'm the one who feeds him, and he sleeps with me," said Minnow.

"So if I started to feed him, and he slept with me, would he think he was my dog?"

"No," said Minnow. "He'll always be my dog. We take care of each other."

"So it wouldn't matter if I fed him and slept with him?"

"It would matter some. Maybe he'd be a little bit your dog then, just like he'll always be a little bit Sam's dog. She saved him when he was a puppy, so when he visits her it's kind of like when a person visits his mother after he grows up. She'll always be his mother and he'll always love her, but she doesn't take care of him anymore. He knows he's my dog now because I love him so much."

"I'd like him to be a little bit mine," said Sadie.

"I think he'd like that too. I'll show you how to feed him when we get back."

Sadie proudly held the leash on the way back, the tired, muddy dog almost sedate for the moment. When they entered the driveway, they saw the van was there.

Minnow said, "Looks like Mom's back with the food."

"Yippee!" said Sadie. "I'm hungry."

They heard the blare of the TV from the front porch.

"Football. Yuck," said Sadie.

Dirk was where they had left him in the recliner. Katrina had joined him in the living room on the sofa with her feet on the coffee table. There was a cardboard box on the kitchen counter that had Marsh written on the side with black felt marker. One of the three wine bottles Katrina had purchased the day before was open and empty.

"About time you two got back," said Katrina. "Where've you been, out rolling in the mud?"

"We've been playing in the orchard with Bonkers!" said Sadie. "It's really fun."

Bonkers chose this moment to walk underneath Katrina's outstretched legs, leaving a wet, muddy streak on her calves.

"Fuck!" she said. "Get that filthy dog out of here! And get your muddy clothes off too." She stood up and wobbled into the kitchen where she dampened a paper towel and wiped off her legs.

"What about dinner?" asked Minnow.

"What about it?" said Katrina. "It's all right there, in that box."

Minnow took Bonkers out to the porch and gave him a thorough rinsing with the hose, sending mud in brown rivulets off the wooden planks. Then she wrapped him in a towel and held him until he quit shivering. In her bedroom she stripped off her own sodden clothes and dressed in the new jeans her mom had bought for her.

Sadie was on her bed playing with two Barbie dolls. Her own wet clothes were in a heap on the floor. She was now in the purple and pink outfit she had worn to the courthouse the day Minnow's life had shifted.

"Do you want me to fix your hair?" she asked Sadie.

"Okay," said Sadie. "Fix it how?"

"When I went to school I had a friend named Amanda and we used to fix each other's hair."

"What happened to her?" asked Sadie.

"Nothing. She just went on to middle school and I started doing homeschooling with my Uncle Billy because Granny Vi died, so we didn't play together anymore."

"That's sad," said Sadie. "I have a friend at school named Marcie. But I've never been to her house."

"You know, I just thought of something," said Minnow. "He's your Uncle Billy too. And she was your Granny too. I never thought of that before. Did you ever meet Granny Vi?"

"No. At least I don't remember if I did," said Sadie. "Who is she?"

"She was our mom's mom, and she used to take care of me, but then she got sick and died. So then Uncle Billy took care of me. You would have liked Granny Vi. And you would like Uncle Billy too. He's really smart, and he teaches me about all kinds of things."

"Where did he go?"

"I don't know," said Minnow. "He used to live here with me, and he's with our friend Sam for Thanksgiving, but then I don't know where he's going. He's Mom's brother, but they don't get along very well."

"Is he a pervert?" Sadie asked.

"Who told you that?" demanded Minnow. "Don't say that about him."

"What's a pervert?" said Sadie.

"Never mind. But it's not a nice thing to call someone, and you shouldn't say it about Uncle Billy."

As she ran the brush through Sadie's tangled blond hair, Minnow imagined Thanksgiving with Billy and Sam, or with the Foster Family. She could almost smell the food cooking, feel the warmth of the kitchen, and hear the voices of people around the table together. "C'mon," she told Sadie. "Let's get dinner out of that box and put it on the table."

The two girls put silverware on the table and pulled four white boxes out of the large cardboard box. Minnow opened one of the white boxes. It had slices of turkey, a mound of mashed potatoes, a jumble of green beans, and a red smear of cranberry jelly. A dinner roll sat on top of a puddle of congealing gravy that covered everything, including the piece of pumpkin pie that was turned on its side at the edge of the box.

"Let's put these in the microwave for a couple of minutes," she told Sadie.

After heating the boxes, they put one at each place at the table and called to Katrina and Dirk.

"We put the dinner on," said Minnow.

"Well look at my two little domestic wonders!" said Katrina. "They've made our Thanksgiving dinner Dirk."

She got out the second bottle of wine and poured glasses for herself and Dirk. The girls each had a can of Coke.

"Cheers!" said Katrina, raising her glass. "To our first family holiday together." They raised their respective drinks, the girls rather awkwardly.

While they ate, Bonkers placed himself strategically at Minnow's feet. She cut off a small piece of turkey and held it down by her leg where he snatched it. Sadie giggled and picked up a large piece from her white box and dropped it to the floor. Bonkers scrambled after it, licking the floor and then looking up expectantly for the next treat. Suddenly Dirk's hand appeared from nowhere and Bonkers was swept off his feet and hurled across the room where he thankfully landed on the sofa.

"Don't feed that damn dog at the table," he growled.

"Don't treat him like that!" said Minnow, running to the sofa and cuddling the dog.

"Sit back down," ordered Dirk. "We didn't make this food so you could waste it on that mutt."

"You didn't make it at all, or even pay for it," she flung back. "It was free food. The Salvation Army made it!"

"And don't sass," he said. "If you want to keep that dog, you better learn some respect."

"Mom!" Minnow looked to Katrina for support.

Katrina's facial expression said, *What do you want me to do?* She shrugged her shoulders and took another swallow of wine.

Minnow took Bonkers and shut him in her bedroom, then returned to the table where they finished the meal in silence. She stole glances at her mother, studying her face for a sign that somehow the longing she had always felt might be assuaged.

That night in bed Minnow held Bonkers tightly to her chest, feeling a sadness she had not felt since Granny Vi had died. Tears seeped down her face and into his fur. He licked her cheeks and neck. After a bit, Sadie crawled into the bed and they held the dog between them.

"Minnow?" she said.

"What?"

"Do you remember what Mom said about because we're sisters we can stay up at night and tell each other secrets?"

"Yes."

"If I tell you a secret, will you promise not to tell anyone?"

"Yes," said Minnow.

"It's about Dirk," Sadie whispered.

November 28

Maggie's sleep was troubled by anxious dreams. In one, she was taking care of an infant Eric and she was sitting on the sofa with a pitcher of margaritas. Eric started to crawl toward the stairs, and she picked him up, but then she tumbled on the stairs herself. He flew from her arms. She awoke with a start.

"Enough," she said, getting out of bed.

She went through her normal morning ritual: shower, coffee, breakfast. After she had eaten it occurred to her that she should probably have skipped breakfast so that the food wouldn't slow the absorption of the pills into her bloodstream.

"Oh well," she thought. "I'll just take more of them."

She dressed in her favorite blue slacks and matching hand-knit sweater and then went to sit in the living room, looking at the view out over the city. She and George had often sat here, but since he died, she had avoided the room. Other than the bedroom, it was where she felt his absence most strongly.

There was a steady November rain with a southwest breeze pushing swift-moving clouds.

"How I've loved this place," she thought. "How I've loved my life! I just can't love it anymore."

She pulled out her phone to look through her photos from yesterday's dinner one last time. There were Toby and Heather, Eric beaming with his autographed photo, Amy with her book, Maggie and Ceci, arms around each other, Maggie and the kids, Maggie and Toby. Then she noticed that there was a new text message she hadn't seen yesterday. It was from Minnow. She opened it.

Hi Maggie, I hope u r having a gd Thanksgiving. Mine is not great, but that's OK. Jenny told me about your husband and Jason. Wow, no wonder u were upset when we drove by Winter Hill Rd. Just wanted to say I'm sorry all that happened, and I'm sorry about your husband. Sometimes people make mistakes, but it was still an accident. Please txt me back Minnow

Maggie sat thinking for a moment. Then she typed into the phone:

Dear Minnow, I'm glad you know about George and Jason. I'm sorry I didn't tell you that day. I have felt so responsible for what happened. Please tell Jenny that I am sorry beyond words, beyond life itself. If I could trade my life for Jason's, I would do it without hesitation. I wish I could have done more to help you and do hope things work out with your mother. I'm glad we met. You've been a bright spot in these difficult last months of my life. Give my best to your uncle Billy and give Bonkers a hug for me. Your friend, Maggie.

She hit the send button and heard the text go through.

With a sigh, she got up and repeated her ritual from the prior month with one small change; she drew a full glass of water from the tap.

This time I have water, she thought.

She opened the bottle of pills and swallowed them four at a time until they were gone. She rinsed and dried the glass and put it away in the cupboard. Leaving her phone on the counter, she went up the stairs to her bedroom to lie on the bed and wait for oblivion to finally come.

Minnow awoke after a restless night and lay in bed thinking about Sadie's revelation of the night before. The little girl must be already up judging by the pajamas in a heap on the floor.

"Should I tell Mom?" Sadie had asked her.

As Minnow had pondered the question, something had shifted. The right answer was yes, a child should be able to tell her mother if something bad like this had happened. Isn't that what mothers did? Comfort and protect you?

In her mind, she saw herself at age six, crying after Brett jerked the tooth from her mouth, her mother watching passively.

She saw her mother at Thanksgiving dinner, watching passively as Dirk grabbed Bonkers and threw him at the sofa.

"No, don't tell her yet," Minnow had said. "Let me think about the best thing to do. But until we figure it out, let's just keep it our secret. But don't be alone in the room with Dirk. Make sure either I'm there or Mom is there."

Now, in the morning light, she mulled over the options. She could tell that caseworker, Helen Lafferty, but she feared that she and Sadie would then be taken and put into foster care with families neither of them knew. There was Maggie, she might know what to do but Minnow had not heard back from her. There was Jenny. She would want to help, but Minnow felt bad involving her when she was still struggling to deal with losing Jason.

What she most wanted to do was to find Uncle Billy and Sam and ask them to come get her and Sadie.

She called Maverick's Store. Donovan again.

"No Minnow, I don't expect them until tomorrow night. Are you sure you're all right?"

"Yeah, I just want to talk to them is all," she said.

"Okay, well I'll tell them you called."

"Thanks Donovan."

Bonkers was whining at the bedroom door to go outside. She put on her old jeans, a sweatshirt and tennis shoes and slipped out into the yard. The van was gone. Maybe they were all out.

Back inside, she poured some cold cereal and reveled in the quiet, sitting at the table and scrolling through her phone. She heard a text come through. Maggie's message.

Minnow slipped her phone into her back pocket and stood at the sink looking out the window. It was raining. Sodden leaves tumbled across the grass in the wind, piling up against the house. Minnow started to work her way through the jumble of dirty dishes from last night's dinner while Bonkers curled up under the kitchen table. It was the first time she'd been alone in the house since Katrina and Dirk had moved in and she felt the tension from the past few days begin to ebb.

She heard a door creak. Billy's bedroom door, only no longer Billy's.

Not alone after all, she thought, a tightness returning to her chest. She heard slow, heavy footsteps in the hall, then the bathroom door, the toilet flushing and the heavy footsteps again. When they reached the living room, the smell came with them—sweat and tobacco.

Bonkers gave a low growl. She didn't turn. She heard the groan of the recliner's springs followed by the footrest mechanism. The TV blinked to life; sports announcers and cheering fans.

Minnow was suddenly aware of making every movement

slow and deliberate, nothing to call attention to her presence. Of course, he had to know she was there. The chair was less than twenty feet away, squarely behind her, in full view of her position.

She heard the tap tap of the cigarette pack, the flick of the lighter, and wrinkled her nose as the smoke made its way to the kitchen. She wondered if this was what it was like to have a father. A plastic cereal bowl slipped from her grasp and landed in the sink with a loud clatter that caused her to jump. *Just finish the dishes and go back to your room,* she told herself.

Dirk came into the kitchen in his bare feet. She noticed that dark hair sprung from all of the openings in his clothing. He was several days past a shave and stubble spread outward from his wiry mustache to his chin, cheeks and neck. Minnow had the impression that some kind of hairy beast was slowly taking over his body.

He sauntered to the refrigerator, pulled out a bottle of beer, and plopped back in the recliner. Minnow heard all of these sounds but did not turn around. She could feel him looking at her back.

"Don't you talk?" he said.

She shrugged her shoulders.

"That ain't talkin'."

"Good morning Dirk," she said.

"That's more like it."

"Where did Mom and Sadie go?" she asked.

"Lawyer's office," he said. "The little brat pitched a fit about being left behind, so your mom took her along. Seems like she didn't want to stay with me. Any idea why that would be?"

Minnow shook her head and continued rinsing dishes.

"Y'know, I know a thing or two 'bout raisin' kids. One o' the things I know is that they gotta learn to show some respect, an' some appreciation. An' they need to give as well as get. If you give 'em somethin' like a roof over their head, or a Thanksgiving dinner, they oughta return the favor."

Minnow didn't respond.

"Whada you think of that?"

Minnow shrugged her shoulders again, still facing the sink.

"Look at me when I talk to you," he growled.

She turned, holding a bowl and spoon. He massaged the neck of the beer bottle slowly between thumb and fingers, exhaling smoke through his nose before crushing the cigarette butt into an overflowing ashtray on the broad arm of the chair.

"That's better," he said.

He fixed her gaze with his eyes, the whites watery and bloodshot. "Now how do you think you ought to return the favor?"

She shrugged again, feeling suddenly like there wasn't enough air in the room. She turned back around and gently set the bowl and spoon on the counter, and then ever so slowly started to move toward the back door. She heard him rise heavily from the chair.

"Now didn't I tell you to look at me?" he snarled. "I got a favor to collect."

She turned again. He stood close, facing her, the beer bottle no longer in his hand. In its place he grasped something red and raw-looking, thrusting upward through the opening in his jeans. For a moment she didn't know what it was. It looked like an alien creature, not a part of him. Then she knew.

Her breath started coming in short gasps, almost whimpers. "No Dirk, please…!" It was a soft wail. She sprang toward the door.

Freeing his hand, he lunged for her, catching her ankle like a snare. She crashed to the ground landing on her stomach, the air driven from her lungs.

He dragged her toward him across the linoleum. She was mute, struggling to draw a breath.

"I'll teach you how to show some gratitude you little bitch." She smelled his rancid breath. He grabbed the waistband of her jeans.

She clawed at the floor with her fingers, trying to free herself. Then from under the kitchen table she heard a guttural sound. With a furious snarl, the tan and white creature flew at Dirk's throat.

Dirk bellowed. He scratched blindly at the dog, his flesh tearing. He found the dog's throat and squeezed, pressing on the small windpipe. The jaws released.

"You fucking mutt!" he roared. He flung the small body like some filthy rag against the kitchen wall.

Minnow was on her feet in an instant. She scooped up Bonkers and bolted out the door.

She ran without seeing, thinking only of escape. She kept looking back, but no one followed. When she reached the parking lot of her old elementary school, she stopped to catch her breath and looked down at the motionless bundle of fur in her arms. His head lolled loosely on his neck, his eyes rolling back so just the whites showed. His pink tongue draped from the side of his mouth like a wet rag and blood trickled from the side of his mouth and nose.

Minnow's heart shredded.

"No, no, no!" she said, sinking to the damp pavement, curled over the dog and gasping for breath as though she'd been kicked in the gut. She remained like that, huddled in a ball, emitting a high, keening sound, blind and deaf to all except the body of her one true friend now stiffening in her arms.

She didn't know how long she cried.

It felt like days.

But eventually her initial grief was spent, and she had to face the reality of what to do next. Still holding Bonkers on her lap, she pulled her phone from her pocket and looked at her meager list of contacts. Billy and Sam were still gone. She tried Maggie. After all, Maggie had sent her a text that morning. The phone on the other end of the line rang until it went to voice mail.

"Maggie?" she said. "It's Minnow. I need your help. Please call me as soon as you get this. Please." Her voice quavered. "I need help."

Then she tried Jenny. After two rings she heard a familiar voice.

"Hello, Minnow!"

"Jenny?" she said, and then was racked with sobs once again.

"Minnow? What's happened sweetheart. What is it?"

Minnow managed to squeeze out four words between sobs. "Bonkers—he killed him!"

"Who did?" said Jenny. "Where *are* you Minnow?"

Gulping for breath, Minnow said, "Dirk, my mom's boyfriend. He killed him."

"But why?"

The answer was a wail. "He was protecting me! Dirk was trying to hurt me, and Bonkers wouldn't let him. And now Bonkers is dead!" She dissolved into painful sobs.

"Minnow, where are you?"

"At my old school, in the parking lot. At East Orient."

"Sweetheart you stay right there. It will take me a half hour, but I'm coming to pick you up. Just stay there, okay?"

"Okay," said Minnow, weeping more quietly now.

When Jenny Foster arrived twenty-five minutes later, she saw Minnow's rain-soaked, crumpled form, still curled over the dog, against the one-story building.

"Come on honey," she said, helping the girl to her feet. "Can I take him?" she reached toward the dog.

Minnow shook her head.

"Okay then," Jenny said. She could see that the small body was stiffening. "Well you hold him on your lap. But get into the car. It's warm in there."

Once Minnow was in the car, and the heat was cranked up, Jenny said, "Tell me what happened Minnow."

Minnow told her everything. About Dirk, about Sadie, about Bonkers saving her, about not knowing who to call, about trying Maggie and getting no answer and then finally reaching her.

"Oh Minnow, I'm so sorry!" she said. "I'm going to take you to our house honey. You'll be safe there, and then we can decide what to do."

Minnow nodded, tears still leaking from the corners of her eyes. On the drive, she told Jenny Foster more of her story. Her painful history with her mother, her years with Granny Vi and Uncle Billy, and the tragic reuniting with her mother.

"I should never have agreed to go back with her," she said. "I just thought maybe it would be different. I just wanted to have a mom like other people have." She was crying hard again.

When they pulled into the garage, Jenny shut off the car, reached across to the passenger seat and held the girl, smoothing back the hair that curtained her face, letting their tears merge and drip together onto the leather seat.

Jenny was thankful that her husband and daughter had gone downtown so that she could have some time to figure out what to do without having an audience.

"How about if I find something soft for him to lie on?" she asked.

Minnow nodded. Jenny found an old beach towel and made it into a blanket. Minnow let her take the dog to swaddle him in the blue and yellow towel. They laid him in an open cardboard box on the workbench.

In the house, Jenny gave Minnow a blanket to wrap around herself and then sat beside her on the sofa.

"I want you to know, Minnow, that there's nothing I'd like more than having you stay here as long as you want. But there are some other considerations that are important."

"Like what?" asked Minnow.

"For one, there's your sister. We need to report what happened to the authorities so that she's no longer at risk from your mom's boyfriend." Minnow nodded.

"And when we report what happened, they may not let you stay here, just because Rob and I aren't certified to be foster parents. I'll ask if we can be, at least until we get things sorted out, but agencies have their rules and I don't know what they'll want to do. Was there a caseworker involved when your mom got custody?"

Minnow nodded again. "I want Sadie to get out of there."

"Yes, that's important. What about Bonkers? Do you want to do something with him now in case you can't stay here right now? We can bury him in our yard if you like. I know a good spot under our beautiful maple tree."

Minnow shook her head. "I want him to be buried at Maverick's store. My friend Sam has a cemetery especially for pets she's rescued."

"Okay. How will we get him there?"

Minnow thought for a moment. "If we could reach Maggie, she'd take him. She knows where it is."

Jenny was silent for a moment. "Well you know, Maggie and I have something of a difficult history…"

"I know," said Minnow. "I just remembered something. Maggie told me to give you a message."

"To give *me* a message? That's surprising." Jenny Foster's image of Maggie was limited to that day in depositions. She had come to the hearing room prepared to hate this woman who represented a loss so staggering that it had left her feeling nothing but pain. Maybe if she could trade the pain for hate it would be a relief. But it hadn't worked. When she'd held up Jason's photo and seen the devastation on Maggie's face, she hadn't felt either hate or relief. She had just felt more sorrow. There was no comfort in that.

"Here," said Minnow. She showed Jenny the text message she'd gotten from Maggie earlier that morning. Jenny read and then re-read the message.

"Oh no…oh my God Minnow!" said Jenny. "When did

she send this?"

Minnow looked at the phone.

"Ten fifteen – two hours ago," said Minnow.

"Where does she live? Do you know?" Jenny had sprung to her feet.

"No, I don't know. I just have her phone number."

"Call it. See if she answers."

"Okay," said Minnow. The call went to voicemail.

"Wait a minute," said Jenny. "I know where she lives. It's in the court papers."

She ran to the corner desk and started throwing papers to the floor, madly searching.

"What's happening?" asked Minnow. "What's wrong?"

"Just call her honey."

"I am," said Minnow. "She's not answering."

Jenny found what she was looking for and grabbed her own phone. "Oh please don't let this be too late!" she pleaded.

Helen Lafferty had planned to take the Friday after Thanksgiving off to go shopping with her daughter, but at the last minute changed her mind and went to work. She knew things would be quiet and it would be her chance to catch up on paperwork without interruptions. When the phone started ringing, she puffed out her cheeks in an exasperated sigh. It can go to voice mail, she thought.

But two minutes later it started ringing again. She picked up. When she heard the name Minnow Marsh, her heart sank.

As she listened to Jenny Foster, and then Minnow, relay the events of the past two days, she knew she'd made a mistake. She should have listened to her nagging doubts about the boyfriend. She should have probed more about the younger child's situation.

She pushed her paperwork aside and shifted her efforts to getting these kids out of harm's way.

Katrina turned up the oldies radio station in the van and started singing along to Michael Jackson, gesturing with her free hand.

> *Just beat it, beat it, beat it, beat it*
> *No one wants to be defeated*
> *Showin' how funky and strong is your fight*
> *It doesn't matter who's wrong or right*

She turned to Sadie who was giggling at her antics. "We got it made, kid!" she said. "And I got the papers right here to prove it." She patted the thick envelope sticking out of her purse.

She did a Michael Jackson dance imitation from the driveway up onto the porch and into the house, still singing.

"Dirk?" she called. "We got it made now baby!" There was no answer. She searched until she found him in the shop putting tools into a box.

"What are you doing?" she asked.

"Just getting together some stuff I can use."

"Why wouldn't you use it here? This is where we live. Look! It's official now."

"Just in case I need it for work," he said.

"Where's Minnow, and what happened to your neck there?" she pointed to the ragged tear in his skin.

"Took off," he said. "Along with that fuckin' mutt. That's what happened to my neck. The damn thing attacked me."

Katrina searched his face. "Why would he attack you? And what do you mean she took off? To where?"

"Dunno why. Dunno where she went. Probably the library. She'll be back when she gets hungry."

Katrina frowned and went back to the house.

Her suspicions were confirmed late that afternoon when the police, together with a CPS caseworker came to get Sadie and informed her that Minnow was also in protective custody due to reports of sexual abuse by Katrina's live-in boyfriend.

"You fucking idiot!" she shouted at Dirk as they drove away with Sadie. "You goddamn fucking idiot!"

"You don't have to believe…"

"Oh I know what to believe," said Katrina. "I believe you can't control your damn dick. I believe that after everything I've done to get us a place to live and money, you've just pissed it all down the drain because you're a stupid bastard. I believe that these papers I just signed aren't worth shit now. I believe you're probably gonna end up in prison for being a pervert."

She grabbed her purse and stomped to the van, her spinning tires spraying gravel as she sped away.

Dirk watched her go. Then he pulled a six-pack from the refrigerator and carried it to the recliner along with his cigarettes and matches. He turned on the television. She would come back. The rest would all go away. It always did.

Toby stood outside of the emergency room bay, trying to stay out of the way of the people going in and out of the room. He had gotten there just minutes after the ambulance. He'd already been on the freeway on his way to the gym when the call came. The doctor had just explained that his mother was in severe respiratory distress and they were going to administer a powerful antidote to try to reverse her symptoms. Then he had rattled off a series of potentially terrible side effects before disappearing back into the room.

"I can't believe she would do this," he said to the woman standing next to him. "She was just at our house for Thanksgiving yesterday. We had a great time. She brought pies, and presents for the kids." That's when the realization hit him. "Oh shit," he said. "She was planning this all along. That's why she brought those things yesterday. Why didn't she say something?"

He sank into a chair, his head in his hands. He'd always felt lucky to have been born to Maggie and George. They were such solid, stable people. So predictable. Now a drunk driving death and an attempted suicide. The roller coaster of the past months had left him feeling like he could no longer count on anything happening as expected.

The doctor came out of the room. "You can go in now Mr. Berry," he said. "Your mother is responding to the medication. She's very alert, but a bit jittery and shivering, not unexpected, and there is no sign of embolism or the other things we worry about most. We're getting her some warmed blankets, but I think we've escaped the worst of the possibilities."

Toby stepped into the room. Maggie was propped up in bed, eyes open, an oxygen tube under her nose. He grabbed her hands. They felt dry and cold.

"Mom," he said, "you terrified me. Why did you…what were you…I'm just so glad you're still here."

"I didn't want to be," she said, shivering slightly. "How did you figure it out?"

"I didn't," said Toby. He motioned for the woman in the hall to come into the room. "She did."

Jenny Foster's eyes held concern and compassion. Then with a shock Maggie realized who she was.

"You? But how…?" said Maggie, continuing to shiver.

"Your text to Minnow," said Jenny. "I called 911 and sent them to your house. And then I called your son."

"Minnow? Is she here too?" said Maggie. "I thought I'd be long gone when she got that message."

"That's a story in itself," Jenny said, "which I'll tell you about when you're more recovered. I'm just relieved that you're not long gone."

"You are?" Maggie said. "I can't believe it was you who sent the ambulance. I would have expected you to be glad I was gone."

"Oh, no," said Jenny. "It just would have made everything so much worse. When I saw your message, I was terrified."

"But at the deposition…"

"I know," said Jenny. "I was angry. So very angry. But it wasn't that I blamed you. Well, perhaps I did. But mostly I just wanted you to know what I'd lost. I wanted you to see Jason. I felt that he was fading away from me, being forgotten. I couldn't bear that he was gone, but I could bear it even less if he wasn't remembered."

"You *should* blame me," said Maggie. "I let it happen. I didn't stop George from driving that night."

"I wanted to blame you," said Jenny. "But mostly I've blamed myself. In fact, if I didn't have another child at home,

I think I would have done what you tried to do."

Maggie frowned, trying to clear her head, to make sense of this. "I don't see how you could possibly be to blame," she said.

"That's just the thing," said Jenny, "what I've come to understand about blame. There are always plenty of places to pin it."

A nurse came in with two heated blankets and tucked them around Maggie. Maggie settled back onto the bed while the nurse checked her blood pressure and pulse. Once they were alone in the room, she said to Jenny,

"What do you need to tell me about Minnow?"

"It's a long story," said Jenny. "Call me after you're released and when you feel like talking." She scribbled her phone number on a notepad from her purse and handed Maggie the sheet of paper.

Toby came back into the room from the hallway.

"They're going to discharge you in an hour," he said, "as long as you don't show any complications from the drug. And they're referring you for psychiatric follow-up. And by the way, you're coming to our house. I'm not going to have you home alone after this experience. They said you should try to get some rest now."

"I don't need psychiatric follow-up," said Maggie. "And I used up all my pills, so what else would I do? My plan's been foiled."

"Thank God," said Toby, "and thank Jenny. You're still coming to our house for tonight – just for my peace of mind."

Jenny said, "I'll leave you now. But I need to fill you in on Minnow. Will you call me later, when you're feeling up to it?"

"Yes, but I don't have my phone," said Maggie.

"We'll stop by the house and get your phone and a change of clothes," said Toby. He turned to Jenny.

"I can't begin to thank you enough. If you hadn't done what you did, it would be…I'd be…" His voice faltered. He walked her to the door and hugged her.

Maggie called Jenny Foster two hours after leaving the hospital.

"I have to get this straight first," she said. "You said you blamed yourself for Jason's death. I don't understand."

"I blamed myself because I didn't feel right about Jason going out with Cameron that night. I knew how that boy drove. I was uneasy. But then I put those fears aside and let him go. And now I have the rest of my life to think about how life would be different if I had said no. Or if I had called to check in with him, delayed when they got in the car by 30 seconds. Or if I'd insisted that he be home earlier."

"But you couldn't have known," said Maggie.

"No," said Jenny. "But blame is all in hindsight. It's taking what we know now and applying it to what we did then. And we all come up short when we do that. So I've let it go. It was just making me hate myself and everyone else. Ironically, it was Minnow who made me see it."

"But I thought you hated me."

"I wanted to," Jenny replied. "And I know it seemed that I did. When I showed you that photo of Jason, I just wanted you to know what we'd lost—to acknowledge it. I needed to know that you saw what was taken from us that night."

"I did see," said Maggie. "And it tore me apart. And the lawsuit…" said Maggie.

"The lawsuit was my idea—not Rob's. He didn't want to

do it. I realize now that it was my attempt to get out from under my own guilt. If I could get confirmation that your husband was at fault, then maybe I would be off the hook. But it didn't really work. I think I will always feel guilty."

"But you…"

Jenny went on. "And then, when I saw you react to that photo, as much as I wanted to hate you, I couldn't do it. I realized that you were just a person suffering from a terrible loss, feeling tremendous pain, like I was."

"I never imagined…" said Maggie.

"I know. I wanted to reach out to you sooner, but didn't know how to do it," said Jenny. "But when I saw your message to Minnow and guessed what it meant, I just couldn't have that weighing on my soul."

"What's wrong with Minnow?"

"She was here until thirty minutes ago," said Jenny. "CPS just came and picked her up."

She then told Maggie the rest of the story.

"She wouldn't even let me bury the dog," said Jenny. "She wants it buried at some friend's store so I had to put it in the freezer until we can arrange that. She said you would know where the store is."

"Maverick's," said Maggie. "In Connor. Yes of course that's where she'd want him buried. I can take him there."

Both women were quiet for a moment.

"The poor child. She deserves so much better. What happens to her now?" Maggie asked.

"Rob and I asked if we could be certified as short-term foster parents for her, but they were not encouraging because of the recent trauma in our own lives. I guess I understand. We are still working through so much after losing Jason. So for now she's in some kind of teen emergency group home situation."

"That could be good, or it could be bad," said Maggie, "depending on the home. I hope it's better than what she just left. What about the other child?"

"I know they picked her up, but that's all I know. What about you, Maggie? Would you consider fostering?"

"I would, but I hardly think they'd find me a suitable candidate after today."

"Then who's out there for her?"

"Billy," said Maggie.

"Her uncle? I thought he was somewhat strange, and there was a reason she was taken from him. Does he want her back with him?"

"Oh I would think so," said Maggie. "From what I know, it was not his choice to have her placed with her mother. I think he loves her deeply. Let me take the dog tomorrow and see what I can learn about his situation and why he lost custody."

"Minnow did ask me to tell you something," said Jenny. "I don't really understand the message, but she said to tell you that she understands the title now. She said, 'Tell her that Bonkers is the mockingbird of my story'."

"Well, well," said Maggie. "So he is. I wish some of my high school seniors had been as insightful as she."

"What did she mean?" asked Jenny.

"It's from Harper Lee's *To Kill a Mockingbird*. In the story, the mockingbird represents the idea of innocence—a songbird that does nothing but sing its heart out for our pleasure. The killing of a mockingbird is the killing of an innocent. In this case, the innocent was Bonkers."

"Oh my goodness," said Jenny. "I so want to help that child."

"As do I," said Maggie. "Jenny, I didn't say this at the hospital because I didn't yet know it was true. I want to say thank you. I'm ever so grateful to you for rescuing me."

"I just did what any decent human being would have done."

"No, you did more. Thank you."

Minnow perched on the edge of the well-worn sofa in the living room of Karen and Randy Archer's sprawling, ranch-style house. She was trying to absorb the words spoken in her direction. Ashley Nichols, the same CPS caseworker who had been assigned to her when she was placed with her grandmother at age six, sat beside her.

Karen was a stout woman in her forties with kind eyes. Randy towered over her by at least a foot. His booming voice matched his size.

"We want this to feel like your own home," Karen was saying. "We have eight kids here, now that you've arrived, four girls and four boys, all between the ages of twelve and seventeen. There's a girls' sleeping room and a boys', and two separate bathrooms."

"And we keep them separate, despite what some of the kids might like," boomed Randy.

Minnow nodded numbly.

"Do you have any things that you brought with you?"

Minnow shook her head, looking down at the jeans, baggy sweatshirt and tennis shoes that she'd put on when she dressed that morning.

"Well I've got a box of clothes kids have left here where I'm sure you can find something to wear until someone can bring your own clothes. Is there someone who could do that?"

"Probably," said Minnow, "If my mom will let them into the house."

"Okay, well we'll see where we are in a couple of days on that. Meanwhile, if you want to change out of those clothes, I'll wash them for you."

"I can change but I don't want you to wash them," Minnow said.

"Why is that?"

"I can still smell my dog on them. It's the only thing I have to remind me of him," she said, tears seeping from her eyes.

"Okay sweetie, I understand. We can't introduce you to the other kids yet, except for Brittany. Everyone else is with family or friends over the Thanksgiving holiday, but they'll be back tomorrow and Sunday."

The girls' room was at the end of one wing of the single story house. It was a large, open room with four beds, four dressers, four small desks, and one table with a computer. Three of the beds were surrounded with posters and miscellaneous items. The walls of the fourth held only small holes, evidence that this was someone else's home first.

"This is your bed," said Karen, pointing to the pock-marked wall. "And this is Brittany." She gestured to the large girl seated on the bed opposite Minnow's. She looked to be seventeen, had a nose ring and was carefully painting her toenails a blue that matched the streak in her hair. "Brittany, this is Minnow," said Karen.

"Minnow? That's a new one."

"Hi," said Minnow.

"Welcome to the home for the unwanted," she said.

"That's no way to welcome someone," said Karen. "Why don't you show Minnow around and help her get settled?"

"Will do. Where's your stuff Minnow?"

Karen shook her head.

"Oh, left in a hurry. Been there, done that."

"Show her where the extra clothes box is and see if you can find some things that fit."

"Okay. C'mon then." She screwed the cap back onto the nail polish bottle and bounced off the bed, motioning for Minnow to follow.

Dirk didn't notice when the cigarette fell from between his fingers sometime after midnight. He was five beers into the six-pack and past worrying about Katrina, about being arrested, or about the cigarette smoldering on the arm of the recliner. Perhaps he woke up briefly when the smoke started to fill his lungs, but if so, it did him no good.

When they found him, he was still seated in the chair surrounded by his empty bottles. The TV remote had become a blob of melted plastic fusing together his right hand and thigh.

It was the neighbor who had called in the fire. She had gotten up to use the toilet at 2 a.m. and seen the flicker of flames in the frosted glass of her bathroom window.

When Katrina arrived home at 2:30 the fire department was already there, but the house was fully engulfed. She stood at the perimeter set up by the firefighters and watched it burn, tears of frustration trickling down her cheeks.

"That fucking idiot," she said.

November 29

Maggie awoke in Toby and Heather's guest room with the phrase *Today is the first day of the rest of your life—make it a good one* repeating in her head.

The rest of her life, a life she had wished to escape, to throw away.

A life now redeemed.

The gift of wanting a future was like a rebirth. For the first time since the accident, there were things she wanted to do. Not things she was *expected* to do, but things she *wanted* to do.

Her first order of business that morning was to convince Toby that she could be trusted to operate on her own. She knew the doctor had told him to keep a close watch on her, but she also knew it was unnecessary. She found him in the kitchen with Amy.

"How can I know what you're going to do after yesterday?" he asked.

"You can never know what I'm going to do, nor is that your job," she replied. "But I promise you I'll not try to hurt myself again."

Amy started to cry. "Why did you want to die, Granny. I don't understand."

"Oh sweetheart," said Maggie, "It's not really that I wanted to die. I just couldn't bear to *live*. I think if I'd really wanted to die, I would have done a better job of it."

"What's so different today from yesterday?" asked Toby.

"Jenny Foster," she said. "If she can forgive me, there's a chance that I can forgive myself, or at least live with myself. I didn't think that was possible yesterday. This may be hard for you to understand, but it makes all the difference. Besides that, I have work to do."

"What work?" he asked.

"I've got to get a child out of harm's way and back with someone who loves her."

"Oh, the kid from the coast. Ceci told me about her. Speaking of Ceci, she was going to come up here yesterday, but I told her to hold off."

"Thank you for that," said Maggie. "I'll talk with her. And yes, that child needs my help. She needed it on Monday and I let my own issues get in the way. That's not happening again. I just had to get over myself."

"Okay," he relented. "Just don't do anything foolish—anything else foolish that is."

She smiled a sad smile and nodded. "I'm ok now."

Thinking of Minnow, she had no idea how to proceed, only that she had to try. She called Minnow's cell, feeling trepidation about what she might find out.

"Maggie?" came Minnow's voice.

"Oh Minnow, I'm so glad I reached you. Are you all right?"

"Yeah, sort of. Are *you* all right?"

"I am now. Where are you honey?"

"I'm at some group home in Southeast. I don't know exactly where it is," Minnow said.

"Are you safe? Are they treating you well?"

"I haven't met all the other kids here yet, but the people who run it are okay."

"Minnow, I'm so sorry about what happened. About the whole thing with your mom and her boyfriend and Bonkers."

"I miss him so much Maggie," she started to cry. "I just can't believe he's gone."

"I know. I wanted to tell you that I'm going to pick him up from Jenny today and take him to Sam's store so she can bury him in her cemetery. Is that okay with you?"

"Yes," said Minnow. "She can bury him but tell her that I want her to wait for a funeral service until I can be there."

"I'll tell her."

"And Maggie," Minnow said, starting to cry again, "if Uncle Billy is there, tell him I'm sorry I didn't stay with him. Tell him I miss him so much, and I miss Sam. I shouldn't have gone with my mom."

"I will. Is there anything you need, that I can bring or send to you?"

"I need my clothes, if there's any way to pick up my clothes. And some books to read."

"I'll see what I can do. You'll need to text me the address where you are. And you can call me anytime."

"Okay Maggie. Thanks."

She quickly told Toby where she was going, grabbed her keys, and was gone.

The Fosters' house was a modest, two-story 1920s bungalow with a wraparound front porch. Maggie pictured the family relaxing together on summer evenings on the porch swing and two rockers to the left of the front door. She wondered what they did now that there were only the three of them.

As soon as Maggie rang the bell, Jenny opened the door and put an arm around her to escort her in.

"Sit down for a moment," she said.

A mission style sofa and chairs circled the fireplace, which was framed on each side by built-in bookshelves.

"Who's the reader?" Maggie asked, surveying the titles.

"Both of us," said Jenny, "But really Rob more than I."

"Than me," said Maggie automatically.

"More than you too?" asked Jenny.

"No, I meant…no, never mind," said Maggie.

"I've been thinking about what you said about redemption," said Jenny sinking into one of the chairs. "In a way, I think you did that for me as well. You and Minnow."

"That's hard for me to fathom," said Maggie.

"Like I said," Jenny went on, "I blamed myself for Jason going out that night. I spent hours playing the 'if only' game. If only I'd said no and he'd stayed home. If only I'd delayed his departure by a few seconds. If only I'd told them to take a different route home. If only I'd let him take our car like he'd asked instead of riding with Cameron. And on and on." She dabbed at her eyes.

"I met Minnow one day, about two or three weeks after he died, when I stopped at his roadside memorial to leave fresh flowers. She was just standing there with the dog looking at everything, and she wanted to know all about Jason. I needed to talk about him—wanted to talk about him—all of the time. I had this feeling that if I didn't talk about him, his memory would be lost to the world and his life wouldn't matter somehow. But our friends seemed to want to talk about everything but Jason. They felt so bad for us, and they didn't know what to say. I know they were afraid of making us sad, so they just wouldn't mention him. For some reason, it made it seem like I shouldn't mention him in their presence either, like we all needed to pretend that this horrible thing hadn't happened. Even Rob and Emmy, our daughter, couldn't handle me talking about him all the time."

"Minnow wasn't that way. She asked me everything. I offered to buy her lunch. Her uncle was waiting nearby with their camper and he gave her permission, so we sat over lunch and I told her all about Jason. What he was like as a baby, his favorite foods, how he used to tease his sister, what he'd wanted to do when he grew up, his friends, everything. And she absorbed it all, was fascinated by it all. It was the most healing conversation I'd had since he died. Even though she was just a kid, it didn't matter. She gave me such a gift. That's how we became friends."

"And you stayed in touch?" asked Maggie.

"She would send me Facebook messages and emails, and we met a couple of times at the same place for lunch when she and her uncle were in the area. Over one of those lunches, I told her about the photo, about holding it up so that the wife of the other driver would see Jason too. She was silent for a long time after I told her, puzzling about something. Then she said, 'You must have needed her to know how beautiful he was so that she would feel the same sorrow you feel.' And I knew that was it, and that you had felt it, that I had seen it in your face that day. But knowing I'd caused you pain didn't make me feel better. That's when I realized that we were on the same journey, you and me, two women dealing with a terrible loss. That's when I let go of my anger."

"Would you tell me about him? About Jason?" asked Maggie.

She did.

And when she finished, she turned to Maggie and said, "Now it's your turn. Tell me about George."

"Seriously?" asked Maggie.

"Yes," said Jenny. "I'd like to know."

She did.

They talked for another hour.

Of all the things Maggie had imagined were even possible following George's death, being in this woman's house having this conversation was not one of them. Nor had she imagined that she would ever feel the easing of the burden of guilt she carried. And she certainly couldn't have predicted the sense of camaraderie that had grown between Jenny Foster and herself in the space of a day.

Although it wasn't only a day. As Jenny had said, they had been on this journey together all along. They just hadn't walked side-by-side until now.

"Do you want to come with me to take Bonkers?" asked Maggie. "The dog. If Minnow's uncle is there you can get a sense of him and we'll both find out his status as far as resuming custody of her."

"Yes, I'd like that," said Jenny.

"The only thing," said Maggie, "is we need to go by the house in Boring to try to get Minnow's clothes. I don't know what we'll encounter with the mother and boyfriend."

"I don't even want to be in the same county as him, much less the same house," said Jenny. "But for Minnow, I'll do it. But they have surely arrested him by now."

So together they loaded the small body in its blue and yellow beach towel shroud, nestled in the cardboard box coffin, into the car and set off for Boring.

Flocks of geese winged across the pale blue sky, and people were out with rakes clearing piles of maple leaves from front yards and storm gutters. The two women continued their conversation as they traveled, and it seemed mere moments before Maggie was turning onto the road to the crooked house. When she reached the driveway, their conversation froze in mid-sentence.

At first Maggie thought she had turned in the wrong driveway. But then she saw the metal sculptures whirling and dancing along the walkway leading to the charred remains of the crooked house.

Yellow caution tape waved in the breeze.

"Oh my lord," said Maggie.

She and Jenny got out of the car and walked up to the tape, gaping at the blackened shell. They both startled when they heard uneven footsteps crunching on the gravel. A short, podgy woman emerged from around the back of the house. She looked to be in her late seventies and walked with a crooked gait that caused her to dip with each step like a three-legged dog.

"Quite the mess, isn't it?" she said to the gaping women.

"What happened?" asked Maggie. "Do you know?"

"Oh yes," she said. "I live in that green house right over there." She pointed to a one-story house with a backyard adjoining that of the crooked house.

"It was me who called it in," she continued. "I was in the bathroom—see that frosted window there—and I was seeing this orange flickering light. So I went and looked out the back bedroom window there and I see this place just ablaze, so I called 911. The fire department, they got here real fast, but it was already mostly gone when I first saw it."

"Was anyone hurt?" asked Maggie.

"Oh yes," she said. "Not just hurt, killed. The man who was living here with that Katrina. I never met him, but I guess he was just sittin' in there in the chair, dead. It was probably the smoke what got him. That's what they say isn't it? That it's usually the smoke more than the fire that kills people."

"What about Katrina?"

"Oh, no she weren't home. I saw her later standing by her van there, just watching it burn. That one's too mean to kill is what I think. Do you know her?"

"I've met her," said Maggie. "We're friends of her daughter, Minnow, and I know Billy as well. I'm Maggie, this is Jenny."

"Pleased to meet you. I'm Lettie. Now Minnow, she's a rose among the thorns," said Lettie. "Her and that little dog of hers. She made Vi so happy. But that Katrina, she was trouble from the start. She's like one of them wildcats that goes after the weakest animal in the herd. She wouldn't let up on Billy, on account of he was different. She always resented Vi giving him special attention. She was the same age as my Mary, but I didn't want Mary to have nothing to do with her. Mary wasn't weak, but she was kind, and to someone like Katrina it's all one and the same."

"Vi didn't deserve a daughter like that, but I guess we gotta play the hand we're dealt. And then Billy, we had some trouble with him too. But Vi, God rest her soul, she told me how he couldn't help it on account of he had the Ashbergers. So I didn't blame him if he couldn't help how he was. I mean everyone's got something. Me, I've got the diabetes and a bad hip. And you all probably got something too. Anyway, seems like Billy took good care of the girl after Vi had her heart attack. But then one day last week he's gone and Katrina's back here with that fellow and another little girl. Do you know what happened to those two girls?"

"They're both safe, in foster care," said Jenny.

"Thank the Lord. Nobody could tell me last night. I told the firemen that they lived here, but they didn't find no sign of them. I tell you, some people's lives are just a heartbreak."

When the two women reached Connor, Donovan told them that Sam and Billy were expected back within the hour, so they settled down to wait in the chairs by the woodstove. The cardboard coffin remained in the car. Donovan was at the cash register and his son Gil at the pumps outside. It seemed that every customer asked after Sam.

"What did you do with Sam? She doesn't get the weekend off does she?"

"When's Sam coming back? She wasn't here when I came in Wednesday either!"

As if in answer to the many inquiries, Maggie heard steps on the porch and Sam's musical laughter. Surprisingly, she heard Billy laugh as well. She realized it was a sound she'd not heard before. It wasn't a deep belly laugh, but a laugh nonetheless.

All laughing stopped, however, when they came through the door and he spotted her in the chair by the stove.

"Why didn't you come?" he said without preamble. "You promised to come and now Katrina has her."

"I know, I'm so sorry Billy. There are no excuses."

"I warned you about her," said Billy. "You didn't listen to me."

"Whoa, hold on here," said Sam. "Let's rewind this a bit. First, hello Maggie, it's good to see you again." Turning to Jenny she said, "I'm Samantha—Sam. I don't think we've met."

"I'm Jenny Foster," Jenny replied, reaching out to shake hands. "I'm a friend of Minnow's."

"My friend too then," said Sam. "Now tell us, has something happened? Why have you come all the way to Connor?"

"A great deal has happened," said Maggie. "It's a long story, so perhaps you should take a minute to get settled and then we'll tell you."

"Why don't we go to the apartment, just behind the store," said Sam. "That way we won't be interrupted."

Sam's place was just as Maggie would have imagined it. The worn and shiny wood-plank floors held an oval braided rug in the single room that served as kitchen, living, and dining room. The chairs had large, square seat and back cushions and wide, flat wooden arms. It felt like a lodge in miniature.

Maggie and Jenny alternated in the telling of the story of the past two days. At various times in the telling, Billy paced and swore, and Sam wept. She held his hand between episodes of pacing.

When they were finished, Sam said, "I want her here with us. She needs to be here."

"I think so too," said Maggie. "I'm afraid I don't understand why they took her out of Billy's custody to begin with."

Now it was Billy's turn to tell his story. He did so, painfully, haltingly.

"It was wrong, I know now," he said. "I just didn't understand then. But Katrina will never let it be forgotten."

"I don't think Katrina has any moral ground to stand on at this point," said Maggie. "But convincing the courts is another thing entirely. You were arrested, but then not convicted.

Correct?"

"Yes. The girl's family didn't press charges, and my mom explained to the district attorney about my Asperger's and so they let it drop."

"Was the girl named Mary by any chance?" asked Maggie.

"Yes. Do you know her?"

"No, but we met her mother this afternoon when we went by the house, or what's left of the house."

"There's also the matter of your other niece," said Jenny.

"My other niece?" Billy frowned.

"Sadie, Minnow's half-sister. Minnow has become very attached to her."

While Billy had known that Katrina had a second child, he had not until this moment recognized that he, too, was related to her.

"We need them both here," said Sam. "Of course, Minnow should have her sister. And who knows what all that poor little kid has been through. Minnow is all she's got."

"But how…?" said Billy.

"Forgive me for prying into your business," said Maggie, "but am I to understand that Billy is here on a long-term basis?"

Billy looked down, embarrassed.

"Damn straight he is," said Sam. "We decided this past week. All we need now to make it the perfect family is a couple of kids. So how do we make that happen?"

"You need legal help," said Maggie.

"I don't even know a lawyer," said Sam. "Billy, do you?" Billy shook his head.

"And I doubt we have enough money to pay a lawyer," she added.

"I know a lawyer," said Maggie. "Let me see what I can do."

It was turning to dusk by the time the group of four retrieved the small dog's body from the back seat of Maggie's car. Sam lifted him from the box and cradled him, stroking the springy hair around his face.

"You're my little hero," she said, tears streaming. "You saved her. Sacrificed yourself to save her."

She turned to Jenny.

"Do you have his collar and tags?" she asked. "I'd like to make a marker with the collar and tags."

"He wasn't wearing it," said Jenny.

"Minnow always took it off when he was home," Billy said. "It's probably at the house, although I guess that means it's gone."

Billy dug the hole.

"Sam, could you give me a lock of his hair? A bit of each color?" asked Maggie. Sam went back to the house and got some scissors and snipped off a bit of brown and another bit of white hair. Then she laid him to rest.

"We'll honor you properly when Minnow is with us," said Sam.

Billy filled in the hole and mounded the dirt on top.

November 30

Minnow was terrified. They were taking her to start middle school the next day. She hadn't been to school since fifth grade, two years ago. She didn't know anyone at this school. The other three girls at the foster care home were already in high school. One of the boys went to middle school, but he was sullen. She wanted to crawl under the covers of her bed and stay there forever.

She opened the dresser drawer to look at the clothes she'd gotten from the foster home—a couple of ill-fitting tops and a pair of jeans. Then she pulled out her phone to call Maggie in hopes that Maggie could deliver her own clothes in time for school. That's when she discovered that her phone service had been cancelled. "Thanks Mom," she said to the empty room. She threw the phone into the back of the dresser drawer.

At least the house had Wi-Fi, so she went to the computer and sent a text to Maggie.

"Mom cancelled my phone service so I can't call. Did you get my clothes?"

Maggie responded immediately.

"I've been trying to call you. Now I know why I couldn't get through. Am I allowed to visit you? I have things to tell you in person."

Minnow asked Randy who checked with her CPS caseworker. He said she could have visitors, but the visit would be supervised. She texted the address to Maggie.

Both Maggie and Jenny arrived two hours later. They stood in a three-way embrace in the home's entryway, then pulled back, each of them wiping tears but smiling. Minnow introduced Karen who joined them in the living room.

"I'm sorry to intrude on your visit," she said. "It's just our policy, especially when kids have been removed from a home against the will of the parent. You can't always know who visitors are or their intentions."

Jenny handed Minnow a large shopping bag.

"These are some clothes that Emmy outgrew. I think

they'll fit you."

"You couldn't get my own clothes?" Minnow asked Maggie.

"No, Minnow, we couldn't. That's part of what we came to tell you about."

They proceeded to narrate the events of the past two days—the fire, Dirk's demise, their visit to Connor and Bonker's burial. Minnow took it all in with a controlled, grim-faced expression, occasionally dropping her head into her hands. But when they got to the part about Billy moving in with Sam, she broke into a grin.

"Wait, what? No way!" she said. "Really? Living together as in *living* together?"

"It appears so," said Maggie.

Minnow started laughing for the first time in the past three days. "That's so awesome!"

"They want you with them. One thing I wanted to ask is whether that is something you would want."

Her laughter turned into a sob. "Yes," she said through her tears. "Yes, it's what I want. Can I go there right now? Please?"

"I wish you could honey," said Maggie, "but unfortunately, it's not that simple. It's going to take some time. I think you know Billy's not allowed to see you right now."

"But you can do it? It's possible?"

"I don't know," said Maggie. "But I hope so. We're going to do everything we can."

"Just hurry," said Minnow. "I want to go back to Uncle Billy. No offense," she added, turning to Karen. "You and Randy are nice people, but this isn't my home."

Before they took their leave, Maggie reached into her purse and pulled out a tiny white box. "I brought this for you," she said, handing it to Minnow.

Minnow opened it to see a gold, heart-shaped locket on a chain, resting on a bed of cotton. "It was a gift from my husband," she said.

"That's so sweet of you," said Minnow, "but don't you want to keep it? It's beautiful."

"No, I want you to have it," replied Maggie. "Open it."

Minnow used her thumbnail to pry open the heart. Spreading the heart open, she found a tiny photo of her and Bonkers in one half of the heart, and a tuft of brown and white hair lining the other.

"Oh, my Bonkers," she said through tears, stroking the bit of hair with her index finger. She clung to the two women in a long embrace, and the three of them stood together, entwined, reluctant to let go. Finally, she straightened, sniffing and wiping her cheeks with the backs of her hands.

"I'd better get ready for school tomorrow," she said. "Thank you for the clothes, Jenny, and please don't forget about me. And if you see Uncle Billy and Sam, tell them I love them."

"Stay strong," said Maggie. "We'll be in touch."

December 1

Minnow crawled into the passenger seat of Karen's dull brown Honda Civic. The rhythmic squeak of the car's wipers and hiss of its tires were the only sound as they drove the mile to Monroe Middle School. Nothing in Minnow's life was familiar. This was the loneliest she had ever felt. Her stomach clenched as the school came into view.

Karen parked the car on the street and guided Minnow past the groups of boys and girls, gathered in knots in the rain-sheltered portico.

"New girl, check it out!" she heard one of the boys say to his friends as she passed.

In the office, a stout woman with dyed blond hair and a take-no-prisoners attitude, introduced herself as Mrs. K and filled out the enrollment forms. She and Karen talked like old friends, and Minnow realized that this wasn't Karen's first time ushering an abandoned kid through this process.

"Minnow, now that's an unusual name. What was your previous school, Minnow?" she said.

"East Orient Elementary," said Minnow. "But I've been homeschooled for the past two years."

"Homeschooled. In that case, we're going to need to do some testing to determine the best placement for you in English and Math. Have a seat over there," she pointed to the wall across from the counter, "and I'll see if Mrs. Hansen in the library can administer the tests." Then to Karen she said, "I think we're all set here, you can take off. I'll make sure she knows which bus to take to get home this afternoon." Karen gave Minnow a smile and wave and exited the office.

Minnow took the empty plastic chair next to a gangly boy slouched in his chair with his head resting on the wall behind. His black hair was gelled into spikes, and despite the slouch, his jiggling legs and darting brown eyes betrayed his discomfort.

"What are you here for, Brady?" asked Mrs. K.

"Mosier sent me," said the boy.

"That's *Mr.* Mosier," she admonished. "And why did Mr.

Mosier send you?"

"He said I was being disruptive, but really it wasn't me. I was sitting between these two guys in that class who were wadding up paper and throwing it at each other. I was just trying to get them to cut it out, and I'm the one that gets nailed for it."

"Okay, well you can make yourself useful. This is Minnow sitting next to you. She's new today. I want you to help her find her locker and make sure she can open it." She held out a slip of paper to Minnow. "Then take her to the library where Mrs. Hansen is going to administer some tests. After that, come back and wait until your next period class."

"Minnow?" he said, looking to his right for the first time. "Like a fish?"

Minnow nodded.

"What were your parents thinking? What kind of fish? Are you like a salmon, or a trout or steelhead?"

"I don't know," said Minnow. "I never really thought about that."

"If I was a fish, I'd be a puffer fish. They are so cool. When something threatens them, they blow up into a ball and puff out spikes all over so nobody gives them any crap." He puffed out his cheeks and bulged his eyes.

"Enough Brady," said Mrs. K. "Get going."

"Okay, okay," he stood up. "C'mon fish girl, let's go find your locker."

Back in her CPS office after the long weekend, Ashley Nichols was in her cubicle triaging the foot-high stack of files on her desk, sorting out the most urgent. The phone interrupted her process, the receptionist saying, "I've got one of your foster moms, Mercedes Diaz, on line two for you."

She picked up the line. "Good morning, Mercedes. What's up?"

"Hello Ashley. It's about that new little one, Sadie, that you brought to us on Friday. I'm worried about her. She won't eat. She just wants to stay in her bed and suck her thumb. I tried to get her up to start school today and she just curled into a ball and started to cry, so I let her be. I don't think she's sick, but that one's had some real trauma. All she'll say is that she wants her sister."

"Oh boy, I was afraid of that. The sister's in another foster situation for tweens and teens. You're at your max with Sadie and I don't have any options to place them together. Maybe I can arrange a visit with the sister to see if that settles her down. And I'll put in a recommendation for therapy for her. Meanwhile, let's just try TLC and see if she pulls out of it. Thanks for the heads up."

Maggie left her car at the Park and Ride and took the MAX train downtown to meet with Pete Benson. No point in hassling with parking. She hadn't been in touch with Pete or Ginger since last summer, although they had recently invited her to a gathering at their home, and on another occasion to the symphony. Both times she had declined, citing previous commitments. In truth she had felt incapable of facing past friends. No one knew how to act around her, and she couldn't seem to find the path to any kind of new normalcy. And then when she had decided that suicide was her only option, she didn't want to rebuild connections.

She had kept to herself, making do with her family and the surface interactions with the grocery clerk and gas station attendant. Now, wrapped in Pete's warm hug of greeting, she felt a lump in her throat. She had missed the presence of compassionate friends.

"To what do I owe this pleasure Maggie?" Pete asked, escorting her to a seating area with leather chairs and coffee table. A well-scrubbed young man in shirtsleeves and tie brought in a tray with water pitcher and glasses.

"My secretary," Pete said. "Ginger loves it that I hired a guy, and in truth he's the best I've ever had."

"I'm actually here on a business matter," said Maggie.

"You're not dealing with more litigation from the accident are you?"

"No, that's all settled," said Maggie. "This is a different matter entirely. It's a child custody case involving friends of mine. I want to help them out."

"Hmm, well domestic relations law is not my specialty as you probably know. But I do have a partner who's among the best. Her name's Yolanda Morales. I'll introduce you. But before I do that, I want to know when Ginger and I are going to cash in that rain-check on dinner."

"I imagine you're both pretty busy through the holidays," she said.

"Not too busy for you. How about next week?"

"Well, I guess I could do that. What night?"

"I'll talk to Ginger and she'll give you a call. Now, let me introduce you to Yolanda."

Yolanda Morales was Maggie's height, solidly built, with a round face and olive complexion.

"Maggie Berry," she said. "I think I remember reading something about you in the paper, maybe last spring? A tragic accident?"

"You have quite a memory," said Maggie.

"It's a curse sometimes," said Yolanda. "But in my profession, it's a blessing. I don't tend to lose track of information. Anyway, I'm sorry for your misfortune in the accident. Is your visit today related to that in any way?"

"No, not at all. I'm trying to help some friends with a child custody case, and I know we need legal help."

"Tell me about the situation," said Yolanda.

Maggie described the events of the past weeks. Whenever she glossed over a detail, Yolanda stopped her and probed for more information. At the end of the story, Yolanda said, "So given your experience with the people involved, what do you think is the most desirable outcome?"

"If I could wave a wand," said Maggie, "I would terminate the mother's parental rights over both girls, and I would place them in custody of the uncle, Billy Marsh and his girlfriend Samantha Maverick."

"And what are the obstacles that you see to this?"

"Several things. The mother will never willingly agree to termination. Whether she wants the girls or not, she will fight it just to keep them from her brother. Then there's Billy's arrest record, although that doesn't seem wholly fair given the circumstances." She explained as best she could about Billy's Aspergers and his unconventional way of parenting and home-schooling Minnow. "Currently there's no relationship between Billy and the younger child, Sadie. But that child has had a painful and lonely existence, and to be placed with her sister would seem the best thing."

"Well," said Yolanda, "it's an interesting case. I like interesting cases. It's difficult, but in my view, not insurmountable."

"Then you would take it on?" asked Maggie.

"We would have to establish some things. First, Billy and Samantha would be my clients so they would need to agree to work with me."

"I'm sure they would," said Maggie.

"That means that I wouldn't be able to share information with you without their permission. Are you all right with that?"

"Of course. But I'm the one who will pay the bills," said Maggie.

"Have them schedule a time to meet with me. If it looks like we can work together, I'll pull together an agreement for you to sign."

December 3

Billy sat in the pickup staring at the blackened remains of his childhood home. The yellow caution tape remained, but investigation of the fire was complete. Everything pointed to the smoldering cigarette on the arm of the chair.

He got out and walked around the yard, thinking of his father throwing a baseball to him, and then calling him a sissy when he couldn't catch it. His dad had been a long-haul truck driver, so those father-son sports sessions were sporadic, but no less painful for their infrequency.

The window to his sister's childhood bedroom was broken out, the frame a corona of black radiating points. Steeling himself, he went up to his old bedroom window and peeked inside. He was startled to see a woman's hairbrush on the dresser. For a moment his mother seemed present.

He thought about how lucky he was that it was his father who had died when he was young, and not his mother. Viola Marsh had little formal education, yet she had understood him, and carved out space in an otherwise hostile household so he could grow up.

Billy had come to pick up his sculptures and metalworking equipment. In the shop he found tools loaded into a cardboard box and other things tossed on the floor. He put every tool away into its proper place and swept the floor. After he was satisfied that things were in order, he started to pack the shop's contents for moving.

When he was finished, the pickup bed was full. He tied down the load and took one last walk through the ruined house, being careful not to step where floorboards were charred. The living room furniture was reduced to pieces of charred wood, springs, and ashes. He started back out the front door but stopped when a blackened piece of metal caught his eye. He picked it up. It was bone-shaped and connected with a ring to another round piece of metal. The word Bonkers and a phone number were stamped into the bone-shaped piece. Billy pocketed the tags and walked to the pickup.

Ashley Nichols had arranged to meet Minnow when school let out to take her for a visit to her sister.

"What's wrong with Sadie?" she asked as soon as she got into the car.

"It's not uncommon for a young child to have trouble

adjusting to a foster situation, especially when they've been through hard things. Speaking of that, even though you're older, I'm concerned about how you're adjusting. How are things going with Karen and Randy? How is school?"

"Karen and Randy are nice, but I don't really have anything in common with the other kids there. And school's okay. I scored high on the tests they gave me, and I met one guy, Brady, who showed me where things are. And I met the librarian, Mrs. Hansen, and can go to the library during lunch. But, Mrs. Nichols, can't I just go back to Uncle Billy? He's staying with our friend Sam in Connor, and Sadie could come too. Please? I should never have gone with my mom. It was a big mistake. I just want my old life back."

"I understand," said the caseworker. "I can make recommendations, but the decision is out of my hands now. It's really a matter for the courts. Let's just start with trying to help your sister adjust to her situation. Can you do that? She needs you to be the grown-up right now."

"I can try," said Minnow. "But please, please will you try to get me back to Uncle Billy?"

"I can't promise anything. But I'll do what I can."

They found Sadie on her bed, hunched into the corner where it tucked into the wall under the eaves. "Minnow!" she cried, springing from the bed and running to her sister. They hugged and cried for a long time, Sadie's sobs triggering Minnow's tears.

Mercedes brought them a box of tissues and talked quietly to the caseworker.

"That's the most life I've seen in that child since she got here," she said.

The two girls sat on the bed. "I don't want to stay here," said Sadie. "I don't know anyone here. I want to go with you."

"I know," said Minnow. "I want that too. Mrs. Nichols is going to try to help us get back together and get with Uncle Billy."

"Can't I go with you now?"

Minnow glanced at the caseworker who shook her head.

"I'm sorry Sadie, but you can't. We have to wait until things get straightened out. Until then, I need you to be brave and strong. That means going to school, and doing what Mrs. Diaz says until we can be back together. Can you do that?"

"Is that what you're doing? Being brave until we can be back together?"

"I'm trying," said Minnow. "I think I can do it if you can. How about it?"

Sadie looked at the two women watching her, and then at her sister. She nodded.

December 5

Sam parked her faded red Toyota pickup in the Smart Park lot and she and Billy hunched under the hoods on their jackets to walk the three rainy blocks to Yolanda Morales' office. Neither of them came to downtown Portland often. And neither of them had much experience with lawyers, with a few unpleasant exceptions.

They shook the rain off their jackets and took the elevator up seven stories to the offices of Harcourt, Benson, Smith and Morales. Yolanda came to the lobby to greet them.

"I'm Yolanda Morales," she said, holding out her hand.

"Samantha Maverick, but call me Sam," said Sam, returning the gesture. Yolanda's grip was warm and firm.

"This is Billy Marsh." Sam nodded to Billy who looked at her quizzically, then he said, "Oh…" and extended his own hand.

Once they were seated in her office, Yolanda started. "Your friend Maggie told me a bit about your situation. It sounds like you want to see about regaining custody of your niece, Mr. Marsh, and perhaps your other niece, as well."

"That's it in a nutshell," said Sam. "Do you think you can help us?"

"Perhaps," said Yolanda, "but first I want to hear about the situation in your own words. Starting first with you, Mr. Marsh, and then from Ms. Maverick."

They told her their story, and as with Maggie, she stopped them to probe the details, taking notes throughout.

"Billy, the best situation for these girls, and the one the court would look on most favorably, is adoption—that is if we can get the court to terminate the mother's parental rights. I think that's a possibility after the most recent incidents with your sister's last boyfriend, especially if Minnow is in favor of termination. Would you consider adoption?"

"Would that mean I would be considered their father in a legal sense?"

"Yes it would."

"I would like that," said Billy.

"I think for the court to look favorably on an adoption, you would need to be home with the girls, not on the road in a camper, and would possibly need to think about school rather than homeschooling."

Billy stood and paced.

"I always go out with the camper. People are counting on me to come. I...I need to..." He cast a panicked look in Sam's direction.

"I would be at home with the girls," said Sam, "even if Billy was out on the road sometimes."

"Yes, from a practical standpoint that makes sense," said Yolanda. "But in the eyes of the court, it's the adoptive parent who is responsible. You would have no legal ties to the girls."

"Hmm," said Sam. "Would it be viewed differently if Billy and I were married?"

"Entirely differently. Then you would both be adoptive parents and the court would have no problem with Billy traveling part time, as long as you were home."

"Looks like Billy and I have some things to discuss," said Sam, smiling.

December 7

Maggie and Jenny walked single file along the overgrown, shrub-lined path to Lettie Herman's front door where Maggie knocked. They could hear movement inside, but no one opened the door. She knocked again. This time the door opened a few inches, but she could see that it remained latched with a chain.

"Lettie? Do you remember us? It's Maggie Berry and Jenny Foster. We met you the day after the fire next door. We're friends of young Minnow."

Lettie pulled back the chain and swung the door open.

"Oh, I remember you, yes certainly. I thought you was some of those people who come round all the time tryin' to sell their brand of religion. I believe in the Lord and all, but those people annoy me."

"You and most of the U.S. population," said Maggie. "Could we possibly come in and talk to you for a few minutes?"

"Oh, where's my manners," said Lettie, "leavin' you standin' out there in the cold. Of course you can. Come in."

She moved away from the door and bade them enter.

Maggie had the sense of being transported back to her own grandmother's house. The two visitors removed their coats in the sudden warmth, and Lettie bustled to take them. She hung them on hooks by the front door.

"Would you take a cup of coffee?" she asked. "I was just fixin' to have one."

"That would be lovely," said Jenny, "if it's not too much trouble."

"No trouble," replied Lettie. "I keep the pot goin' all day. We can sit at the table if you like."

She put out china cups and saucers, and unplugged a percolator on the kitchen counter. The pot wavered with the tremor in her hands, causing some of the coffee to spill into the saucers.

"Drat," she said. "Can't even pour a cup of coffee these days without half of it endin' up outside the cup." She mopped the saucers with a dishcloth and joined them at the table. "Now what can I do for you ladies?"

"Well, Minnow is in foster care, but it's not a good situation for her, and her uncle wants her back with him. He wants to formally adopt her."

"I think Vi would have wanted that," said Lettie. "Get that Katrina out of the picture altogether."

"The thing is," said Maggie, "when Katrina was trying to get Minnow away from Billy, she brought up the incident that happened with your daughter many years ago, and the courts used that incident as a reason to take Minnow away from him."

"Hold on a minute. Are you saying that spiteful mother of hers got her back because of what happened with my Mary?"

"Apparently so."

"Well I never...that's just plain wrong. I told them at the time that I wasn't pressing charges once I understood about Billy. He didn't mean no harm. That don't mean it was okay to do that, and it scared Mary half to death. But he never did it again, and that was the end of it. Or at least it should have been."

"Billy has a lawyer who is going to try to get the decision reversed," said Jenny, "so that he can adopt Minnow and her sister as well. The reason we came to see you is to ask if you would be willing to testify in court that Billy has not caused any problems since that one incident. And also to tell them anything you've observed about how he's cared for Minnow since her grandmother died."

"Well, I ain't never been to court," said Lettie. "But I've seen a lot of court stuff on TV. I guess if it would help Minnow, I could do that. What would I have to say?"

"You'd just have to answer the lawyers' and judge's questions truthfully," said Maggie.

"The whole truth and nothing but the truth?" Lettie said.

"So help you God," Maggie said.

"When's this court thing going to happen?"

"We don't know yet, but probably sometime in January."

"Well, you can tell that lawyer that I'll come, as long as I can get a ride to the courthouse. I don't drive these days with my bad hip and bad eyesight."

"We'll make sure you get there," said Maggie. "Thank you for being willing to help Minnow."

"It will be a pleasure," said Lettie. "Especially if it gets her out of the hands of that mother of hers."

December 23

The group of four that gathered in the judge's chambers at the Clackamas County Courthouse made up in nervous energy what it lacked in size. Billy, dressed in a suit and tie for the second time in his life, could not stand still and kept leaving the group to walk the perimeter of the judge's office. Sam was radiant in a peacock blue dress that made her hair shine like gold. Donovan and Maggie beamed like proud parents.

When the judge was ready, Sam corralled Billy and held his hand through the brief ceremony. Once the judge and witnesses had signed the official documents, the group took the newly minted license and adjourned to a restaurant overlooking the Willamette River for lunch. With Christmas music playing in the background, the staff and diners were in a holiday mood. Billy sported the expression that he had worn all morning, some combination of shock and amazement.

"Well, we did it!" said Sam, laughing in her musical way. "Can you believe it?"

"No," said Billy. "I never expected to be married."

"Are you sorry?" she asked.

"No, I just never expected it. I used to think it would be nice, but I never thought anyone would want to marry me."

"I guess you thought wrong then, didn't you?" She held up her ring finger with its modest adornment.

"Yes, I did." He smiled and looked at his own left hand.

Donovan offered a toast. "To the bride and groom, a beautiful couple we hope to soon be the parents of two beautiful girls."

They all lifted their glasses.

December 24

Minnow stood looking out of the window at the wet pavement under the streetlight. A family walked by, the four of them trying to share one umbrella, squealing and laughing when the umbrella's edge would send a stream of water down someone's neck. Karen and Rob were gone to visit grandparents for the holidays, leaving Simone, a twenty-something-year-old woman who played video games on her phone all the time, to supervise the two girls who had nowhere else to go for Christmas.

"This sucks," Brittany said as she entered the room. "Is this your first Christmas in a foster home?"

"Yeah," said Minnow. "My Uncle Billy would have me with him, but the court won't let him. And my friend Jason's mom would have invited me, but they went out of town for Christmas, and they wouldn't let me go with my friend Maggie because she's friends with my Uncle Billy."

"Right," said Brittany. "Well I can't wait. Another eight months and I turn eighteen then I am so out of here. What about you? How many years have you got?"

"I'm only twelve," said Minnow.

"You're on the long-haul girl. Six years ahead of you."

"I'm out of here next month," said Minnow.

"How do you figure?"

"Uncle Billy is going to try to adopt me. He just has to get the court to agree. So then I can get out of here for good."

"Dude," said Brittany. "Do you have any idea how many times some freakin' relative was going to adopt me? And look at me, still here. They make all these promises, and then something happens in their lives and it's no longer convenient," she made quotation marks in the air with her hands. "Or the court doesn't approve, or your birth parent steps in and messes it up. I mean, it's a nice fantasy to hold onto and all. But take it from me, don't get your hopes up 'cuz it's a mighty big crash when it doesn't happen."

Minnow went back to her book. Instead of keeping her company, this girl just intensified her loneliness.

January 15

Katrina chose a barstool next to the most muscular of the three lone drinkers at Harry's Hideaway. He wore a tight-fitting black tee shirt with cut out sleeves under a leather jacket, worn Levis and scuffed up cowboy boots. He had sandy blond hair, and a three-day growth of beard that only partially obscured the pits from acne scars on his cheeks and chin.

"I don't remember seeing you here before," she said.

"Just moved to the neighborhood," he replied.

"Well, let me be the first to welcome you. I like to show people around if that interests you at all."

"It might."

"What brought you here? Do you have a job nearby?"

"I'm a truck driver," he said. "I can live pretty much anywhere I can park my rig. I just liked the looks of the area. What about you? Do you live around here? Work around here?"

"My dad was a truck driver," she said, "before he died. That's probably why I've always been attracted to guys that drive big rigs. I've always lived around here."

He raised his glass to her.

"Hey, I know some livelier places to go nearby if you're up for a change of scene," she said.

"Sure, why not."

"I'd like to see your rig too, if you want to show it to me. Big trucks turn me on."

"Lead the way," he said, slapping a two-dollar tip on the bar and stepping down from the stool.

January 26

When Billy and Sam climbed into his pickup and headed to the Multnomah County Courthouse, Billy remarked that he had been to court more in the past two months than in all of his previous life.

"At least the last time it was to get hitched with me," she said. "So it's not all bad. And I'm counting on this being good too."

Yolanda Morales had told them that she thought they had a good case, both for requesting termination of Katrina's parental rights, and for approval of adoption by Billy and Samantha.

"Your decision to marry has helped us a great deal," she said. "I hope you didn't do it solely because of this case, though."

"I've loved this guy for years," Sam had said. "If the case gave him a little push, then I don't see anything wrong with that."

Billy blushed in response.

But then, as attorneys are wont to do, Yolanda had gone on to tell them all the ways things could go wrong. Those were the things that cycled through Billy's thoughts as they drove down the freeway.

They met Yolanda in the vestibule outside the courtroom. She said, "I see that your sister and your niece are both here already. As difficult as it may be, I need you to avoid reacting emotionally to them."

Neither Katrina nor Minnow were under similar restraints. When Katrina saw Billy and Sam, she spat out, "You're not getting away with this you Goddamn S.O.B."

Minnow couldn't contain herself either, she jumped up and down and waved, wiping tears from her eyes.

Despite Yolanda's admonitions, they both smiled and waved back. Billy was startled by how much she'd changed in the past two months. Her face was more angular, more grown up. She would officially be a teenager in two months, but she already looked the part. Sam held up both hands with crossed fingers, and then cupped her hands together over her heart.

They spotted Jenny Foster, who had come to support Minnow. Billy was looking around for Maggie, who was to bring Lettie Herman. He jumped when the cell phone in his jacket pocket rang. Sam had insisted he get a cell phone so that she could call him when he travelled. He wasn't sure he would ever grow accustomed to the sound.

"Hello," he said.

"Billy, this is Maggie. I didn't want you to think I was a no show again. We're just parking the car. I have Lettie and we'll be there in ten minutes. Would you let Yolanda know?"

"Yes," he said.

"All right. See you in a few minutes."

Once the hearing began, Maggie sat with Lettie, reassuring her that it was a simple matter of answering the questions truthfully. As she watched Yolanda Morales work, Maggie felt that the lawyer was worth every penny she had paid her.

While Katrina talked tearfully about her love for her children and wanting to restore her family, Yolanda dispassionately took the judge through Katrina's numerous historical failures to protect and care for her two children. She made the case that the issue was not what Katrina wanted, it was what Minnow and Sadie needed, a stable, safe and loving home and family. She proceeded with testimony from Lettie, Maggie, Billy, and Sam, to show that such a home was available, waiting for them. The clincher, however, was when she asked Minnow to take the stand.

"Do you understand," she asked, "what is being decided here today?"

"Yes," said Minnow. "It's about terminating my mother's rights as a parent, and whether my uncle and Sam can adopt me and Sadie."

"Correct," said Yolanda.

"Do you understand that once your mother's parental rights are terminated, that's a permanent decision and she will no longer be recognized as your parent in a legal sense?"

"Yes."

"How do you feel about that?"

"It's what I want," said Minnow. "I want to be adopted by Billy and Sam. And I want my sister with us."

"Are you prepared if this means severing all ties with your mother?" asked the judge.

"I don't have any ties with my mother. I've never had any, even though I used to wish I did," said Minnow.

Minnow kept her eyes on the judge and avoided looking in her mother's direction.

The judge's decision was swift and sweeping. Katrina's parental rights for both girls were terminated.

Billy and Sam were given temporary custody of both Minnow and Sadie, pending adoption proceedings.

The emotional release among the small group supporting Minnow, Billy, and Sam was immense. Minnow and Sam both thanked the judge through tears of relief. Then Sam and Maggie hugged Yolanda Morales. Everyone thanked Lettie. Minnow and Jenny joined the group where Sam folded her new daughter into a lengthy hug. Billy couldn't contain himself and had to walk the length of the courtroom and back several times.

No one noticed when Katrina slipped away.

Outside the courtroom they discussed logistics. "We can go pick up Sadie now, right?" Sam asked Sadie's caseworker who had represented her at the hearing.

"Yes," she said. "I'll contact her foster mother so that she knows the outcome. She knew this was a possibility, so should be prepared. If you want to head that way, Sadie should be home from school in an hour and you can take her home with you.

"We only have the three seats in the pickup," said Billy. "What about Minnow?"

"How about if I take Minnow with me?" asked Maggie. "Is that ok with you?" she asked the teary girl.

Minnow nodded.

"We will go get your things first, and then take Lettie home, and head out to Connor."

"To home," Minnow said.

"Yes. To your home," Maggie repeated.

"Perfect," said Sam. "I'm just beside myself. I never thought I'd get to be a mother, and now I have two daughters!"

"And a husband," said Billy.

"And a husband," she said, putting an arm around Billy, and the other around Minnow.

With that, the joyful group went their separate ways.

Katrina parked the van behind the school grounds and walked to the narrow passageway between the two portable classrooms that were used for kindergarten and first grade. The flimsy wooden buildings that had been placed there twenty years ago as temporary solutions to overcrowding at the school no longer seemed temporary. Students in the portables had to walk to the front of the main school building to be picked up by parents and buses at the end of the school day.

Katrina was ready.

Within seconds of when the dismissal bell signaled the end of school, the doors of both buildings flew open and a herd of five and six year olds streamed down the steps. The air filled with their squeals, chatter, and laughter. Katrina spotted Sadie wearing her pink, princess backpack.

"Psst! Sadie!" she called.

Sadie looked around, unsure of the source of the sound.

"Sadie!" Katrina called again.

"Mama?"

Katrina beckoned to her.

When Sadie reached her, Katrina grabbed her hand and said, "I need you to come with me. I've got a treat for you."

The two of them ran across the school grounds and to the parked van.

Maggie, Lettie, and Minnow were nearly to Lettie's house after leaving the foster home with Minnow's belongings when Maggie's phone rang. She pulled over to take the call.

"Hello there Billy," she said.

"She took her," said Billy. "She went to the school and took her!"

"Who took whom?" said Maggie. "What has happened?"

Sam came on the line. "Katrina. She went to Sadie's school and snatched her and drove off with her."

"No!" said Maggie. "She wouldn't try to…"

"She already has," said Sam. "We're on our way to file a police report. I just pray they can stop her. She's probably heading out of town. Anyway, we'll see you back in Connor when we're done. Can you stay with Minnow until we get there?"

"Of course."

Maggie's hands were shaking when she set down the phone.

"What happened Maggie?" asked Minnow.

"Katrina has Sadie. Billy and Samantha are afraid she's going to leave town and hide out somewhere."

They sat in silence for a moment, processing this turn of events. Then Minnow said, "I know where she gets her gas."

"And?"

"She'll probably need gas if she's heading out of town, right? Well I know where she gets it. She steals it from this guy's field near our old house."

"True to form," said Maggie. "Tell me where to turn."

When they reached the barn with the drum of gasoline on a stand, there were no cars in sight. Maggie parked at the side of the barn so that they were hidden from the road. They could see the gasoline drum through the shrubbery at the side of the barn, but the car was well camouflaged unless someone looked directly through the bushes. They settled down to wait.

"This is just like I seen 'em do on TV," said Lettie, peering eagerly out the side window.

"So she steals gasoline from this place?" Maggie asked Minnow.

Minnow nodded.

"That's just like her, I tell you," said Lettie, "from the time she was your age Minnow. Always lookin' for a way to take advantage of a situation. It near killed your grandma, wantin' to raise her right and all. But some people just get made crooked I think. I sure do miss your grandma, though. She was one special lady."

"Yeah, me too," said Minnow. "What if we are too late," she squeaked out.

Just then Maggie shushed them, listening to the sound of a car engine approaching. The sound grew louder, and then ceased. Through the shrubbery they saw the brown van, and then Katrina getting out and approaching the pump.

"I don't believe it!" said Maggie.

"What'll we *do*?" said Minnow.

"Can you sneak around to the other side of the van? The one opposite the gas tank? Sadie knows you. If you can open the door, she'll come to you and you can run back here to the car. Be careful. I'll follow behind you, just in case you need backup."

"Okay," said Minnow, opening her door silently and creeping around the back of the barn.

Minnow approached the van in a crouch and coaxed the door handle downward. She slowly swung the door open a crack and poked her head inside. A moment later she opened it fully. It protested with a loud groan, but at that point the two girls were running at full speed for Maggie's car.

"What the…?" said Katrina, turning in shock. "Minnow!" She ran toward Maggie's car. "Don't you fuck with me this way!" she screamed.

Maggie made it back to the car barely two steps ahead of Katrina.

"Shut the doors!" she yelled. "Lock them!"

Katrina pounded on the hood, and then the windows.

"Give me back my fuckin' kid, you meddlesome old bitch!" she shouted, her face a portrait of fury.

Maggie started the engine and was about to pull away from Katrina when Minnow said, "Wait, where's Lettie?"

Maggie realized that the passenger seat where Lettie had been sitting was empty. She looked in her rearview mirror and saw Lettie hobbling around the barn toward the car as fast as she could move, a step and a dip, a step and a dip. Maggie slammed the car into reverse and it lurched backwards towards Lettie, sending Katrina sprawling as she tried to hold on to the door handle.

"Get in," said Maggie, unlocking the door.

Lettie plopped into the seat and shut the door, breathing heavily, just as Maggie locked it again. Maggie was twisting the steering wheel to speed away when Lettie said, "Hold on a minute there. Before we go, I think we should call the police."

"They'll never get here in time," said Maggie. "She'll be halfway to Idaho before they can get a chase started. And since Sadie's with us, they may not even bother."

"Oh, I don't think she'll go far," said Lettie, grinning. She jingled a ring of keys in the air. The key ring was a fist with a raised middle finger.

The panic turned into a chuckle, and then a laughing fit.

"Why Lettie, you devil." said Maggie.

"I seen 'em do it on the TV." Lettie chuckled, sending the group into hysterics again.

Maggie picked up her phone and dialed 911, ignoring the angry woman putting small dents in the hood of her car.

February 1

Donovan was hosing off the concrete around the gas pumps when a petite girl wearing black leggings and a lime green rain jacket road up on her bicycle, her long, blond hair escaping beneath her bike helmet.

"Hi Donovan," she said.

"Well hello Miss Carrie. Do you need some air in those tires?"

"No, thank you. My Mom told me there's a girl my age living with Sam and Billy. I want to meet her."

"That would be Minnow," said Donovan. "She's in the

apartment behind the store. They're getting ready to do a little ceremony for her dog. Why don't you just go around back and knock on the door. I'm sure she'd like to meet you."

Carrie peddled up the driveway and leaned her bike against the porch rail. Before she could knock, the door swung open. A tiny girl of six with short blond hair, missing front teeth, and freckles, stood silently in the doorway.

"Hi," said Carrie. "I'm here to see Minnow."

The little girl ran back inside calling, "Minnow, there's someone here to see you."

Minnow appeared from the hallway.

"Hi!" said Carrie. "I'm Carrie. I live just down that road." She pointed behind her. "My Mom said you were living here now and that you're my age, and I said 'OMG, that's so cool!' I was, like, so excited. There's no one else my age close by, except Trevor Wilson, and he's a jerk. Anyway, I just had to come meet you."

"Cool," said Minnow. "Come on in. You're the first person I've met in the neighborhood. I have another friend named Carrie. She really likes Kit Kat bars and Dr. Pepper, and soccer. Do you like those?"

"I like Reese's Peanut Butter Cups. And I played soccer in grade school, but not in middle school. Do you play soccer?"

"No," said Minnow. "But I'm glad you came over. Do you want to hang out for a while? We're going to do a funeral for my dog that died. It's just in the Furry and Feathered Friends Cemetery behind the store."

"Really? Awesome. I've never been to a dog funeral before. When my cat Misty died, my Mom just buried her and that was that. What was your dog's name?"

"Bonkers because he always went bonkers over everything. He was the best dog ever. Sam gave him to me. Donovan rescued him and Sam took care of him in the Critter Spa, and then when he was all healthy, she gave him to me."

"What's the Critter Spa?" asked Carrie.

"I'll show you. Come on," said Minnow leading the way to the room attached to what was now Billy's metal shop.

Billy was at his workbench hammering on something that he secreted under a cloth when the girls walked in.

"Uncle Billy, this is Carrie. She lives right over there," said Minnow.

"I met Billy once before in the store," said Carrie.

Billy gave a little wave.

"I'm showing her the Critter Spa," Minnow told him.

Minnow opened the door carefully, making sure no one was poised for escape, then motioned for Carrie to enter. There were six puppies barely old enough for their eyes to be open, huddled together in a corner of a pen. And there was a jay with its wing in a splint, hopping along a shelf at the back of the room.

"Sam likes to rescue animals, so people bring her ones they find around here. Somebody found this jay with a broken wing. And someone dumped these little puppies in the woods. We have to feed them from a bottle right now because they're too little to eat dog food." She pointed to the miniature-sized baby bottles lined up on the shelf.

"Can I hold one?" asked Carrie.

"Sure."

Each girl picked up a puppy and stroked its soft, short fur. The dogs swung their noses around, searching and mewling, and started sucking on the girls' fingers.

"That feels so funny!" said Carrie, laughing. "So if Billy is your uncle, does that mean Sam's your aunt?"

"I guess so," said Minnow. "But they're going to adopt me and Sadie, my sister. So then they'll be like my mom and dad."

"Lucky," said Carrie. "I think Sam would be the coolest mom ever. My mom's okay though. She's just really busy all the time 'cuz she has a job and she's a single mom. She and my dad are divorced, and he lives in California."

"Do you have any brothers or sisters?"

"I have a brother, but he's seventeen, and he lives with my dad, so it's just me and my mom."

"C'mon," said Minnow, nestling the puppy back with its littermates. "Let's see if they're ready to do the funeral."

The dirt that Billy had mounded over the small grave was still visible in the center of the circle of people. Billy held the cloth-covered object from his workbench. Minnow and Carrie stood side-by-side. Sadie held Sam's hand.

Sam spoke first.

"Bonkers," she said, "you were such a sad, scruffy character when Donovan found you. You were dirty, matted, smelly, and scrawny. You didn't trust people, and who could blame you the way you'd been treated, and I didn't know if you would even survive. But you did, and you brought such joy to everyone, especially Minnow." Sam's voice choked and tears puddled in her eyes. "And you died much too soon, much too soon. But you died a hero. Our little lopsided hero. We'll miss you forever." She gave Sadie a bunch of flowers and directed her to place them on the grave.

"Goodbye Bonkers," Sadie said. "It sure was fun playing with you in the orchard."

Minnow held a wooden cross with Bonkers written along the crosspiece. She placed it at the head of the grave and pushed the base into the soft earth.

"Bonkers," she said, crying, "I'll love you forever. You made me so happy. And you saved me. You shouldn't have had to die. I love you so much Bonkers." She could say no more.

Sam pulled Minnow next to her, held her and kissed the top of her head.

Now Billy walked to the foot of the grave carrying his cloth-wrapped object. A thick metal spike projected from beneath the cloth. He pushed the spike firmly into the ground. When he removed the cloth, the object spun into life. Unlike his other sculptures that rotated with a graceful symmetry, this one had a short side and a long side. While it spun smoothly, it gave the illusion of wobbling out of balance. Some of the pieces were silver, and some copper, but not in a discernable pattern. It had one piece shaped like a dog tail that worked like a weathervane to rotate the sculpture so that it always caught the wind. The metal plate in the center held a slightly blackened, bone-shaped tag engraved with the name Bonkers.

There was a silliness to the way the device spun. It tricked the eye into following its trajectory, and then plunged and wobbled, like a sudden dip in the road. Sadie was the first to giggle, and then Carrie joined in. Soon Minnow and Sam were laughing as well.

"It's perfect," said Minnow.

May 2

It was the kind of Oregon spring day that made a person want to sing.

Rhododendron bushes were in full bloom splashing pinks, whites, and reds in front yards everywhere. Yellow tulips were giving way to purple irises, dogwood trees were laced with white and pink blossoms, and evergreens were covered with bright green spring growth. Everything looked alive and new. The cool, fragrant air carried hints of warmer days to come.

Along Winter Hill Road, a small group of people clustered silently for a few moments. Then each person walked forward and added an object to the shrine. Jason's photo had faded over the past year. His father replaced it with a new one in a plastic sleeve. Jenny nestled a toy truck from his childhood among the other objects. Maggie and Toby laid fresh flowers next to the photo. Eric added a pair of soccer shoes, and Amy a CD cover from her favorite band. Minnow and Sadie had each woven friendship bracelets that they dropped over the top part of the small wooden cross. A clumsy black and white puppy followed Sadie on a leash. When everyone had finished, the group wrapped arms in a lengthy hug.

Toby led the way as they proceeded fifty feet down the hill where a second memorial had sprung up. It had a photo of a middle-aged man in a University of Oregon football jersey, giving the camera thumbs up. There were other objects as well: a golf ball and tee, a Peace Corps tee shirt, a service award from the Rotary Club.

Again, the group stood quietly for a few moments, then repeated the ritual of each adding to the site. When it was done, they pulled together into another lengthy hug.

As they started to disperse, Jenny said, "Next year, same time, same place?"

"Next year, same time, same place," said Maggie.

www.ingramcontent.com/pod-product-compliance
Lightning Source LLC
Chambersburg PA
CBHW032012310726
48972CB00002B/382